PART OF THE FURNITURE

Also by Mary Wesley

JUMPING THE QUEUE
THE CAMOMILE LAWN
HARNESSING PEACOCKS
THE VACILLATIONS OF POPPY CAREW
NOT THAT SORT OF GIRL
SECOND FIDDLE
A SENSIBLE LIFE
A DUBIOUS LEGACY
AN IMAGINATIVE EXPERIENCE

MARY WESLEY

PART OF
THE FURNITURE

BANTAM PRESS

LONDON · NEW YORK · TORONTO · SYDNEY · AUCKLAND

TRANSWORLD PUBLISHERS LTD
61-63 Uxbridge Road, London W5 5SA

TRANSWORLD PUBLISHERS (AUSTRALIA) PTY LTD
15–25 Helles Avenue, Moorebank, NSW 2170

TRANSWORLD PUBLISHERS (NZ) LTD
3 William Pickering Drive, Albany, Auckland

Published 1997 by Bantam Press
a division of Transworld Publishers Ltd
Copyright © Mary Wesley 1997

A catalogue record for this book is available from the British Library.

ISBN 0593 041151

Typeset in 12/13 pt Baskerville by Phoenix Typesetting, Ilkley, W. Yorkshire.

Printed in Great Britain by Mackays of Chatham PLC,
Chatham, Kent.

For my granddaughter Katherine
and Prisoners of Conscience

ONE

A full moon lit the street stretching ahead; it was a long street and empty. The houses had blinded windows and secret shadowed doorways; only an occasional polished door-knocker or the radiator of a car parked by the pavement reflected the moon.

There was no sound of traffic and, although the air-raid siren had wailed its alarm an hour before, she could hear no planes.

'You'll be all right?' they had questioned. 'Find your way across to Paddington? Better take a taxi.' Their minds were already ahead on their journey.

They kissed her goodbye, fumbled hurriedly with last-minute inspiration into inside pockets, 'There, take this, pay for the taxi, take care of yourself.' They humped their luggage into the train, forcing their way into its crowded corridor, merging without backward glance into the crowd of khaki and blue, the smell of tobacco, damp uniforms and sweat. The notes now held between freezing fingers had been warm from their bodies; she pushed the crinkled paper into her bag and snapped it shut. There had been no taxi.

'If there's a raid,' one of them had said, 'take cover, go to a shelter or take the tube. You'll be all right in the tube.'

Aware of the cold, she thrust her hands into her pockets and doing so found her gloves, stood still as she put them on and, looking up at the moon, tried to see past its brilliance to the stars.

'London looks wonderful by moonlight,' one of them had said, 'an austere mix of charcoals and greys, secret, mysterious—'

Already the memory of their voices was fading.

There was the distant crump of guns and simultaneously the sound of bombers droning up the Thames, guided to their target by the treacherous moon. Shivering, she turned up the collar of her coat.

New shoes pinched her toes; she had been on her feet all day and was unused to hard pavements. Taking them off, she stood in her stockings. The pavement was smooth and ice cold; the warmth of her feet melted the frost and wet her feet. As she moved on, the street seemed endless.

In the distance a group of hurrying figures rounded a corner to vanish into a house, letting a slice of light flash out as they opened and closed a door. Perhaps if she reached the turning where these people had appeared she would find her bearings, see where she was. There might even be a taxi, or better still a tube station? To have decided to walk so that nobody would see her tears did now seem pretty stupid.

Suddenly the bombers were immediately overhead and from close by a battery of guns fired and a man's voice yelled, 'Bloody fucking moon!', whooping up the scale, infecting her with his fear.

Walking was a lot easier without shoes; try not to think of the bombers.

Their train would be free of the city by now. They would be clear of the suburbs, chugging fast through open country. She began to hurry and, almost running, pretended, as they had taught her all those years ago when she was a child and gullible, that she could catch her shadow. ('Hold your breath, keep quiet, run as fast as you can, see, I have caught his, you can catch yours, it's easy, easy.') They had played the game, the last week of August, running and leaping by the light of the harvest moon among the corn stooks, before the declaration of war, both over six feet, their shadows weird and wonderful beside

8

hers so puny. They had seemed even taller tonight boarding the train, bending briefly to hug her goodbye, their minds elsewhere but minding their manners. 'Take care of yourself.' 'Mind you take a taxi.' 'Better go by tube.'

When the stick of bombs fell she cowered by the railings, holding her shoes and bag by her ears. When the last bomb dropped, she began to run; she must reach the end of the street. Running, she avoided the cracks in the pavement, shortening and lengthening her stride like a wounded bird. When the man caught her by the elbow and jerked her up steps into a house, she yelped with a mix of terror and indignation. She caught her breath to protest as he slammed the door shut.

'You will find it healthier in here,' he said, letting go of her arm, 'and warmer. Have you far to go?' he asked when, after her initial protest, she stayed mute. He was divesting himself of an overcoat, letting it fall onto a chair.

She said, 'I am on my way to Paddington.'

He said, 'You would have been safer travelling by tube. What's your name?'

'Juno.'

He did not laugh, which was the usual reaction, or remark that she had a long way to go to grow into the part, but said, 'Nice. And your surname?'

'Marlowe.'

'Fine combination.' He was tall but bent and frail, with hair faded almost white. He breathed hard, gasping and catching his breath with evident effort. 'This will go on all night,' he said as another stick of bombs began to fall. 'That lot sounds near Wigmore Street.' He watched her wince. 'They sound as though some giant was ripping up sails or sheets — Oh, there goes the best linen! Joke? Not very funny? Do you always carry your shoes?'

She said, 'They pinch my toes. It's easier to run.' She wanted to ask his name, having given him hers, but did not.

He said, 'Sensible. You had better stay here until the raid is over. Do you want to tell anyone where you are? Telephone?'

9

She said, no, thank you, she did not need to telephone.

'In that case,' he said, 'let us check who else we have in the house, they will be in the basement. There is a stout table in the kitchen which seems to inspire confidence, though personally I have a phobia about getting trapped underground and buried alive. I spend these nights on a bed I've had moved into the drawing-room, but you are welcome to the basement if that's your preference.'

She was impressed by his courtesy. He looked ill by the muted light in the hallway. She raised her voice above the thump of guns to shout that she too feared being below street level. This was not the moment to tell him that this was her first experience of an air raid.

He said, 'Right then, upstairs it shall be. I don't undress,' he said, leading the way to the basement stair. 'There is something undignified about being dug out of the débris in one's pyjamas. But first let's just see who is here, what the congregation is tonight.'

The people in the kitchen lolled round a table. A man in naval uniform dozed with his head on his arms. Two women sat knitting on upright chairs and a broad-beamed lady stood by the stove, stirring the contents of a saucepan. There were two girls in party dress and their escorts in Guards' uniform sipping wine, grouped close and vulnerable. The woman by the stove said, 'Hullo, you're very late, we thought you might have got stuck. Soup?'

'No thanks.' He shook his head. 'But you, Juno?'

Juno said, 'No, no, thank you.'

'What's that you're drinking?' he asked.

One of the girls said, 'Wine. Want some?'

'No,' he said. 'I've got whisky upstairs, I'll have that. That sounds near the Zoo,' as another stick of bombs dropped.

The girl who had not yet spoken said, 'I wonder where they have evacuated the penguins?'

Her Guardsman shouted, 'Whipsnade?' hurling his answer above the sound of guns. 'Must be Whipsnade.'

In a corner of the room a man sneezed, blew his nose,

said, 'I have the most God-awful cold, I shall give it to all of you, I apologize for the infection in advance.'

With apparent prescience the second Guardsman remarked, laughing, 'That will hardly matter if we get killed in this.'

His girl exclaimed, 'Oh, Nigel, honestly! We were on our way to the Café de Paris, we want to dance. It's Jonathan's last night on leave,' she explained. 'We've only popped in here until it eases off.'

Her voice had a whining note which grated on the ear but it was blotted out by another bomb.

The woman stirring soup said, 'That was close.'

But the man with the cold blew his nose and said, 'I think it was farther away. What do you think, Evelyn?' and they all turned to look at Juno and the man who had brought her into the house.

Juno thought, Evelyn, what a nice name, I've never met anyone called Evelyn. So that's his name.

Evelyn said, 'Hard to judge. Come on, Juno, let's get ourselves some whisky.' As they turned to go upstairs he called over his shoulder, 'The Café de Paris has a glass roof, I suppose you know?'

Everybody laughed, even the man who had supposedly been asleep, and one of the Guardsmen shouted, 'You are pulling our legs, the Café de Paris is underground.'

Evelyn muttered, 'Even so,' leading the way upstairs into the hall and on up to the first floor, pulling himself up by the banister rail, walking slowly into his drawing-room to sit heavily in an armchair, breathing wheezily, chasing each breath. She noticed that he was deathly pale.

He said, 'Well, it's better here. Could you pour me a drink? The decanter's on that table, there should be glasses. Pour one for yourself, it will do you good.'

Juno poured a finger of whisky into each glass and gave Evelyn his. He swallowed a mouthful and thanked her, leaning back and stretching his legs. Balancing the glass on the arm of his chair, he said, 'It's very cold, don't you feel it? Could you turn on the fire?'

11

She knelt to light a gas fire which popped and gurgled among imitation coals.

He said, 'There's a lavatory across the landing, should you need it. Do you think you could ease off my shoes?'

He looked exhausted, she thought, glancing up as she unlaced his shoes.

He said, 'Thank you, Juno. All those people are my neighbours, they like sheltering in my kitchen.'

'Not your family?'

'No, no, they come to comfort me.'

'I had an impression of fear,' she said.

'Of course, but crowding together helps. I have plenty of booze and the neighbour with the soup brings it with her, it gives her right of entry. You should have had some, it's excellent soup.'

'I was too frightened.' And too miserable, she thought, and looked at the beautifully coloured whisky in her glass.

Watching her, Evelyn said, 'Then drink your whisky, courage is not confined to the Dutch. Go on, lap it up.'

She swallowed obediently, tried not to show surprise; she had never tasted whisky, though she knew its smell. As the spirit burned her throat and ballooned into her head, she looked for a chair, but there was only one by the fire and he was in it, so she crouched and sat cross-legged on the floor with her back to him.

Evelyn said, 'Presently, when I have caught my breath, I shall get onto my bed over there and you shall lie beside me, listen to the bombs and tell me the story of your life.'

Juno did not answer but watched the fire glowing as red as the whisky glowed in her chest.

He said, 'So where were you running from on your way to Paddington, pursued by demons?'

'Euston.'

'What were you doing at Euston?' He smiled, realizing why her gait had been so curious when running towards him; she had been avoiding the lines between the paving-stones. 'How old are you?'

'Seventeen. I was seeing them off.'

12

'Them?'

'Jonty and Francis.'

'Who are?'

'Friends.'

'Off to the war.'

'How do you—?' She turned her head to look up at him.

'History repeats itself.' He closed his eyes, leaning back, husbanding his breath.

'So they won't come back.'

'I did not say that,' he snapped. 'I, for instance, came back from the last lot, and if it's any comfort to you the casualties in this war may not compare with the last.'

'But they will be just as agonizing.'

'So you are determined to see the black side. Drink your whisky and tell me about yourself and this Jonty and Francis – brothers?'

'Great friends, and they are also cousins.'

'And you are in love with them?'

'It feels like it.'

'And they with you.'

'No! No. I am a – a person who is, sort of, around.'

'But they took you along to see them off. Drink up, Juno, you are neglecting your glass.'

Surprised by his use of her name she obeyed, swallowing hastily so that the whisky stung her nasal passages and made her cough.

'Dry your toes.' He pulled himself upright, reached for the whisky, sat back with a gasp, then carefully poured a shot into her glass before leaning back, eyes closed.

She stretched her feet towards the fire, watched her stockings steam; her Aunt Violet, she remembered, watching the steam rise, had told her that to do this engendered chilblains. She sipped cautiously at her drink.

Evelyn said, 'Go on.'

She said, 'They would not allow their families to see them off, they said it would depress them.' (Boring, Jonty had said.) 'But then suddenly, as a joke, they took me along.' ('Why not take her part of the way? As far as

13

Euston? A last whiff of home.') She tugged at the toes of her stockings, feeling their damp warmth. 'We came up to London last night,' she said, 'and today they had some shopping, last minute socks and things. Then we went to a movie, Ingrid Bergman; have you seen her?'

'Yes.'

'We had lunch before the movie at Wilton's, lots of oysters and brown bread and butter, they drank stout. I suppose you know it?'

'Yes.'

'Then, after Ingrid Bergman, we had an early dinner at Quaglino's. I'd never been there either. I suppose you know it, too?'

'What did you eat?'

'I can't remember.'

'Go on.'

'Then it was time to catch the train so — Uhh!' She put her hands over her ears and shuddered back against his legs as a stick of bombs whistled and shrieked to fall nearby, then further and further away. 'Gosh, it's noisy.'

'Not this time. Go on, you got to Euston.'

'Yes. Well, that's about it. They said take a taxi, they both did. They each gave me ten bob and they said take cover if there's a raid, or better still go by tube, and they got into the train.'

'Contradictory.'

'They weren't thinking, not really. In their minds they'd already left. I've seen them like that before, going back to school or university.'

'You are half grown up.'

'What?'

'Have you a father?'

'He died.'

'Mother?'

'Gone to Canada.'

'Expecting you to join her?'

'But I don't want to.'

'When are you going?'

14

'I'm not. I don't want to leave England, and I am scared of submarines, and—'

'You want to stay as close as possible to Jonty and Francis.'

She did not answer, eased her toes in the nearly dry stockings. A fire-engine raged along the street, followed by an ambulance ringing its bell. The guns were firing still but further away; there were footsteps in the street.

He said, 'So what *will* you do? Where will you go? Have you relations?'

'No, no relations.' No relations I can bear; only Aunt Violet, who is stuffy and conventional, kind and interfering. 'No,' she repeated, her tone obstinate.

He said, 'All right, if that's what you want, though relations are customary.' He did not believe her. 'So where were you heading to when you left Euston and were on your way to Paddington?'

'Nowhere. I told them — I made up a cock-and-bull story, I did not want them to worry.'

'Do you imagine Jonty and Francis will worry?'

Stung by the contempt in his voice, she looked up at him, furious. 'Beast.' She tried to stand up but the whisky affected her balance, it was better to sit. She fumbled for her handkerchief and blew her nose. She said, 'Actually, I let them think I was going to Canada. They know my mother took my luggage with hers and that I have only a suitcase left. I shall collect the suitcase and cash my ticket, that will give me time to think what to do.'

'Ah.'

'I know,' she said stiffly, 'that they won't write.'

'M–m–'

'They will not be allowed to, where they are going. They are both bilingual French and German, they will train—'

'Jonty and Francis should not have told you.'

Jonty and Francis will not survive long, he thought.

'Jonty and Francis did not tell, I eavesdropped,' Juno articulated carefully. 'I must be drunk, you shouldn't have given me whisky. I've never drunk it before.'

'How was I to know?'

'Now I have betrayed them!'

'Try not to be stupid.' He was weary, closed his eyes, breathed carefully.

The gas fire popped in the grate; the raid was moving away across the city. Downstairs there were voices in the hall, doors opened and closed, a lavatory flushed, footsteps clattered out into the street. The front door slammed.

He said, 'Gone dancing,' got carefully to his feet and, moving to sit at a desk, drew writing-paper towards him, wrote, folded the paper, put it in an envelope, licked it, sealed it, came back to his chair. 'For what it's worth,' he said, 'I have written to my father. He will help you if your relations fail—'

'But I have no—'

'So you said, no relations, but should you get stuck, need help, take this, put it in your bag. Go on.'

Juno put the letter in her bag.

He said, 'Now give me your hand, you are drunk and it's time to sleep.'

He pulled her up and led her to the bed, where he lay down fully dressed. She felt dizzy and sat beside him, holding her head in her hands.

He said, 'Lie down, you'll feel better.' She lay down. He pulled a blanket over them both, 'Lie quiet, go to sleep.'

She knew she would not sleep, the room was swooping about. She cried out, 'I—'

He said, 'What is it now?'

'Nothing, nothing.'

He said unkindly, 'There will come a time when Jonty and Francis are just a bad dream.'

She shuddered away from him but he pulled her back, letting his arm lie across her body. She was drunk. She would wait until he was asleep then slip away, let herself out of the house and run. But when the All Clear sounded she slept on, breathing deeply and sweetly through her nose.

The cold woke her. Cold feet where the blanket had

16

slipped. The chill weight of his arm across her waist and the chill pressure of his body along her back. She slid free, tiptoed to the door, crossed the landing to the lavatory, sat to relieve herself, listened to a surreal silence, raised the blackout curtain a fraction, saw daylight and snow falling, the street already white.

She went back into the drawing-room to find her shoes lying by the fire and put them on.

'Evelyn,' she said, remembering his name. 'Evelyn, it's snowing.'

She shook his arm; it fell slackly away from him. She touched his face with the back of her hand, held her breath, heard none of his, saw that he was dead.

Five minutes? Ten? A moment later? She tiptoed onto the landing. Listened.

The mahogany banisters led down to the hall. She leaned on them, lifted her feet, swooped, once, twice, sliding down into the hall, opened the front door and let herself out.

In the train Jonty leaned back in his corner seat and stretched his legs as the compartment emptied of uniformed figures, all bent towards the same camp. His destination and Francis's was half an hour further on. They could talk now that the carriage was empty, Jonty thought. He leaned forward to open a window, let in some air, rid them of the smell of too many young men crushed into too small a space. 'That's better,' he said.

On the seat opposite Francis was staring at nothing, pale eyes vacant, face expressionless. Could the thoughts crowding Francis's brain be similar to his own? Would Francis mock if he suggested that it might have been better if, for their very first assay, they had found someone with experience? Would Francis admit to having had a fear, identical to his own, of mockery? To have been laughed at by some strange woman would have been horrible, and belittling; at least that pitfall had been avoided. They had managed without experience. But he was pretty sure

17

Francis would agree that some degree of experience would have helped.

It was strange how silence seemed to enshroud the past twenty-four hours, making it difficult to talk; it was somehow not possible now to discuss their joint adventure. Surely one of the most important things that could happen to a man need not be private from one's most intimate friend, one's cousin? Yet it seemed to be so. Jonty sighed, opened his mouth to speak, closed it, crossed and recrossed his legs.

Perhaps Francis thought it had all gone well? Perhaps, in his opinion, they had not taken advantage? Or perhaps Francis assumed that, because she was in love with them, everything was all right, they had not gone too far? Was it possible Francis's mind was not crammed with niggling regrets? Could it be that Francis was not afraid that their ignorance and clumsiness had put her off? Not that she had known how ignorant they were. No, Francis would probably say, were they to speak of it, that if they had managed to latch on to some experienced lady they would have risked a dose of clap; they had received so many warnings. It could be that in Francis's opinion they had managed very well, their spur of the moment decision had been masterly. Anyway it was over now, what had been done was done, she was in love with them, wasn't she? Jonty glanced at his cousin and glanced away.

On the opposite seat Francis muttered, stood up, made his way out of the carriage and along the corridor to the lavatory. Unbuttoning his flies he noticed that his penis was sore, and thought, 'What we did was crude and rough.' He made his way back to the carriage, said, 'We shall be there in a few minutes,' reached up to the rack for his luggage, was inspired to say something consolatory to Jonty, could find nothing. He would have liked to say, 'She's been our toy, but not any more. We should not have shared,' but Jonty might think him sentimental. Jonty might laugh.

18

TWO

*V*iolet Marlowe stilled the clatter of her alarm clock and in the ensuing silence waited five minutes before getting out of bed. Last night's raid had been fiendishly noisy, yet she had managed five hours' sleep, a small but important victory to be savoured. She had, too, slept without stuffing her ears with cottonwool, another plus. It was amazing what one could get used to, given a bit of gumption.

On the floor above boards creaked as her lodgers padded about. Presently they would tiptoe downstairs, gather up their overcoats and gas masks, wheel their bicycles into the street, close the front door and pedal off to breakfast at their club on their way to their offices in Whitehall: John Baines, limping from a wound received on the Somme, to the War Office; Bill Bailey wheezing from mustard gas, the contact never clearly explained since he had served in the Navy, to the Admiralty.

Congratulating herself on their consideration and tact, Violet pulled back her curtains and, looking out into the snowy square, noticed the narrow lines which marked the bicycles' passage towards the Brompton Road.

John and Bill, while not exactly boring, were certainly reliable; they had been friends of her husband Dennis, killed in 1918. Their wives were confident that, lodging with Violet, they would stay clear of mischief, while she for her part was grateful for unobtrusive masculine company during the raids. Though none of them was craven enough to shelter in the basement, should a bomb fall uncomfortably close, one or other might call out something along the lines of, 'Bad shot, Jerry,' or, 'Close shave, that one,' or even, 'Anybody feel like a drink, hot or cold?' should they be awake.

Running her bath, Violet remembered that both men had returned the night before from weekending in the country with their families, bringing garden produce not yet unpacked and put away; this she must do before setting off to her work for the Red Cross. With this in mind she bathed quickly, dressed in her uniform skirt and blouse and, carrying her jacket, went down to the basement. There, hanging her jacket on the back of a chair, she set the kettle to boil for coffee and examined the contents of the country hampers.

Both Eleanor Baines and Joan Bailey had sent eggs, Eleanor's brown, Joan's white; there were vegetables, sprouts, potatoes and beetroot, boring but seasonal, and surprisingly, since neither woman kept a cow, a luscious lump of yellow butter weighing a good two pounds. This, thought Violet as she stowed it in her refrigerator, hinted at hanky-panky if not Black Market, but 'Who am I to question?' she said out loud as she made herself coffee and sat to munch a bowl of cereal.

Hardly had she swallowed a mouthful when the doorbell rang. She exclaimed, 'Blast!', pushed back her chair, put on her jacket and went upstairs. 'Goodness,' she said on opening the door, 'it's Juno! What are you doing here? I thought you were in Canada.'

'How smart you look in uniform.' Juno stepped back, feeling unwelcome. 'Did you have it specially made?'

'Of course, I don't believe in off the peg. But don't just stand there, it's been snowing, come in. Just look at your feet! Why can't you girls wear sensible shoes?' She drew her niece into the hall and shut the door. 'You must be freezing.' When had she last seen the girl? Ages. She looked white, tired too. 'Come in,' she repeated, leaning forward to kiss her niece.

'I came' – cautiously Juno returned the kiss, noting her aunt's scent, Elizabeth Arden's Blue Grass – 'to see you, I . . . You smell delicious,' she said.

'I understood you were joining your mother in Canada,' Violet quizzed her uninvited relation. 'I am off to work, you have only just caught me, I was eating my breakfast. Have you had breakfast? Like some coffee?'

'Coffee would be heavenly.' Juno followed her aunt.

'These days we eat in the kitchen.' Violet strode down the hall. 'I encouraged the maids to join up.'

Juno said, 'Oh. And did they?'

'Cook is making Spitfires but Bridget, you remember Bridget?'

'Yes.'

'Well, Bridget went back to her family in Cork, said the war had nothing to do with her, that she was a Fenian, if you please.'

Juno laughed. 'And is she?'

Violet said, 'How would I know? Help yourself to coffee and tell me why you are not in Canada.'

Juno poured herself coffee and, sitting opposite her aunt, drank, closing her eyes and shivering. It had been so cold walking through the snow, her feet were numb. 'I don't want to go,' she said.

Violet had been eating All Bran when Juno rang the bell; it had now grown soggy but would, she told herself, still do its job. She must not throw it away, not in time of war. Juno looked awful. What was the matter? The girl was watching her.

'I suffer,' she said, 'from constipation, this stuff is supposed to help. It tastes of cardboard.'

Juno smiled and swallowed coffee. The girl needed help, talking about constipation was not exactly helpful. How should one talk to girls? Being childless, one didn't know how to start. One was afraid of being clumsy. John and Bill would know, they both had girls, not as old as Juno, but girls.

'So you don't want to go to Canada, but would rather

21

join one of the services? Do your bit? That it? Am I guessing right?'

What had the girl been up to? How old was she? Seventeen?

'You are too young to get a commission but I'm sure I can help, you had better join the Wrens. I do know of some splendid girls who have become F.A.N.Y.s, but there again it's officers only and again you are too young. Tell you what, we'll discuss it with my lodgers, John Baines and Bill Bailey, old friends. They work in the War Office and the Admiralty, they will know what the form is, what strings to pull. Are you sure you won't eat anything? Did I offer? How awful of me. Would you like an egg?' (I am making a dog's breakfast out of this.) 'Poached or boiled? Scrambled?'

'No, no, Aunt Violet, just coffee, it's lovely.' Juno wondered what had possessed her, what crazy impulse had landed her here at Aunt Violet's mercy.

'So which service shall it be? I work for the Red Cross, but I can't see you there somehow. Mine is executive work, of course.'

'I don't want to join any of the services, Aunt Violet.' Juno's eyes met her aunt's.

'Don't tell me you take after your father!' Violet was aghast.

'What do you mean, Aunt Violet?'

'My dear, he was a conchie.'

'I am proud of him.' Juno bristled. 'He was a brave man.' She put her cup back onto its saucer.

'My dear girl, he went to prison!'

'Yes.'

'Prison!'

'Where he contracted TB, which later killed him.'

'Ignominiously.'

'Was there not ignominy in the trenches? I barely knew my father but I admire him. He did not believe in violence.'

'What would you know about it? He was influenced by that awful man, Lord Russell.'

'May I have some more coffee?'

22

'Help yourself.' Violet stared at her niece. 'Have I got this right? You do not want to join your mother in Canada and you do not want to work for your country in time of war. I simply don't understand you.' If Dennis had not been killed, if Dennis had lived and they had had children – 'a pigeon pair' Dennis had wanted, what a curious old-fashioned expression – if one of this 'pair' had been a daughter, would she, Violet, have been able to cope? Violet stared at her niece while envisaging Dennis's daughter; she surely would have wanted to fight for her country? Juno with lowered lashes was pouring coffee; her hand was not steady. Some splashed into the saucer and she added milk.

Violet pushed the sugar bowl towards her niece. 'Sugar.'

'No, no, thank you.' The coffee was good but her feet were still numb with cold.

'So why are you here?' Violet heard herself ask. 'Are you short of money?'

'I wondered whether you would let me have a bath. I have some money, thank you. I was caught in the raid last night, I missed my train back – I feel so filthy. There was a man who died, at least I think that's what he did, I took it he was dead, I—'

'Oh, my dear! Oh, you poor child! How stupid I am rambling on – why didn't you say? You have had a shock. Now finish your coffee and come upstairs. You shall have a bath and I will put you to bed in the spare room with an aspirin. You'll feel much better after some sleep. I have to go to work but I will be back tonight and then, after supper, we can discuss your future. Bill and John will be here and they will help, they have girls of their own. Come along, seeing a man killed is no joke—'

'He wasn't, I didn't, he—'

'Juno, don't worry, tell me about it tonight. Between us we will sort you out.'

'But Aunt—'

'Not now, Juno, later, come along.' Violet put her arm round her niece and led her upstairs. 'Now let's find you a clean towel and if you want to wash your hair, there's shampoo. Everyone caught in a raid gets dusty. There's plenty of bath water—'

'But I wasn't, there wasn't a bomb.'

'Of course there was, I can see it all, you are disorientated. We see lots of this in the Red Cross. Rest is what you need—'

'Could you lend me a pair of clean knickers?'

'Why yes, of course.' Had the girl peed from fright? People did, one heard of it, but Juno was 'family', could she have? 'Here we are.' They had reached the bathroom. Violet turned on the taps. Juno began to undress. 'I'll fetch you some knickers.'

Violet plumped up the pillows of the spare-room bed, pulled the curtains and, finding a pair of knickers she had bought in a sale before the war, meant to change because they were too small but never got round to it, returned to the bathroom. Juno had left the door open and was submerged in the bath. Her clothes, scattered on the floor, looked dry except for shoes lamentably sodden. Violet said, 'You can keep these, they are too small for me.'

'Thank you very much, Aunt Violet.'

Lying there in the bath, her wet hair clinging to her skull, Juno reminded Violet of her brother; he too had been long and thin, but fair-haired where Juno was dark. 'You have not told me what you were doing in London.'

'I came in for the day, missed my train back. I have to go back to collect my suitcase, it's still in the cottage.'

'But your mother's gone to Canada, she wrote—'

'Yes. The cottage is let to other people.' Juno closed her eyes. 'This water's lovely.' She felt she could lie in it for ever, forget and forget. But her aunt was speaking, enunciating carefully, 'Is your mother going to marry that man?'

'I did not know you knew about him.'

'She made no secret. What do you think she went to Canada for?'

'To escape the war?'

Was the girl being pert?

'Your mother would not run away.' Juno's mother, her

24

sister-in-law, whatever else, was, Violet intimated, no conscientious objector. 'I think she has decided to marry again. The man is rich, got some sort of business.'

'He has a name.' Though not fond, Juno felt protective towards her parent.

'Jack something.'

'Sonntag.'

'German.'

'Might be Dutch?'

'Possibly,' Violet conceded. 'Do you approve of him as a step-father?'

'Mother likes him. Personally I don't care if I never see either of them again.'

'Juno! What an unnatural thing to say!'

'No more unnatural than admiring your brother, my father, and desperately wanting—' (oh so desperately wanting Jonty and Francis). Juno sank down into the water to hide a rush of tears. Coming up to breathe, she said, 'You are being so very kind, Aunt Violet, considering you do not really like me.'

Violet breathed in, held her breath, let it out. 'You are my niece, of course I like you, blood is thicker than water.'

'What a remarkably silly expression that is,' she would say later that night, when regaling John Baines and Bill Bailey with an account of Juno's visit. 'The very fact that a person is a relation can be irritating. If she were not my niece, I am sure I would like her more. She looks like my poor brother. I could never approve of his ideas, they were so – well – embarrassing.'

Munching a Brussels sprout, for they were at supper, Bill Bailey said, 'Perhaps it's as well she left before you got back from work.'

Violet said, 'No, Bill dear, no. I feel I should have stayed. I could have rung the office, told them to manage without me. I could have reasoned with her.'

John Baines said, 'Girls like that do not see reason, it's a waste of breath.'

25

THREE

Squashed into a corner on the crowded train, Juno read the *Evening Standard*. The bomb which had fallen on the Café de Paris had killed a great many people. Had those girls sheltering with their boyfriends in the basement kitchen, frustrated from their fun by the raid, reached it in time to get killed? Crushed against her neighbours, swaying with the movement of the train, she remembered the party tiptoeing out, suppressing their laughter, closing the street door, their footsteps receding along the pavement.

'I like to catch a train before the raid starts,' her neighbour was saying to a friend. 'My daughter and Fred worry less—'

'It says here,' said the friend, who was reading the *Evening News*, 'that the roof was of glass. What can the authorities have been thinking of? Just imagine, glass!'

Another voice chimed in, 'Direct hit, wannit? Can't have known much.'

A man standing between the crowded seats, retaining his balance with a hand on the rack, said, 'Society folk ain't got no nous,' and then placatingly, 'Not a bad way to go, dancing. I like dancing.'

'I think my Fred would rather know,' said the woman who liked to catch her train before the raids started. 'Fred doesn't like surprises and, society or not, they can't have known.'

But they had known, Juno remembered, had been told,

and they had not listened, had not believed; they were intent on some fun on the last night of Jonathan's leave, whoever he might be. The man had told them about the glass roof. What had been his name? Sitting squashed in the train, chugging along in the gathering dusk, blinds drawn claustrophobically, she tried to remember. She could remember the weight of his arm across her body and that he was dead and that she, freeing herself, had slid down the banister into the hall, a quick exhilarating slide.

Aunt Violet's stairs had a similar rail of polished mahogany; she had slid down that on rare duty visits with her mother – 'Don't do that, darling, you might pitch onto your head,' – but today she had walked decorously down, left a polite note on the hall table thanking for the coffee, the bath and the knickers, silk-knit elasticated at the knee. Quite unlike the pair they had eased off her gently, determinedly, well, not so gently perhaps; those were now crushed into her bag, slightly torn.

She was glad she had left a note, though it had been a mistake to visit Aunt Violet, who was kind and conscientious and would now do her utmost to keep in touch and inveigle her, if not into the services, into some form of worthy war work.

She must collect her suitcase and escape, Juno told herself, shrinking from the prospect of returning however briefly to the house she had lived in for so long with her mother. It was too close to Jonty's and Francis's homes, did in fact belong to Jonty's parents, who were now renting it to another family. She had been a fool to leave her suitcase there – all her other belongings had gone to Canada with her mother – but she had not wanted Jonty and Francis to be burdened with it on their last day in London. (Stupid, I could have left it in the left-luggage at the station.) She had been riding on some sort of wave, carried away.

Carried away, she could hear her mother's voice, 'You get so carried away, darling, do try to be sensible.' Who was she to talk? Falling in love at her age, she was nearly forty! It was ridiculous; how could a woman of that age fall in love? And with Mr Sonntag, a man of fifty.

'Do call him Jack, darling, Jack is his name. You will learn to love him as I do; we will be a proper family at last, not just you and me. Think of it, a whole new life in Canada.'

Juno clenched her teeth and twisted her toes in her damp shoes, torn between embarrassment for her mother and affection.

If she could retrieve the suitcase, she could change her shoes for a more sensible pair.

'Nearly reached Reading,' said a woman's voice.

'Will Fred be meeting you?'

'Either Fred or my daughter,' said her neighbour.

'Nice to get out,' people were saying as they gathered up their bags. 'Trains get so stuffy in the blackout, can't get used to it. You getting out here, love?' nudging Juno.

Juno said, 'Two more stops.'

'There's Fred,' said Fred's wife, 'standing under the light so I can see him. Don't these wartime lights make people look like corpses! Fred, here I am.' She waved. 'Here!' she shouted.

Evelyn, the man's name was Evelyn. Evelyn Copplestone. He had not looked like Fred, but he had been dead.

'Will you be all right, dear?' Fred's wife was opening the train door, letting in a rush of icy air. 'You all on your own? You look a bit funny.'

Juno said, 'Yes, thank you.' She was all right, she said, 'Goodnight,' and pulled the train door shut. Two more stops, and a three-quarter mile walk to the cottage. There were dry clothes and shoes in the suitcase, the house would be empty, she could sleep and tomorrow – well, tomorrow she would decide what to do. No need for the moment to think of Evelyn Copplestone, whose mouth had been open as were his eyes, but he was dead. Dead bodies lack glamour.

FOUR

*T*wo stops on from Reading Juno left the train, surrendered her ticket and started walking. She forgot Evelyn Copplestone; more immediate thoughts crowded a mind so choked with love for Jonty and Francis and the surprises they had sprung on her that there was room for little else. It would be much later that it would occur to her that finding a man dead she should have dialled 999, asked for an ambulance or a doctor, or even rung the bell of the house next door and roused the neighbour who had stirred soup in his kitchen. But she had not; she had slid down his banisters and hopped it.

Later she would be filled with shame, aghast at her selfishness, would question whether he had really yet been dead. Could she not have held a mirror to his nose? Had she had a mirror handy in her bag? Had she even felt for his pulse? She had done none of these things.

Yet it would have been the height of folly, when she visited her Aunt Violet, to inform her of Evelyn Copplestone's plight. He was past answering for himself and she, Juno, would have been bombarded with awkward questions. The truth would have been abstracted, the situation relished, the police called, an endless delay enforced and her life messed totally up. Callous though her lack of action had been, it had served towards her survival. Now, walking in her damp, wretchedly uncomfortable, high-heeled shoes, she looked forward to reaching the cottage which had been home for the major part of her life.

Though since her mother's departure to Canada, of course, it no longer was.

So, stepping out as best she could along a road slippery with snow, and only fitfully lit by a moon which, unlike the night before, dodged constantly behind clouds, Juno's thoughts, those she could spare from Jonty and Francis, concentrated on the thick shoes, warm socks and dry clothes waiting in a suitcase left in the scullery cupboard at the cottage.

The cottage would be empty but warm; she would change her clothes. If the water was hot, as perhaps it might be, she could have a bath. Perhaps she could sleep? Then, tomorrow, she would return to Reading, surrender her ticket to Canada at the travel agent, be given a refund, and with this be in a position to decide what to do next.

Yet as she walked the cold was so intense, and her physical state so miserable, that at moments she regretted the cavalier refusal of her aunt's offer of help. She must find a job, the refund would not last long; her mother, expecting her in Canada, had left her with the minimum of money. She must support herself. Her aunt was her only relation; had her refusal been too hasty? There were other jobs than those in the forces, she had heard of them. Then what about her mother's friends, Jonty's and Francis's parents? Would Susan Johnson and Margery Murray not help? Were they not old family friends, had they not always been kind? There were several families in the neighbourhood with daughters doing war work, girls whose parents were friends of the Murrays and Johnsons and in some cases of her mother, girls working in munitions or in jobs they called 'hush-hush', girls whose fathers were retired military men and in one case a judge. True, her own father having been a conscientious objector was of little help, but he was dead, need not be mentioned. She could try.

As she slid and slithered along, she decided to go and see Jonty's and Francis's parents and enlist their help. They might even, she told herself optimistically, ask her to stay the night, give her a meal if the cottage had grown cold, help her bypass Aunt Violet. With this in mind, Juno quickened her step and, reaching the cottage, circled round to the back. Fumbling under the boot-scraper for the key to the back door, she felt it lie familiar in her hand.

With the key in the lock she pushed and the door creaked as it always had, a loud teeth-on-edge creak. It was said that her father, years ago, had tried to cure the creak and failed. The local carpenter was equally unsuccessful and her mother, growing used to it, either ignored it or suggested the noise would deter burglars, alert her to their entry should such unlikely persons invade a house with so little to steal. To Juno the creak was customary and welcoming; almost she expected her mother to call out, 'Is that you, Juno?' She stepped inside and felt for the light switch.

There was an alien smell of Jeyes Fluid and Mansion Polish. Her mother never used either, insisting that Mrs Haley from the village use beeswax and, if necessary, tear-jerking Scrubbs Ammonia for the drains. Juno sniffed and, remembering that the house was empty and that the curtains might not be drawn, forbore to press the light switch.

There was no familiar scent of wood smoke. The house felt cold. She detected a whiff of soot and remembered that Jonty's mother had ordered the sweep. Outside the wind was rising, whooshing through the Scots pines behind the cottage. The house sighed and creaked, cooling, unoccupied. She heard a faint rumble of water in the pipes leading to the tank in the attic; the bath water would be cold.

There was the sudden noise of the front door being opened, a crack of light under the kitchen door, voices and the door slammed shut. She slipped off her shoes, crossed the scullery in stockinged feet and shut herself in the broom cupboard with her waiting suitcase.

Margery Murray and Susan Johnson were twin sisters; their voices, loud, confident, uninhibited, could carry in a force ten gale. Juno's mother had once explained this

31

phenomenon as having to do with large families; if you did not shout, you were not heard. From the enclosed space of the broom cupboard Juno could hear every syllable.

'It all looks clean and cosy. D'you think they will be happy?'

'Of course they will.'

'When do they arrive?'

'The Cooksons?'

'Yes.'

'They said before dark. They may have been held up, but I suppose we should expect them any time—'

She could hear both women breathe. They were no more than a couple of yards away; if she emerged from the broom cupboard, what would they say? What explanation could she give? Better not.

Jonty's mother said, 'James said, if they have not arrived by now to turn off the electricity.'

'It's pretty late. Why is James fussing?'

'He is afraid that, not knowing the house, they might shine a light, splinter the blackout. We'd better do what he says.'

'The house is blacked out, isn't it?'

'Of course it is, but you know James and what he's like since he became head of ARP. The Cooksons are new. The Marlowes were habituated.'

'I wonder how she is getting on in Canada?'

Francis's mother moved away.

'Haven't heard yet. I shall miss her.'

'So shall I. Did the child go?'

'Juno? Hardly a child—'

'What?' Francis's mother was back close to the cupboard.

'Not a child, but not grown-up either. Where's this mains' switch?'

'James said under the scullery sink.' The sisters' footsteps slapped across the floor. They were wearing gumboots.

'What an inconvenient place.' Juno could hear Jonty's

mother shuffling to her knees and muffled a laugh. She was a large woman.

'Can you reach it?' Susan Johnson asked. 'Want me to try?'

'No, I've got it. Switch on the torch, Margery, while I turn this off.'

The light under the cupboard door turned from yellow to blue.

'Gosh, we look comical in this light,' the sisters chortled.

'What happened to Juno? I thought she had gone with her mother?' Susan Johnson breathed hard from her efforts.

'I'm a bit vague. Staying with her aunt? Following on in the next ship? There was some difficulty about getting a passage. The war makes everything so complicated.'

'D'you think Jack Sonntag will cope with her?'

'He struck me as an able sort of man.'

'But Juno—'

'Oh, he will manage—'

Margery and Susan stood for a moment, then Margery said, 'She was always under the boys' feet.'

'Tagging along like a puppy, poor child.'

'All very well when they were younger, but they need girls of their own age now.'

'They were both so kind and patient with her. She must have got in the way—'

'Her mother being such a friend, one couldn't say anything. I must admit her departure eases things.'

'Eases things.' The sisters had a trick of repeating what the other had said.

'We must organize lots of pretty girl visitors for their leaves.'

'. . . their leaves. What they'll need most is girls and fun.'

'. . . and fun. It's called sex,' said Francis's mother, Margery.

'What do our darlings know about sex?' Susan was amused. 'Sex is called love at their age.'

'Oh, Susan, it's still sex.' Margery laughed outright. 'And

33

I hope it will be with girls we like, girls who will make suitable daughters-in-law, girls with a bit of money.'

'A bit of money.' Susan laughed too. 'How awful we are, there's time enough. Did I tell you that I told Jonty to tell that child they were going off on such secret missions they would probably never come back?'

'Wasn't that a bit much?' Margery sounded surprised.

'I thought it would stop her hanging around. I thought she was capable of not going to Canada—'

'A bright idea, but was it kind?'

'What about being cruel to be—'

'Even so. Oh well, done now, I suppose.'

In her cupboard Juno could hear the agreement in Francis's mother's tone.

'You said yourself,' said Susan Johnson, 'that you were afraid if she did not go to Canada, you would be asked to keep an eye on her.'

'An eye. One could not have refused, and it would have been a chore,' her sister murmured.

'Exactly, and she would still be hanging around.'

'Hanging around.' Margery sighed. 'So she would, you're right there.'

Their feet slapped across the scullery floor and into the hall. The front door opened and slammed shut, the light from their torch flickered down the path, their voices diminished. The pain from the surprise they had provided did not.

FIVE

*E*merging from the cup-
board, such a charge of rage pulsed through Juno's body
that she felt quite hot. Fumbling in the dark, she stripped
off her clothes and dressed again in the clothes from the
suitcase; vyella shirt, woollen sweater, corduroy trousers,
wool socks and heavy walking-shoes. Then, feeling about
in the case, she found handkerchiefs and, taking one, blew
her nose.

'Bloody women, bloody women.'

She folded her London clothes and, with the ruined
high-heeled shoes, slammed them into the case, banging
it shut, thumping the case as though she were blacking the
eyes of her lovers' parents.

'How could they? How could they? All those years? So
smarmy, so kind, so charming, so bloody patronizing.'

She did not cry; the humiliation was beyond tears. She
washed her face and hands at the sink. The water was cold
and bracing. What if she turned up on one of their
doorsteps?

'Oh, Juno, my dear, how lovely to see you. Have you
forgotten something? Did you come back for it? Is there
anything we can do? Are you hungry? D'you need a bath?
A bed? A meal? Come along in, my dear, don't stand there
in the cold.'

She could hear their voices, visualize their smiles. Both
sisters were famous for their hospitality, prided themselves
on keeping open house in spite of the war, stretching their
rations.

Juno shook with anger, felt warm and energetic, forgot the soreness and discomfort, the bruised ache between her legs engendered by her first sexual encounter.

Though she had on occasion seen little boys naked, and once or twice, when they undressed when they went swimming, caught brief glimpses of their parts, she had thought little of it. No-one, least of all her mother, had thought to tell her that those dangly bits of Jonty and Francis could expand telescopically into something quite else, something which could force an entry, and hurt.

Had they tossed up as to who should go first? Had she exclaimed, 'That's never going to get inside me!' Had they heard? Had they listened? Was it Francis or Jonty? They had said several times that they loved her and she, while experiencing no pleasure, had cried out that she loved them, and laughing, for it had been better to laugh than to cry, had caused one of them to grunt, 'Don't laugh, I haven't finished.'

Afterwards she had been happy when they petted and kissed her, nuzzling her neck, smoothing her hair, closing her eyes with their tongues, tracing fingers over her mouth, saying, 'You are lovely,' 'A sweetie,' 'We didn't hurt you,' 'We did not mean to,' 'We have never done it before,' murmuring as they fell asleep and she, not sleeping, had lain between them listening to their sated breathing.

Standing in the cottage scullery, shaking with anger, Juno forgot all that. Later she would remember the texture of their skin, the hardness of muscle, the life in their hair, their lips and exploring tongues, the strange smell of semen, but now she detested their mothers with her whole being.

Should she set fire to one of their houses? Where were the matches? Why not set fire to both houses?

She felt her way to the kitchen and, reaching up to the shelf where the matches were habitually kept, found no matches; the bitches had tidied them away. They had lied, Francis and Jonty. They would come back. No, it was their mothers who had lied, their mothers who would invite

36

girls to stay, more sophisticated, older girls than herself, girls with money, suitable girls, girls who, even though they might not practise it, would know about sex, worldly girls who would not get under the boys' feet or tag behind them like puppies.

There was no point, really, in setting fire to their houses; no matches, anyway.

The wind was dying in the trees behind the house. A plane droned overhead; the siren wailed in far-away Reading. Juno picked up her suitcase, opened the cottage door, locked it and threw the key far into the dark.

SIX

*T*here now arose the immediate question of an overcoat.

The inside of the cottage had been pretty chilly; outside
it was freezing with a knife-like wind and, thanks to her own
perversity, she had no coat.

There had been an argument with her mother. There
was the warm and lovely houndstooth tweed with satin
lining which had used up all her clothes' coupons, and the
serviceable old overcoat worn every day in holidays and to
school.

'There is wear in it yet,' she could hear her mother say.
'This new one I shall pack so that in Canada, where you will
really need it, you can start afresh.'

Starting afresh played a major part in her mother's
thoughts.

'I shall want you to look your lovely best when beginning
your new life.'

She had grumpily watched her parent fold the houndstooth tweed, lay it in the trunk, close the lid and lock it. She
could have protested more vehemently had she not just
uttered a slighting and derogatory remark about
Jack Sonntag, a reference to thinning hair coupled
somehow with his occupation, which was that of an arms
manufacturer.

Wounded, her mother had spurted a tear and, shamed,
Juno had capitulated.

'Oh, all right, pack the bloody thing.'

She waited ungraciously for the usual protest, 'No need

38

to swear,' or, 'Where *do* you pick up such language?' when she knew perfectly well, but her mother had held her tongue, tied a label on the trunk and moved smoothly to another task.

Juno had left the despised old coat accidentally-on-purpose in the room where she had spent the night with Francis and Jonty, an action she now regretted.

Pacing as briskly as was safe in the dark, Juno thought of her mother and did not blame her for wanting to flee to Canada, or for wanting the love and security offered by Jack Sonntag, who was large, rich, capable and kind, so different from her father, the frail irritable conscientious objector who had gone to prison and wrecked his health out of sheer perversity, her mother had once murmured, though he had, come to think of it, kept a thick thatch of hair right up to his premature death. Had he perhaps been a bit of a prig? The idea amused Juno. Had his particular form of morality got up her mother's nose? Was his conscientious objecting some form of inverted snobbery? Might this account for her mother never having been quite able to disguise a certain awkwardness when the subject of her late husband's past cropped up, as it sometimes did, in conversation with local friends whose husbands had won a Military Cross at Passchendaele, a DSO in the Dardanelles, lost a leg or a life at Loos. Then she would edge the talk towards some blander topic, make no mention of Pentonville or whatever prison had harboured her husband.

That her mother had loved her father Juno was sure, but due to this latent embarrassment she had tactfully refrained from asking her parent for details. The little she knew was gleaned from Aunt Violet's derogatory remarks and a withered newspaper cutting discovered years after his death, when ferreting in a desk drawer for an elastic band.

Her mother, a parson's daughter, should surely have sided with the peacemakers, but when Chamberlain came back from Munich she had vilified him, called him lily-livered. Left to herself, she would have 'bombed Berlin to put a stop to Hitler's cheek.' Had her father been alive,

39

Juno wondered, would her mother have been so outspoken? She had a sweet soft voice; remembering it, Juno chuckled.

So was it so very odd that when the war did come and she met Jack Sonntag, this bellicose woman should cleave to him? But to allow herself to be removed from the theatre of war? When they discussed her parent and Sonntag, Francis and Jonty had attributed her behaviour and actions to sex, a theory Juno had dismissed as absurd. It was inconceivable, she thought as she trudged along, that her mother could do with Jack Sonntag what she had done two nights before with Jonty and Francis, it was plain ridiculous.

But what was conceivable, she thought with a jolt, was that in some horrible way she resembled their mothers, Margery and Susan. Juno drew in her breath. Out loud she said, 'Oh God!', remembering her mother.

'You will love Canada. Quite a lot of people have sent their children, quite a lot of people have gone. Not only the poor Jews, the Princess of the Netherlands is there, for instance. You will love it, you will meet lovely people, it's a wonderful country to grow up in. There will be so many new friends for you—' and so on.

Had she noticed her friends' objection to her hanging around their sons like a puppy, being 'always under their feet'? Had that weighed the balance, made her decide to go to Canada? Had she not also said, 'I am doing this largely for you'? She had.

'Damn her,' Juno whispered in the frosty night. 'I love her, but I will not go,' and then cheeringly it occurred to her that now she understood something which had long puzzled her. Jonty's father, watching the taxi driving off to the station taking Francis and Jonty to catch the train back to school, would rub his hands together and say, 'Distance lends enchantment.'

The fact remained, though, that she had no coat; the houndstooth tweed was probably in Canada by now. And it was freezing cold.

SEVEN

*W*alking from the station in her hopeless, high-heeled shoes it had been necessary to stick to the road, but returning sensibly shod Juno did what came naturally, she took short cuts. First she walked across the rectory paddock, then through the churchyard at an angle, weaving between the headstones to the rectory lane which she followed as far as the inn, cutting through its backyard to the Johnsons' boundary wall, where she turned left into their kitchen garden and across that to rejoin the main road and on, for another quarter-mile, to reach the Murrays' back drive, where she paused to consider the feasibility of the final lap.

Short cuts had been a speciality of Francis's and Jonty's, a game they had taught her. Any new short cut had to be proven and tested. The distance concerned must really be shorter than the accepted route before it counted on their list. Short cuts could lead across country, through woods and fields. In towns it was permissible to navigate through buildings as well as streets and alley-ways; a simple example was to cut through Harrods from the Brompton Road into Hans Place or Basil Street, or through Fortnum and Mason from Piccadilly into Jermyn Street. Three days ago they had taught her that from Berkeley Street one could walk through the Berkeley Hotel, cross Piccadilly and zigzag through the Ritz into Arlington Street, so saving several hundred yards.

Another such route through a building was all too familiar, but Juno hesitated before taking it. This was to

41

enter the Murrays' house by the conservatory, cut past the pantry to the kitchen, cross the kitchen into the corridor leading to the gun-room, walk along that and let oneself out by the side door into the rose garden, cross the rose garden and rejoin the road by the gardener's lodge.

Although the doors in the Murrays' house were usually locked at night, Juno knew where to find the keys, knowledge gained, she thought sourly, during the years she had spent doing what Francis's and Jonty's mothers referred to as 'hanging about' and 'following like a puppy'. To walk round the Murrays' house by the road would add mileage to her journey, and the arm which carried the suitcase would ache worse. Besides, there was something she wanted hanging on the row of hooks outside the gun-room. Juno ceased to hesitate, walked swiftly across the Murrays' lawn and let herself in. The conservatory door was not even locked.

The air in the conservatory was still. She listened and heard nothing except a tap drip into the tank from which Mrs Murray drew water for her plants. Holding the suitcase up against her chest for fear of knocking into a flowerpot, Juno stepped forward and, reaching the passage, tiptoed past the pantry towards the kitchen. Through the baize door into the front hall she could hear the tock of a long-case clock and, listening, heard it make its preliminary grinding noise before striking the hour. It struck twice and resumed its ticking. She opened the kitchen door very quietly and went in, closing it behind her. Her arms were aching from the weight of the case. She rested it on the floor.

From his basket near the Aga stove an old labrador heaved himself up and padded towards her, mumbling a greeting. His flailing tail rapped smartly against a table leg.

She whispered, 'Oh, shush, my lovely old boy, shush, please shush.' She stroked the dog, crouching down to feel his cold nose thrust against her cheek and caress his stout flanks. 'Go back to your basket, you naughty old thing, or you will rouse the house.' The dog wagged its tail harder, whimpered with pleasure at the interruption of a tedious night, barked.

In the front hall the outer door slammed shut and a light went on, Francis's father returning from his night shift at the ARP post. Juno skittered across the kitchen into the passage to the gun-room and dived in among a row of coats and mackintoshes hanging bulkily on hooks.

In the kitchen Francis's father spoke to his dog, 'Go back to your basket, you old rogue.' He dumped something heavy onto the kitchen table and yawned loudly. 'God, I'm tired. Basket, I said basket.' The dog barked. 'Shut up. Basket, you'll wake the whole house.'

Juno listened as the dog's claws clicked across the floor and the wicker creaked as it obediently lay.

Margery Murray's voice called from upstairs, 'Is that you, darling? I heard Bonzo bark.'

Francis's father answered loudly, 'Yes, it's me.'

'You are very late, what happened?'

'Old Perdue was late on duty.'

'Oh! Are you coming to bed?'

Francis's father shouted, 'Of course I'm coming to bed. Shan't be a minute.'

Juno listened as he left the kitchen, went back to the hall and into the downstairs lavatory. There was a pause, then the lavatory flushed and his steps came back to the kitchen. Next Francis's father pushed open the door into the passage, letting in a stream of light as he hung a heavy over-coat onto a hook, brushing past Juno's chin. As he did so he farted loudly, then he went out, closing the door.

A beautifully mannered and courteous man, Juno had never heard him fart. Her heart beat violently. She breathed in and out several times to steady her nerves, then, reaching up among the jumble of coats and mack-intoshes, she found what she was looking for.

The coat brought back from their trip to Hungary in 1937 had been a joint present for their mothers. They had only been able to afford the one, Francis and Jonty said. Their mothers wouldn't mind sharing, would they? So often they shared their dresses, borrowing and lending, they could do that with this coat, couldn't they? Wasn't it lovely? Were their mothers not pleased? They were themselves delighted by the originality of their present. It was sumptuous, rather grand, not like those awful embroidered peasant blouses everybody else had bought.

The coat was of dark brown sheepskin leather, the fleece on the inside. It had black frogged buttons from waist to chin, a bell-like skirt. There were deep pockets and an astrakhan collar. Jonty and Francis had been tickled to death.

Margery and Susan had not been so pleased. They concealed their feelings, of course, affected pleasure, but the coat had a nipped-in waist which did not meet round their ample figures and, unbuttoned, it looked ridiculous. And the skirt was too long, they were neither of them tall. With their sons out of earshot they murmured, 'What a waste of their money,' 'It's sort of fancy dress,' 'I suppose one could use it as a car rug, Susan,' and Susan echoed, '. . . a car rug, yes.' And one of them said, 'Well, we can't leave it just lying about, hang it up,' and, hanging on the row of hooks in the passage outside the gun-room, it had gradually been worked to the back and forgotten.

As Juno felt among the fleet of Burberrys, jackets, tweed coats and mackintoshes, they rustled and protested. One fell off its hook but she caught it as it fell. She was sweating when she eventually freed the sheepskin coat, carried it into the kitchen and put it on a chair by the suitcase, which Francis's father had miraculously not seemed to notice.

Breathing deeply to still her fear, Juno became aware that she was ragingly hungry. The air in the kitchen was rich with the memories of meals past. When had she last eaten? In London Aunt Violet had offered an egg, but she had refused and gulped coffee. There had been whisky in that man's house, but she had refused soup. She would give much for that egg now, or that soup. 'Let's just have a little look,' she whispered to the dog in its basket. The dog twitched its tail.

Juno felt her way to the larder door, switched the light on briefly, taking in the content of the shelves, switched it off. Carefully she took a cold potato and ate it, then a meat rissole, rearranging its mates on their dish. Bolder now, she tore the legs off a cold pheasant, ate, gave a bit of skin to the dog, who had followed her, licked her fingers. She drank deeply from a jug of milk, then backed quietly out, closing the door. She could not give the pheasant bones to the dog, they might splinter inside him. She gripped them between her teeth.

From her bag she took a comb and combed her hair. Could she risk the lavatory? She could and did, using the servants' wash-place but not pulling the plug. Only then did she put on the sheepskin coat. It fitted beautifully, as she had known it would. She buttoned it from waist to chin and turned up the collar. She picked up her bag and the suitcase and, letting herself out, whispered goodbye to the dog. When she reached the road she threw the pheasant bones into the ditch and began walking.

She was warm and fed and her conscience had never felt better.

EIGHT

*I*t took several days, later she would not remember how many, to recover the rebate on the ticket to Canada. People desperate for a passage must be contacted, people who would surrender their eye-teeth for her place on the ship, for the shared cabins and the risk of torpedoes, but, 'There's a war on,' the man in the travel agent said. 'There are forms to fill in, I have to work by the book. Can you prove your identity? Have you a passport? An identity card? We have to be careful. Let me see your documents.' Haste was not a word of which his vocabulary was aware.

Juno said, 'It's all on the ticket.'

The man raised his eyebrows and fingered the ticket while staring at Juno through wire-framed glasses. 'I have an uncle in Canada,' he said, 'my mother's brother went there to live. He seems to like it. He used to work on the railway, coast to coast. I wouldn't care for it myself, don't know what he does now. We lost touch.' He looked down at the ticket. 'How d'you spell Marlowe?'

'As it's spelt on my passport.' She pushed the passport closer to his hand.

'Ah! And Juno? Funny name.'

'That's on the passport, too, and on the *carte d'identité*.'

'The what?'

'My identity card, French, a joke.'

'Foreign? You foreign?'

'She was a Greek goddess.'

'As I said, foreign, huh.' Slowly he filled in the form.

46

'Sign here.' He pushed the form towards her. 'There, in that space.' Juno signed. 'Come back in a couple of days.'

'But—'

The man shook his head. 'As I said, there's a—'

Juno said, 'Oh God!'

'You get in touch with him then, or the Greek tart. It was Greek, you said? Next. Yes, sir?'

'It is unwise to hurry them,' a man who had been standing behind Juno muttered from the corner of his mouth as he took her place. 'I am trying to get a passage to Canada for my wife,' he said to the man who was conscious that there was a war on. 'I don't suppose there is much that you can do to help me, but—'

Juno stood back. Why can't I speak like that? she wondered as she listened to the mix of friendliness and authority. He speaks like Jonty's and Francis's fathers. He knows perfectly well there is a passage, he has been listening; there is a passage, mine. He is pandering to the man's power and frightening him at the same time. How does he manage without being ingratiating, irritating or humble? As she turned to go the man behind the desk was smiling at the man who had taken her place, looking positively anxious to tackle his dilemma even, she suspected, saying, 'Let's see what we can do,' though she was by now out of earshot. She was startled when he called out loudly, 'Miss!'

'Yes?' She turned back.

'Left your passport and identity card.' He handed them to her. 'You should be careful of those, got your ration book?'

Juno said, 'Of course. Thanks,' as she ungratefully thrust the passport and identity card into her bag.

The man said, 'See you Thursday, then,' and smiled complicitly at the man who wanted to get his wife to Canada. 'Where were we, sir?'

In the street Juno checked her bag to see whether she actually did have her ration book. She did; it nestled against the envelope Evelyn Copplestone had given her.

47

His arm lying across her body had been cold, she imagined, though through his sleeve she had not exactly felt it so and now, thanks to the coat, she was warm and must keep warm until Thursday. She would go to the cinema, it was cheap and would be heated. They were showing Laurel and Hardy; she had seen the film, sitting between Jonty and Francis. They had laughed a lot but not as hysterically as at the Marx brothers, who were their favourites. She bought the cheapest ticket and went in. The film was halfway through; she watched it to the end and then watched the News, which showed the bomb damage in London and the king and queen walking about in the rubble, being caring and at the same time not stopping people getting on with their jobs. They obviously had the right touch, as had the man who had stood behind her in the queue.

'I bet he gets a passage before Thursday,' she shouted out loud.

Several people said, 'Shush,' and the woman next to her said, 'Shut up,' but Juno felt a bit better and sufficiently relaxed to sleep through Laurel and Hardy when they came round again, and on through the News for the second time. She was still asleep when they played 'God Save the King' and the cinema emptied. An attendant woke her and she found herself back in the street.

She returned to the station where she ate a horrible but filling bun in the buffet and drank some wishy-washy tea, which was so hot it burned her mouth. Then, finding an empty seat at a table, she sat down to watch people come and go.

There seemed to be an awful lot of hanging about and humping of luggage. When a train came in, people rushed to get seats before those who were getting out had a chance to reach the platform. The windows of the buffet steamed up, but she rubbed a space free to look through. By this time the passengers were mostly soldiers, sailors and airmen carrying sausage-shaped kitbags so tightly packed they looked about to burst. Juno kept her small suitcase by

48

her feet, even though she knew it would be more sensible to leave it in the left-luggage office.

The buffet was relatively warm. It reeked of humanity, buns and tobacco; from time to time she went out onto the platform to gulp fresh air and read the notices, which said, 'Careless Talk Costs Lives', and, more humorously, 'Be Like Dad, Keep Mum'. In the freezing air she congratulated herself on the acquisition of the coat, which was snug and intimate. It did not smell of Francis's and Jonty's mothers; if it had, she would have torn it off and cast it under the wheels of an oncoming train. Instead, as it warmed to her body, it let off comforting whiffs of lanolin and leather.

Back in the buffet she dozed fitfully through the night, waking once to find a group of soldiers sitting round her playing cards while they waited for their transport. Seeing her blink, one of them invited her to join in. She won three shillings, which they insisted she keep. She felt quite sad when they left to clamber onto their train, 'Gotta get back to fucking camp, love, bye.'

Later their places were taken by blue-jackets, who were partially drunk and made remarks she did not understand or respond to, which irritated them so that they pressed her harder and took offence as she withdrew into the folds of her coat. One of them was raising his voice and had become quite threatening, when the buffet doors opened and a pair of military policemen looked in. Their eyes swivelled from right to left, then left to right. The sailors got up and went onto the platform, muttering, 'Bloody Pongos.' Juno was glad to see them board the next train and dozed off again from exhaustion.

When she woke next, there was a young woman sitting opposite her with a baby on her lap. With one hand she drank tea from a thick railway cup and with the other she both joggled the baby and pushed a bottle of feed into its mouth. Juno wished there was a third hand to wipe the baby's nose, which exuded snot like a slug creeping down its lip to join the milk in the aperture which would some day become a human mouth. There was now added to the smell from the buffet of tobacco, buns and humanity, the taint of urine and milk. The baby's mother smiled. 'Woke up, did yer?'

Juno nodded and caught the baby's eye; it was angry and anxious. Expecting it to belch, when it did she was pleased for she had got something right, expected the belch and it had come. She said, 'Bang on cue!'

The child's mother said, 'What?'

Juno said, 'He looks like you.'

'No, she don't, she looks like her dad. She's a she, can't you tell?'

Juno said, 'Not really, sorry.'

The young woman said, 'I sat on this when I came in, it's yours, innit?' She handed Juno a black woollen cap. 'Been seeing your boyfriend off, ain't you? Got a boyfriend in the Navy? He gave it you, I see, real act of love, that. My sister's boyfriend's a sailor, but he wouldn't give her his cap, said it was special issue. She begged him, but no, he said no. Your bloke must be real fond. Look at it, new, brand new.'

Juno turned the woolly cap over in her hands; it was coarse, hard-wearing, still creased where it had come out of its pack. The woman said, 'Put it on. Keep your 'ead warm, that, look nice with that funny coat.'

To please her, Juno put the cap on.

The woman said, 'Lovely.'

Juno felt that to undeceive her would lack tact and later, when she caught sight of her reflection in the buffet door, decided to keep it, for the woman was right, the cap looked fine with the coat and was blessedly warm, but at the time she said, 'Manna from heaven.'

The woman said, 'Haven't seen that one, there's no time for the flicks when you 'ave a baby. Would you like to hold her while I get another cuppa? You want one?'

Hastily Juno said, 'No, no thank you. I'll get you one.' Getting to her feet, she said, 'Do you like milk and sugar?'

The woman, no fool, said, 'You're afraid she'd be sick on yer coat. I'll get it meself, you toffee-nosed bitch,' and walked off, carrying the baby, hardly heeding Juno's cry of, 'I'm sorry, I didn't mean—' (which of course she had, for nothing ponged worse than sick, and she did not want the coat ruined). 'I just don't know anything about babies.'

The young woman shouted, 'Then lucky you!' and then, when she had got her tea, sat at another table with her back turned away, making Juno feel humble and remorseful and at the same time enraged.

At some time during the second day she was asked by a railway official whether she was all right, or was she in trouble? She had been hanging about the station for a long time. She told him she was all right and thanked him, said she was just waiting for a friend. She smiled at him before resuming her watch on the crowd of people, which swelled and shrank according to whether a train was expected.

Conscious of the official's interest she pulled the cap low down her forehead to add dignity and age, telling herself that she must learn the confidence of the man who had taken her place in the queue at the travel office; she must try to look as though Francis and Jonty would spring from the next train, arriving on leave expecting to be met by herself in the guise of a girl approved by their mothers, sexy, suitable and rich. But none of the men in khaki and blue looked like Francis, with his thatch of fair hair and eyes so pale they looked like water; nor did they have Jonty's gypsy eyes and springy dark hair. Only occasionally was there anyone as tall as either. When the railway official walked past her for the third time, she got up and left the station to wander about the town until the cinema opened and she could be lulled to sleep by Laurel and Hardy, forget she was hungry.

Being hungry led to thoughts of her father, whom she barely remembered and had not much liked, and the recollection that somebody, when she was small, most probably Aunt Violet, had remarked in her hearing, in derogatory and scoffing accents, something about 'his ridiculous and show-off hunger strikes'. She had not known what hunger strikes meant but now, years later, she discovered untapped sympathy and admiration. She half wished that she too could be, as he had been, force-fed, but this now became confused with a gruesome description once given by Jonty of the force-feeding of geese to make *pâté de foie gras.*

Turned out of the cinema when it closed, she counted her money and found there was just enough for another bun and cup of tea. Back at the station, however, the buffet was shut and there was nowhere to sit but the ladies' waiting-room, which was cold, stuffy, and smelled depressing, an atmosphere which, combined with her hunger, sapped what confidence she still had.

Sometime in the early hours the station official, who had been off duty but come on again, woke her. He was accompanied by a policewoman. She told them that what she was doing, since they asked, was waiting for the rebate on a passage to Canada and that, until she got it, she had no money but the man in the office had said, 'Come back Thursday.' When Thursday came she would get the money and be all right. Saying this, she pulled the wool cap straight on her head and wrapped the sheepskin coat closer round her knees, which did not prevent the police-woman asking to see her identity card.

Juno said, 'Gosh, I didn't know anyone really had to show them. I thought that was all for Nazi and Fascist countries,' and fished the card from her bag. The police-woman looked at it, handed it back and, without sparing a smile, went off to harass a party of inebriated soldiers who were bothering some superior-looking Wrens.

The station official now remarked that he was the father of a young daughter, that it was Thursday and the travel office would be open presently, but meanwhile if Juno came to his office there was a fire in there and he would give her a cup of tea, please follow. Juno followed.

In the official's office she sat on a hard chair by a coal fire, drank scalding tea and ate a spam sandwich so liberally spread with mustard it brought tears to her eyes, which, until she said 'Mustard,' the official affected not to notice.

Then the official enquired where, when she got the rebate for the passage to Canada, Juno intended to travel.

She, to stop him prying, handed him the envelope given her by Evelyn Copplestone addressed to his father which reposed in her bag, and immediately the station official said he would work out a route for her. She would have to change trains twice to get on that branch line. It was eight-forty now, and the travel office would be open by the time she got there; when she got back he would have her ticket ready, put her on the nine-fifty going west. And what about another sandwich?

So she ate a second sandwich, which again made her spurt tears, and set off through the town to the travel agent. There it seemed quite natural for the surly man to smile as he handed her the rebate on her passage to Canada, and for the waiting to be over.

Back once more at the station, she paid for the ticket the railway official had obtained for her, and to please him – for what else could she have done? – got into the train he told her to and began a journey she had not planned to a destination she did not know.

NINE

'*H*e's in London, me dear, but you'd better come in.' The woman opened the door wider. 'Come in,' she said, ''tis cold. A letter, you said?'

'Yes.' Juno repeated what she had said on the doorstep, a simple variation of the sentences she had composed on the long journey. There had been three or more trains, two changes, two lengthy waits for connections, the unscheduled scramble along the track in open country, looping through soggy fields to regain the rail track beyond the place where a random bomb had scored a direct hit, so that she and the other passengers could climb into another train which had been shunted down the line to collect them from the opposite direction. Nobody had talked much. People had been patient, had not complained or displayed animosity; mostly they had minded wet feet from the tramp through the long grass beside the line. The bomb was a solo, explained an anonymous know-all.

'Must have been chased by a night fighter on his way back to Germany from bombing Bristol, or maybe Liverpool, I'd say it was Bristol. He'd want to get away so he'd lighten his load. That's what they do when they are being chased. It wouldn't have been dropped to annoy. Heard of one which hit a cow, it's open country so it don't make sense.'

A voice sneered, 'Sense!' but otherwise the explanation was accepted without comment; they were all too busy, too intent on not losing their luggage, though some servicemen, already overloaded, were cheerfully helpful.

54

Juno's destination was the eventual end of a branch line; terminus would be too grand a word. The station appeared to be in open country, though it was night by now, too dark to see much. The engine let off steam with a satisfied hiss; she got out and surrendered her ticket.

She would have to wait, the porter said, there was only one taxi and it had been taken by another party. It might come back or it might not, all depended on how it stood for petrol.

'I met your son in London, Mr Copplestone—' She repeated the mantra, standing in the dark with her case at her feet. She wondered what on earth she was doing here, why she had come. She could see her breath freezing as it left her lips. 'I met your son Evelyn in London, Mr Copplestone. There was an air raid and he—'

The taxi was returning; it ground to a halt beside her. 'Where's it to?' She told the driver the name which was written on the envelope. He said, 'Ah,' got out, swung her case into the back of the car, held the door open for her, shut it when she was in, then settled himself behind the wheel and started the engine.

They drove from the station in what seemed to be open country up a hill into a large village, blacked out. The houses loomed in darkened streets. Then they were in open country again, the road nipped in by high hedges.

'I met your son, Mr – I met Evelyn – no – I met Evelyn Copplestone, your son. He said I—' It was slipping from her. At one moment during the journey she had got it almost right, hit the right note, but hitting the right note had only helped to tighten the bonds which knotted the grief, the anxiety and the anger lumped in her midriff and clogging her mind.

Now the taxi wound up a long hill, changing gear with a jerk to twist through another village, a wider street, no lights but dark squat houses, a glint here and there of shop windows and the shadow of a church tower. Then down a steep hill to swoop up again, climbing hard between steep banks or walls on either side with hedges atop to form a tunnel, up and down, but mostly up, the road climbing steeply.

'I met Evelyn, I met your son, there was an air raid and he, and he said, and he—'

The taxi had stopped. There was a gate; the driver got out to open it but the wind was rising and fighting to slam the gate shut.

'I can help.' She jumped out of the car. 'Let me hold it while you . . .'

The man drove through. The gate wrenched free and slammed shut. She got back in the car. The driver said, 'Thanks, miss,' and the car jerked forward and her case, which had posed upright, fell across her foot, bruising the instep.

Now they were driving across open moorland; she could see patches of snow against black heather and a half moon racing the clouds.

'Oh, Mr Copplestone, I met your son in London and he—'

The driver changed gear. They were passing under trees which were being whipped into shape by the wind, then down a dip and the taxi stopped.

Juno got out and the driver put her case beside her and named his fare. She paid him, thanked him, said, 'Shall you manage the gate?'

The man said, 'Yes,' he was not talkative, and drove off.

There was an archway into a courtyard lit by the fitful moon and, across the yard, a porch. She hesitated before fumbling for a bell.

Perhaps she should have asked the man to wait? Arriving like this was bad manners. She was tired and not thinking straight. Fool. When she had delivered the letter she would have to leave. She should have kept the taxi to take her away somewhere when she had handed in the letter. Where?

There was no bell, she could not find a bell. The sound of a horse whinnying across the yard startled her. It stamped its hoof and throttled breath through its nostrils.

Her hand found a knocker; she knocked. Somewhere in the house a dog barked.

She had intended saying, 'I met your son in London, Mr Copplestone, and he gave me this letter for you.' Simplicity was best.

There were explanations, of course, some flowery additions. One for instance, 'The letter was not stamped so I brought it by hand.' Or, 'He told me to deliver it by hand,' which was a lie. Also she had hesitated long whether to opt for brevity or whether she should say, 'I met your son in London and he very kindly sheltered me in his house during an air raid and gave me whisky' – perhaps it would be unwise to mention the whisky? – 'before giving me this letter to give to you by hand,' but he had said nothing about delivery. He had died, hadn't he?

Perhaps he had expected her to stamp the letter? People did, normal people; they stuck on stamps and posted them into pillar-boxes. But it had to be by hand or tear it up, throw it into the waste-paper basket, get no answer.

In the event she held the letter towards the woman who opened the door and said, 'I brought this letter for Mr Copplestone.'

And the woman said, 'He's in London, me dear, but you'd better come in. Come in, 'tis cold. A letter, you said?'

Then when Juno was in and the door closed, she took the letter and looking at it said, 'Mr Evelyn's writing,' and laid the letter on a salver which sat on an oak table.

Juno stood looking at the letter, noticing that the envelope was square, not oblong as were most envelopes, but square and pristine in spite of its long sojourn squashed beside her identity card, ration book and passport.

A dog had appeared, its nails clicking on stone flags. It came across to Juno and snuffled round her legs, sussing her out. Then it thrust an icy nose against her fingers, jerking her hand up for attention. She could feel its whiskers.

The woman, looking closely at Juno, said, 'Soup.'

57

TEN

*J*uno followed the woman across the hall to a large kitchen and sat on a hard chair at a long deal table grooved by many scrubbings. The dog settled on its haunches beside her, leaned against her leg and rested its chin on her knee.

The woman glanced at the animal but made no comment. She was a short woman with thick grey hair pulled back into a bun. Her face was brown from sun and wind and traced with wrinkles. She had very bright, very small brown eyes and a large mouth pursed in an expression of permanent amusement. She wore dark-grey, ribbed, wool stockings and flat-heeled shoes. Her calves, shapely and muscular, emerged abruptly from a heather mixture tweed skirt which sagged round her bottom with the familiarity of long wear. Above the skirt she wore a pale grey cardigan over a dark grey jersey, and covering the lot a loose holland overall.

Moving precisely and without haste the woman fetched a jug from a walk-in larder, closing the door quickly to exclude a blast of cold air. From the jug she poured soup into a pan to heat on the stove. Two cats, so tightly balled together it was impossible to distinguish one from the other, remained wrapped in sleep, ignoring her feet. While the soup heated the woman put bread, butter, salt, a knife, a spoon and plate in front of Juno. Then, when the soup was heated, she poured it into a bowl which she put in front of her.

'Eat that.'

Juno said, 'Oh!' as the aroma of pheasant wafted up

her nose. 'Thank you.'

The woman suggested, 'Take your coat off?'

Juno obeyed, slipping her arms free of the sleeves, letting the coat flop back over the chair-back.

'Eat it up.' The woman watched her.

Juno obeyed, spooning the gamey liquid from bowl to mouth. The spoon was silver, smooth on her tongue, not plate as had been the forks and spoons at Quaglino's where she had last eaten proper food, days ago, sitting between them, listening to their jokes. How could they joke at a time like that? After—

'Like some more?'

'No, no, thank you. It's absolutely delicious, but I—'

'Yes?'

'There are knots in my chest like coiled springs, I—' She pressed her fists against her breastbone. 'I'm sorry, I can't finish it.'

'I dare say.'

Juno laid the spoon in the bowl. There was soup left over; she could eat no more. It was such wonderful soup, she had not eaten much, she was wasting food, it was wartime, it was wicked to waste good food. She could hear Aunt Violet's voice. I hardly know Aunt Violet, she thought. I don't want to, but I know what she would say.

'Jessie will finish it.'

'Oh!'

Juno watched as the woman removed the bowl and poured what was left into a dog-bowl on the floor. (Imagine, Aunt Violet!) The dog removed her chin from Juno's knee and sauntered to the bowl to lap. She finished the soup, scraping the bowl along the stone floor to reach the last drop. Her tail waved at half-mast in rhythm with her lapping. She was either a very fat dog or about to whelp.

'Bed?' The woman was speaking.

'Bed?'

'Those springs in your chest might uncoil. Come along. You won't need that' – Juno had sprung up, snatching at her coat – 'but bring it if you wish. It won't run away, but

59

bring it if it makes you feel safer.' This was a long speech. 'Come along,' she said again.

Juno followed her, carrying her coat. In the hall the woman picked up the suitcase, said, 'No,' when Juno made to take it, and led the way up wide uncarpeted stairs. The dog followed, her paws shuffling and clicking on the polished wood. Juno, climbing behind the woman, felt such immense fatigue she could barely climb without stumbling. The woman led her along a cold dark passage carpeted at intervals with rugs and into a bedroom, where she switched on a lamp beside the bed, saying, 'Got a nightdress?'

'In my case.' Juno looked about her. The room was large, with shuttered windows. The woman was drawing faded chintz curtains. There was a mahogany chest of drawers, an oak armoire, a cheval glass, a bookcase stuffed with books, an armchair with a sagging seat, its chintz matching the curtains, and across the foot of an enormous bed a *chaise longue* onto which the dog was climbing to settle possessively, resting its nose on its paws.

'Bathroom's through that door.' The woman pointed. 'You unpack your nightie and sponge while I put a match—' She knelt by the fireplace and, taking matches from her overall pocket, struck one and applied the flame to kindling in the grate. 'Soon warm up,' she said as the kindling caught and flames drew up the chimney. 'Don't take all night.'

Juno rummaged in her case for nightdress and sponge-bag. The woman was stacking logs in a pyramid over the sticks. A drift of smoke blew back sweetly scented into the room, then was sucked up the chimney. 'Wild night.' The woman stood up. 'Come on now, get undressed.' She reached to pull Juno's sweater over her head, removing the wool cap as she did so. 'Pretty hair. Take all these things off and go and clean your teeth.'

Juno unzipped her trousers, kicked off her shoes without undoing the laces and eased off her socks. The woman dropped her nightdress over her head and said, 'Lavatory,' pointing to the bathroom door.

The bathroom window was shuttered. The bath was huge with a mahogany surround, the basin and lavatory bowl willow-patterned. There were soft, much-mended towels and rose-geranium soap.

Juno cleaned her teeth, bathed her face and, sitting on the lavatory, stared round the room. She had never seen such a bathroom. There was a dressing table, another armchair, more books and still the room looked large.

In the bedroom the woman had turned down the bed and was unlacing Juno's shoes, putting them tidily by a chair where she had laid Juno's clothes. She said, 'Hop in,' pointing to the bed.

Juno climbed into bed. The linen sheets were cold and smooth. In the double bed in the London hotel the sheets had been of cotton and Jonty's and Francis's bodies had radiated fire.

The woman said, 'My name is Ann. What's yours?'

'Juno.'

'Then sleep well, Juno, give those springs a chance.'

Juno said, 'Thank you,' in a strangulated voice. If she could be alone, she could weep if she needed to. She said, 'Thank you very much.'

'Sleep well, then,' the woman said. 'I'll put your light out, the firelight's nice. Come along, Jessie.'

'Oh, can't she stay? Please let her stay.' Juno was almost shouting. 'Please!'

Ann stood in the open door, her hand on the knob, the firelight flickering across her face. 'Very well, if that's what you'd like,' she said gently. Then she was gone.

Juno drew in her breath, thrust her legs down in the icy sheets and laid her head on the pillows to stare up at the firelight dancing on the ceiling. Perhaps tomorrow she would meet Mr Copplestone, explain why she had brought the letter, how she had met his son. If there was an explanation, she would have to think of it tomorrow.

A gust of wind went whump in the chimney; hail pattered on the window-panes. On the *chaise longue* Jessie whimpered, stretched out in her sleep, relaxed.

61

ELEVEN

*R*eaching the porch, Robert Copplestone kicked off his gumboots and pushed the door open, letting it slam behind him. He stood in his socks, grateful to be in from the icy night, grateful to be home.

Hearing him arrive, Ann came from the kitchen. 'You're back.' She took the hat he held in his hand and helped him out of his overcoat, which she shook before hanging it up. 'Still snowing.' She eyed him closely as he pulled off his gloves. 'And you travelled in that suit – 'tis too thin – hot toddy?'

'Please, Ann.'

'You walked,' she accused him, looking at his feet in thin silk socks emerging from black suited trousers. 'Funerals is always chilly, funeral suits should be warm. You should have changed before you travelled. Where are your shoes, then?'

'The taxi couldn't get up the hill, so I borrowed Bert's boots. I left my shoes and case at the farm.'

Ann clicked her tongue. 'In this weather! You don't look fit, look like death—'

'Well, I did, and I'm here.' (And I shan't tell her I was nearly blown over at the moor gate and felt like lying down in the snow and giving up.)

She eyed him anxiously, face drawn with fatigue, usually erect shoulders stooped. She said, 'The fire's lit in the library, go into the warm. I'll bring the toddy.'

'Where's Jessie?' He glanced round the hall.

'She'll come. Go and sit by your fire, you're frozen, don't want you ill. Go on.' Ann pushed him gently.

He walked slowly across the hall to his library, thin-socked on stone slabs, to slump in an armchair, stretch hands towards blazing logs, rest feet on warm rug, lay his head back, close his eyes.

Ann came with hot whisky and water. She had been expecting him for hours; the kettle had been simmering on the hob, whisky and glass ready. 'Drink.' She watched him. He swallowed.

'That's good. Thank you, Ann. Ah, Jessie! Where were you?' He put the glass aside, leaning down to pat and stroke his dog, who was lashing her tail and whimpering with joy. 'Why weren't you at the door? Are you grown deaf, my beauty? I've never known you not be there.'

'Got better things to do.'

'Oh, oh, I *see*! The pups have arrived! Clever girl. How many?' He looked up at Ann.

'Two. Drink the whisky while it's hot.'

'It's scalding. Are they all right? Dogs or bitches?' Obediently he gulped some whisky. 'Just what I needed. Thank you, Ann.'

'One of each.'

'Any clue as to the father?'

'One's brindled and one's black and white.'

'Smooth-haired?'

'Can't tell as yet.'

'Clever girl.' He stroked the dog. 'All right, all right, go back to them now.' The dog was anxious, torn between loyalties, flattening her ears and glancing towards the door. 'She won't want to leave them, will she,' he said to Ann, 'not for long, not for more than a few minutes at first. I'll come to the kitchen in a minute,' he said to the dog, and to Ann, 'When were they born?'

'Yesterday.'

'Ah.'

'And not in the kitchen.'

63

'She didn't have them in the kitchen? Did you move her basket?' He frowned.

'She had them in Mr Evelyn's room . . .'

'?'

'On the *chaise longue.*'

Robert Copplestone looked bewildered.

'She's taken a fancy to the young lady.'

'What young lady?'

'Who brought the letter from Mr Evelyn.'

'Explain.'

'It's on the hall table. I'll get it.' Ann left the room.

Robert drained the rest of his whisky. Ann returned with the envelope, carried so long in Juno's bag. He took the letter, slit the envelope and read aloud, 'Dear Father, Juno Marlowe needs your help. In my present state I can't do much. I suspect you will find her rewarding, so over to you. Lovingly, Evelyn.'

Ann said, 'So that's her surname.'

'Is she here?'

'Yes.'

'Where?' His voice rose.

'I put her in Mr Evelyn's room. It was the only room with the bed made up and fire laid ready.'

'But—'

'She's ill, sir, temperature a hundred and three. I had to do something quickly.'

'I must go and see—' Robert made to rise from his chair.

'Asleep.' Ann pushed him back. 'Been asleep on and off since I put her to bed, she couldn't even finish her soup—'

'But—'

'You can't see her now. Come and have something to eat or we'll have you ill too.'

'The doctor—'

'Couldn't get here in the snow. I telephoned. He said aspirin and hot drinks, keep her warm. As if I didn't know.'

'Ah.'

'Soup?'

'In a minute, Ann. In a minute.' Robert Copplestone

read his son's letter again, quoting aloud, ". . . in my present state I can't do much . . ." Ann, do you think he knew?'

'We all knew, didn't we?'

'Yes. Yes, we did.' Robert sighed. 'But we did not *want* to know, did not want to admit. Oh god, Ann! The doctor in London said he died in his sleep, his heart just stopped. It has been touch and go for years, but when it happens—'

Ann said gently, 'Surprise and shock,' and whispered to herself, 'That cursed gas.'

'His next door neighbour found him. She had the key, used to take shelter with him, make soup, she said – she said, I think she said, he seemed very tired that night, exhausted –'

'Come along, sir, have some hot soup now.'

'Very well.' Robert Copplestone got to his feet.

'Your slippers.' Ann held them out.

Absently Robert fumbled his feet into the slippers. 'Aren't these Evelyn's?' His voice was high with pain.

'Very likely.' Ann waited. Father and son had always interchanged shoes and slippers. 'Come on,' she cajoled.

He made an effort. 'I'll eat in the kitchen where it's warm.' (And where I won't be alone.)

Ann said, 'It's game soup. I gave some to the girl but she couldn't finish it.'

To please her, Robert said, 'But I will finish mine, I am very hungry,' too tired to have an appetite, but Ann was good, kind, had loved, did love Evelyn. He followed her to the kitchen, sat at the table where she laid a place.

He said, 'The funeral was quiet and quick.'

'He would have wanted no fuss.'

'Fuss! What a word!'

She poured soup into a bowl. 'Eat up.' Under pressure she spoke as to a child. 'It's game soup, your favourite, just try—'

He picked up a spoon, tasted the soup. 'It's delicious.' He spooned some more, laid the spoon down. 'He did not

65

want to be a nuisance, he left written instructions with our solicitor, he said the same thing to me some time ago.'

'The same to me, sir, just the once, then no more mention.'

'M–m.'

'Eat it while it's hot.'

'What a bully you are,' he said but he ate the soup.

'And a nice little omelette.' She was breaking eggs into a bowl.

'I couldn't—'

'You could, and when that's inside you, another hot toddy before bed.'

He watched her beat the eggs. 'We could have some sort of service in the village after the war. What do you think?'

'Yes.' She poured the eggs into a pan. 'When—' she said but did not go on. How could she say, 'When we are used to his loss'? She slid the omelette onto a plate. 'Now eat that.'

Between mouthfuls he asked, 'Hens bearing up, are they?', trying to be normal, trying to respond to the woman's courage.

'Everything's all right at the farm. Bert's short-handed, of course, grumbling. Takes the lads being called up as a personal affront, as Mr Evelyn would say.' She watched Evelyn's father eating the omelette. We have to mention his name, she thought, it wouldn't be natural to bottle it all up. Wish he would shed tears. She leaned her bottom against the stove, taking comfort from its warmth. 'And there's been a calf born,' she said.

'Bull calf?'

'Heifer.'

'Good.' He had eaten the omelette. 'Thank you, Ann, I feel a lot better.'

'Hot toddy?'

'If you will keep me company.'

She poured whisky into tumblers, added water from the kettle. We are used to doing without lemons, she thought, as we must get used to doing without Evelyn. Curse this war.

She handed her employer his glass and stood sipping and watching him as he sat nursing the glass between his hands.

Outside the house the wind rose; there was a spatter of rain against the window. Robert Copplestone raised his head. 'It's thawing,' he said, gulped down his drink and stood up. 'I have kept you up late, Ann, you should go to bed.'

'You too, sir.' She rinsed the glasses at the sink. 'You look,' she said, 'done in.'

Robert said, 'Is the door – the door of Evelyn's room open?'

'Ajar so that Jessie can come and go—'

'I'll just peep in—'

'You can see the puppies tomorrow.'

'It's not the puppies I want to see, you silly woman.'

'Thought not, but all you'll see is the top of her head—'

'Let's hope Evelyn was right.'

'How, sir?'

'Rewarding, he said.'

Dryly Ann said, 'He was a good judge.'

'Of blondes.'

They mounted the stair together, walked quietly along the corridor to peer through the open door of what so lately had been Robert's son's room. By the light of the fire it was just possible to discern a head on the pillow. Juno slept, her face turned away from the door. On the *chaise longue* the dog, Jessie, wagged her tail.

Robert whispered, 'This one's dark,' and presently, as he undressed and got into bed, mulled over in his mind his son's suggestion of reward.

TWELVE

Waking in the night, Juno was aware of a change in the weather; wind, bitter and persistent bearer of snow, now gusted with the jollity which presages spring. She got out of bed, felt her way to the window, drew back the curtains and unlatched a shutter.

In later years it might occur to her that, seeing that view for the first time, she saw it without thought of Jonty or Francis and was entranced.

What she saw was a stretch of moor etched starkly by the moonlight above a wooded valley. To the left of the woods lay a pattern of silvery fields round a group of stone buildings. Barns? A farm? A glint of water zigzagged through the fields to a large pond, to reappear wider and swifter on its way through the woods, to a valley, to the sea, perhaps? It was difficult to judge distances. As it cut through the fields she felt a longing to follow.

The curve of the lane up which she had driven in the dark was delineated by high black hedges, but the moor, rising and dipping, hid the gate she had wrestled to hold for the taxi to pass through. In the distance hills rose steeply up, but nearer the house stood an avenue of beeches whose branches bowed to the wind and etched the sky.

Immediately under her window there was a stone terrace, beyond it a garden bounded by walls and over the walls a kitchen garden, walled also. Nose pressed to the glass, Juno tried to remember the name of the house she now found herself in. The address had been written on the envelope she had carried so long in her bag. The letter was addressed to Robert Copplestone. This she remembered, but the name of the house? The place? Village? Town?

The woman who had opened the door had taken the letter, laid it on the oak chest, this she remembered. She remembered, too, rehearsing her speech, 'I brought this letter from your son Evelyn, Mr Copplestone, I—'

What more had she prepared to say? The speech was yet to be made and all she could remember was that the man Evelyn was dead, that she had felt horribly ill when trying to eat soup and that the woman had brought her to this room, put her into bed and that the sheets had been ice cold. Juno yawned, closed the shutter, drew the curtain. Should she try to find her way down the stairs, find the letter if it were still in the hall, find a light, read the address, discover where she was?

Feeling her way, she gripped a bedpost and her knee knocked against something upholstered. She heard a snuffle, a damp nose touched her hand and she remembered the dog who had been there on her arrival. Stroking it, her fingers encountered something else which squeaked and moved. A puppy. The bitch's cold nose edged her hand away, warning her off. Circumnavigating the *chaise longue* she felt her way back to the bed, climbed in, snuggled down, slept.

When next she woke she sensed movement; the house was awake. Steps ran down the stairs, a door slammed; there were distant voices. Water gurgled in pipes. Outside there was the insistent and busy cawing of rooks, a cock crowed in the distance, a cow lowed; there was the sudden clatter of horses' hooves and the crash of a tractor starting up. A man's voice shouted above its din. It was time to get up. It was time to tell Mr Copplestone about the letter. She would feel morally able to make her speech if she could have a bath. She remembered the beautiful bathroom. She would have a bath, get dressed, nerve herself, tell Mr Copplestone about the letter. Be on her way.

* * *

Loud voices in the kitchen could be heard from the yard. Robert Copplestone unsaddled his horse, slipped off its bridle and opened the stable door. The horse clattered in, shuffled through the straw bedding and made for the hayrack. A sturdy Welsh pony poked her nose over from the adjacent box. Robert ran his hand along the horse's back and, feeling it scarcely warm, congratulated himself that to save work he had not had the animal clipped out. He gave the horse an affectionate pat, checked that the water-bucket was full, hung bridle and saddle in the tack-room and, closing the doors, crossed the yard to the house, where a male voice in the kitchen was rising in plaintive crescendo mixed with mockery from deeper accents.

''Tis not as if I'd asked to go.'

'Some has, silly buggers.'

''Tis too much, I say, for one man to be milking eight cows—'

'Hah! 'Tis a chance to see the world, I say.'

'Give over, Bert, we all know you didna want to join up.'

'Reserved occupation, I did think.'

'Thought you was safe, did 'e?'

'You ain't and nor is I—'

'Reserved occupation would 'ave got them cows milked an' no trouble, an' there's the pigs an' the tractor—'

'Tractor needs milking now, does it!'

'You can laugh, young John, but 'tis I be left on my own—'

'Should 'ave been more polite, like, to the landgirl as was tried.'

'She wain't no good, even boss said so, and I say eight cows is too many for one man on his own and you boys galli-vanting off to dress up as soldiers.'

Ann's angry voice broke in, 'It was not gallivanting when Mr Evelyn was gassed in the last lot, and Sir was in it too.'

'We didn't say they wasn't, Ann, but 'twas up to Sir to get us reserved occupation status for this lot, same as Wally at Simpson the Butcher, he's reserved occupation.'

70

'Wally has a gammy leg as well you know,' said Ann tartly. 'Good morning, sir,' she said as she caught sight of Robert.

Robert wiped his feet on the mat, 'Good morning, Ann, and John, Bert. What's up? Some sort of trouble?'

'Come to say goodbye, sir. Dick and I are off tonight.'

'Of course you are. Well, good luck, boys, try and keep out of trouble. We will hope to see you when you come home on leave – and Bert, is something wrong?'

'Morning, sir, no sir. We was just considering the milking—'

'Yes?'

'Eight cows, sir—'

'I can milk.'

Four men and Ann turned to stare at Juno, and Juno, doing a double take, was staring at Robert. So he wasn't dead. He hadn't died. He was here; something funny going on. Alive? Had he been asleep when she – no, this one was older, stronger, frighteningly like. She drew in her breath, she must try again. 'I'm sorry, I could not help hearing. I'd like to help. I can milk a cow.' She looked at the ring of faces.

'You must be Juno Marlowe.' Robert took her hand. 'I hope you feel better.' He was smiling.

'Yes, absolutely. Thank you.'

'Have you had breakfast?'

'No, but please, I—'

'Then we will have it together. There should be a fire in the library. I often eat there. That all right, Ann?'

Grinning, Ann said, 'Right away.' From the yard where Bert and John had removed themselves there was a burst of raucous laughter. Ann grinned. 'That put paid to them,' she said and was pleased to hear Robert laugh out loud as he led Juno away.

71

THIRTEEN

'*I* will just get the fire going, gee it up a bit.'

Robert felt ridiculously nervous of this vulnerable-looking girl, yet she had made him laugh. He knelt on the hearthrug, rearranging logs in the fireplace. They glowed pink, then red on their bed of ash.

'It's fiendishly cold out on the hill this morning, always is when it begins to thaw, don't you agree?'

'Yes.' Juno watched him. 'I—'

'I like to ride out early, see for myself that all's well.' Carefully he laid fresh logs across those already burning.

Watching him, Juno compared his actions with those of a giant playing spillikins, each log balanced with precision to catch alight and meld with the others.

'Like riding, do you?' Robert balanced the last log. 'Fond of horses?'

'I can ride.' She watched a puff of wood smoke blow down the chimney past Robert's head to be sucked back by the draught.

'Then I come in.' Robert sat back on his heels. 'I eat my breakfast with a quiet conscience, or that's what I hope, before tackling my post and the day's minutiae.'

Kneeling, Robert patted the pockets of his shabby tweed jacket. Where had he put Evelyn's letter? What was it Evelyn had said besides that bit which stuck in his mind about reward? Rewarding? Had Evelyn explained the girl? Must have. God help us, I can't remember! Where did I put it? Getting a letter from him when I have just come from his funeral is so – so what? Unbalancing, ghastly, upsetting, mad.

'I got back late last night,' he said. 'That should do now, don't you think? Are you an expert on log fires?'

'I love—'

'I had rather a longer journey from London than is usual after – well, I won't bother you with that, with why I went. No, no need to go into it now.'

Robert shied away from the object of his journey. How could he tell this girl what he had felt as Evelyn's coffin slid into the furnace? He hardly knew himself what his feelings had been.

'I felt numb,' he said out loud, 'perhaps it's a good thing. Perhaps it's nature's anaesthetic, what do you think?'

'I—'

'Then after, the train journey. Really, the people who run the railways these days are magnificent, don't you agree? The station at Plymouth had been hit yet again, so we all walked along the line in the dark, with the Navy and Royal Marines helping people with their luggage. Everyone so cheerful! If it were not so serious, you'd think they were enjoying it, enjoying the war!' Robert lurched to his feet. He was tall, taller than his son.

So I am somewhere near Plymouth, thought Juno. I remember now, the train stopped and voices shouted 'Plymouth' in the dark and the official at Reading had said, she remembered, 'It's way beyond Plymouth, but you change trains further on.'

Robert was feeling in his pockets, frowning. 'I've mislaid it—' he muttered, 'confound it.' Then, louder, 'The worst bit of course was the last. The hill was snowed up, I had to walk, I borrowed Bert's boots at the farm. Did you get through the moor gate when you came? I hope you did not have to walk?'

'I held it against the wind for the taxi to drive through.'

'Good for you. Ah, here comes Ann with our much-needed breakfast, let me help.' Robert surged towards the door, through which Ann was manoeuvring a large tray. 'Let me take the tray. Ann.'

'You'll spill things. Just clear a space on the table, you've cluttered it up again.' Ann bumped the door shut with her bottom and advanced into the room. 'Coffee, toast and scrambled eggs,' she said. 'Hurry up, this weighs a ton.'

Robert sprang to sweep a heap of letters and papers aside. 'It's all unnecessary forms from the Min of Ag. Think of the waste of paper, time and trees!'

'Think of your breakfast while it's hot.' Ann unloaded the tray, placing knives, forks, spoons, coffee-pots and plates of scrambled egg in neat precision. 'Come on now,' she ordered, 'eat!'

Robert drew a chair for Juno and another for himself. 'Please sit here.'

Juno sat.

'Ann, I've mislaid that letter. Have you seen it?'

'You were wearing your London suit.'

'Ah! Of course I was—'

'And Bert's taken back his boots, made a fuss because you got snow in them—'

'It was deep, tell him I'm sorry.'

'Not to worry, he has others which are dry. There's more coffee. Should you want it, shout.' Ann left the room.

Robert poured coffee and handed a cup to Juno. 'Bert is Ann's husband, she bullies us both.'

'Oh.'

'Bert lives at the farm. Ann lives here in the house.' Robert shot Juno a glance. 'They prefer it that way.'

Juno gulped coffee and said, 'Delicious.'

Robert began eating his scrambled eggs. Juno followed suit, discovering as she did so that she was ragingly hungry.

There was silence except for the click of knife or fork on their plates and the gurgle of coffee as Robert replenished their cups.

I have talked too much, chattered from nerves like a young man. He glanced surreptitiously at Juno. She did not look, he thought, at all like the usual run of Evelyn's

74

girls. Come to think of it, there had never yet been a dark-haired girl. He looked away, not wanting to pry yet longing to, afraid she might catch him at it, make him feel a fool.

A log shifted with a crisp whisper; a flame flared and lit Juno's face. 'I hope you were warm enough in . . .' He hesitated, then said, 'in your room.'

'Thank you, it was wonderful.'

'And Jessie has moved in with you?'

'I was so glad to find her there, and the puppies.'

'Animals have good sense. Of course, apart from the kitchen, hall and this room, the house is dreadfully cold, but you had a fire?'

'It was lovely.' It would be easier to talk to this man if he did not look so like his son. 'I woke in the night and looked out at – at the silence.'

'And you saw? Heard?'

'The stream. I wanted to follow it, discover where it goes—'

'To the sea, it winds to the sea.'

'How wonderful.'

What had Evelyn told her? Not much, it seemed. What had he said in the letter? Where was it? There would be an explanation in spite of his habitual brevity. Why can I not remember? I am talking too much. I can't stop. But perhaps it will draw her out?

'We had a bunch of evacuees at the start of the war, but they hardly stayed five minutes. The silence terrified them; they panicked and left almost as fast as they had come. The noise of bombs, it seems, was preferable . . .'

Juno smiled.

'Then we had the landgirl, but that did not work, which reminds me.' Robert began to laugh. 'What inspired you to suggest you can milk a cow?'

'Because I can.'

The Johnsons and Murrays shared a farm run by a manager; Murray and Johnson land adjoined. The boundary between Johnsons's and Murrays's was a turgid, murky stream which harboured coot and moorhen, eels, perch and roach, preyed upon by a heron, who, when surprised, would leap into the air to fly off with slow flaps trailing excessive legs.

Jonty and Francis were not interested in the stream or the heron; when they wanted to fish they stayed with friends in the Test Valley, preying on trout and salmon, and Juno, awaiting their return, wandered solitary about the fields.

It was on one such occasion that the farm manager had shown her 'the new contraption' his employers were 'wasting their money on'. Juno remembered his voice; he came from the North, despising the soft Home Counties. The 'new contraption' was a moveable milking parlour, a thing made of steel struts and bars, propped on wheels.

'Idea is to move it from field to field, save the cows walking back to the milking shed; they don't like it.'

'Why not?' she had asked, egging him on.

Cows enjoyed routine, she was told. It was good for them to walk in and out twice a day from their pasture. The 'new contraption' was draughty and cold out there in the open. Not that he, the manager, objected, the manager assured her as he made clear he did; it was 'chilly too for them as did the milking, it would have shown more sense to give the workers a rise.'

On impulse she asked whether he would let her learn to milk and the manager, perhaps sorry for her solitude, more probably to irritate his employers – she had not known at the time that he was under notice – had deputed one of the men to show her.

When Jonty and Francis returned from their piscatorial trip she had boasted of her new powers and they, disbelieving and teasing, had insisted on immediate proof, hurrying her to the farm at milking-time.

It was dusk, she remembered, the cows in their shed lined up, each chained to the manger chewing the cud, waiting to be milked. Proudly she had picked up a stool, taken a pail and begun milking the first cow. But Jonty or Francis cried, 'That's a very quiet cow, she doesn't count,

76

try another, try this one.' And even when she was again successful they went on teasing, pretending not to be satisfied, 'You will never manage to milk the new beast father bought last week, she's there in that separate box, see if you can milk that one.'

In the half-dark she had taken the pail and stool into the box, run her hand along the animal's flank, settled herself on her stool, reached for its udder.

Arriving at that moment, the farm manager interrupted Francis's and Jonty's laughter. Reaching into the box he had yanked her out to fall on the cobbles, with pail and stool clattering about. What he shouted at Francis and Jonty was unrepeatable, so violent was his anger, 'Bloody fucking young fools, she might have been killed,' was the mildest sentence.

She had not waited for the diatribe to end but taken to her heels, and running across the field had leapt the murky brook and, leaping, misjudged the distance, landing in mud up to her knees. She remembered that, and what a mess the mud made of her skirt. But what she remembered with perfect clarity was the incredible softness, the silky satiny feel of the bull's testicles when, feeling for a teat, she had held them in her hands.

Watching Juno, Robert Copplestone thought, She's far away, gone miles. My God, she looks sad. She is numb, as numb as I am. Then, seeing tears well suddenly up and stream unchecked down her cheeks onto her jersey, he thought, Oh good, that's better, let her weep, wish I could, and reached into his breast pocket for a handkerchief.

But she was already finding her own tucked up a sleeve, taking a deep breath, blowing her nose, wiping her eyes, saying, 'Sorry, I was remembering something. Should we not get on with the milking? Cows hate being kept waiting.' Her voice was almost steady.

Robert said, 'Yes, yes, of course. If you are ready, I will take you down to the farm, show you the way. You had

77

better borrow a pair of Ann's boots, they will probably fit,' and, 'You sure you have had enough breakfast?' and, 'Although it is thawing, the snow is still lying in places,' and, 'My cows are Jerseys, I hope you like them,' and, 'We'd better ask Ann to lend you an overall.'

A little later, as they walked down to the farm, Juno's feet shifting uncomfortably in Ann's too large boots, he said, 'I am talking too much,' and was grateful when she said, 'No.' But all the same he kept silent for several minutes, only asking, as they reached the farm and he opened the farmyard gate, 'How old were you when you learned to milk?'

Juno said, 'About ten. Yes, ten.' Jonty and Francis had been seventeen? Their last year at school? About that. And the moveable milking parlour – she had not thought of it for years – so hated by the farm manager, had stood rusting and despised, unused in the corner of a field. Remembering this Juno giggled, and Robert was reminded of the word 'rewarding' in Evelyn's letter.

Suddenly Juno asked, 'What is the name of this place?'

'Copplestone.' He was puzzled by her question.

'Of course. Copplestone. Like you, Copplestone. Oh, good.' She laughed again. 'I brought you a letter, did you get it all right?'

'Yes. But I can't find it, I forget where I put it. Can you tell me what Evelyn said?'

'No! He wrote something and stuck up the envelope. Is it important? I mean, all I know is that he told me to give it to you.' Juno frowned. 'If he had meant me to post it, he would have stuck on a stamp, wouldn't he?' she queried anxiously. 'I—'

'You'm going to keep those cows waiting till Michaelmas?' Bert shouted from the byre. 'Or not?' His tone was disagreeable.

'Not. We're coming,' Robert yelled back. 'On our way. Bother him.'

'May I go in alone?' Juno's voice was gentle.

78

Robert watched her back as she clumped across the farmyard. One or two of Evelyn's blondes had been dizzy; there had been one who was dumb. This dark girl was neither. He walked thoughtfully back up the hill to the house. As he came within earshot, Ann was shouting, 'Telephone.' He forgot what he had intended to do and hastened to answer it.

Juno told herself there was no need to be afraid, she had offered to help and her offer had been accepted, but she felt uncertain as she walked towards the cowshed. Bert watched her approach, making her sharply aware that she was treading on his territory.

Walking towards the man, she wished she had not parted so abruptly from Robert, long-legged and comforting with a nice rumbling voice; a person she might, unlike her mother, be able to talk to without fear of verbal reprisal. But now here was Bert. He was short and broad and bow-legged. He wore corduroy trousers and heavy boots; his collarless shirt was fastened at the neck by a stud. Above the stud a large adam's apple worked up and down his weathered throat and his half-open mouth showed yellow teeth.

My mother, Juno thought, would make him an appointment with the dentist, she being a stickler for teeth. A stickler for health in general, if it came to that, taking immense care of all that was physical but leaving the spirit to fend for itself. Perhaps if she had not cared so well for my hair and teeth, Juno found herself thinking, I might have been able to confide?

This improbable idea made Juno smile. Bert did not smile in return but continued to watch her, small eyes of blueish grey peering from under a ridge of eyebrow.

Juno said, 'So here I am, tell me what to do. I had better hang this up,' she added, taking off her coat. 'Ann has very kindly lent me an overall.'

Bert did not answer but took a pail from its hook and

79

handed it to her. Unlike his teeth, the pail gleamed spotless; the cowshed too was swept and clean, smelling sweetly of warm cows and hay. Bert said, 'Start there with that one,' pointing. 'Stool's hanging there.'

Juno put on Ann's overall, took the stool, set it beside the cow Bert indicated, sat, leaned her forehead against the beast's flank and began to milk.

FOURTEEN

*T*he sound of milk squirting into the pail was rhythmic. Juno leaned her forehead against the cow's flank and worked in time with her chewing the cud. The warm smell of cow, the rustle of hay tweaked from the rack, the shifting of hooves on concrete, engendered peace.

Once, at the Johnsons's, when learning to milk, she had tried to play a tune, varying the sound, angling the cow's teats, directing the flow to hit the sides of the pail at different angles. The cowman had asked what the hell she thought she was doing, told her to stop mucking about, not to upset the cow.

Across the shed with his back to her Bert was milking, too. From time to time he growled at the cow he was milking, 'Stand still, can't 'ee?', whether she moved or not, and scraped his stool roughly along the concrete floor, 'Ar-r-r.'

When the cow's udder was empty, Juno stood, eased her back, stroked the animal's throat, patted her flank and carried the pail to the dairy to pour its contents into the receptacle Bert indicated with a jerk of his head. Then she went to the cow next in line and repeated the process until between them they had milked seven cows. The eighth, housed with her calf in a separate stall, rolled her eyes when Juno peered over the partition and, lowering her head, displayed her horns, protecting the calf lying in the straw. Juno blew gently, puffing her breath towards the cow, who raised her head and stared. Sensing Bert

81

behind her Juno, without turning round, asked, 'What time do you milk evenings?'

'You coming again, then?'

'Yes.'

'Four-thirty, then.'

'Shall I sweep the stalls?'

'You leave 'un be.'

'All right.'

'Can 'ee make butter?'

'I can learn.'

'Will 'ee be staying, then?'

'I don't know.'

'Huh!'

'See you at four-thirty, then.' Juno hung her overall on a hook. She was resolved not to smile, would not say that she would love to stay or how much she had enjoyed herself.

'Can 'ee carry the house milk up to Ann?'

'I might just manage.'

Bert handed her a covered can. 'Don't spill 'ur.' There was no word of thanks.

Juno took the can and, leaving the farmyard, headed up the hill. As she walked she flexed the muscles of her free hand to ease the ache of unaccustomed use and, doing so, remembered how much her hands had hurt when she learned to milk as a child. Now she enjoyed the slight stiffness. As she walked she looked up to the house, noting how neatly it tucked into the moor and the hill behind, how protectively the walled gardens swept round the building and how, skirting the gardens, tumbling from point to point of rock until reaching the fields, the stream, increasing in size towards the farm, swelled out into the pond then carried on across several fields to disappear into the woods. It would be weeks later that she would discover that, turning on itself like a buttonhook, it circled the hill behind the house to charge down a narrow valley and fan out across a sandy cove into the sea.

As she came up to the house there was a commotion.

Robert Copplestone was hurrying across the yard. He had changed into a dark suit and was humping himself into an overcoat, one arm sleeved, the other groping. Ann bustled behind, carrying a bowler hat and a small case. Garage doors stood open, a car ready.

'How did it go?' Catching sight of her, Robert looked anxious but amused. 'The milking?'

'Fine.'

'Bert has a heart under his – er – his – er –'

'Masculine, superior, proprietorial manner.'

'Oh God! Was he rude?'

'Just grumpy, guarded.'

'Was that all? You must have made a hit.' Robert exploded with laughter. 'He was absolutely terrible to that poor landgirl I tried, reduced her to tears. Here, let me take that can. Oh. He trusted you with that? That's a great compliment, his own special can.'

'Are you catching that train or not?' Ann reached behind her employer to ease his arm into the coat sleeve. 'Thought you was in a hurry.'

'I am.'

'And don't forget your hat.' Ann handed him the bowler.

'Oh, God!' Robert exclaimed. 'All this respectability! Do you think for one second the dead mind?'

'You'll miss the train, you'll miss the funeral.' Ann pushed him towards the car.

Juno said, 'The undertakers mind.'

'Oh! Bright girl. Yes, of course.' Robert hurried towards the car, got in, pressed the starter, slammed the door shut, caught his coat in it, opened it, slammed it again. 'Be here when I get back,' he shouted as the engine started. 'Don't go, don't disappear. Promise?' He leaned out.

Juno shouted, 'I said I'd help with the afternoon milking.'

'But you will be here when I get back?'

Doubled up with laughter, Juno shouted, 'Yes.' Then, as the car sped down the hill, 'What's going on?'

'A friend's daughter has been killed in an air raid. Her father rang up, asked him to come to her funeral.'

Juno looked at Ann, 'Not the Café de Paris?'

'How did you guess?'

'People were talking about it in the train. Oh, how horrible.'

Ann said, 'Yes, it is. His son's funeral yesterday and now this, it's all too much. She was a nice girl, and pretty—'

Juno thought, one of the girls in the basement? One of the girls so eager to go dancing? The girl in evening dress drinking wine? Was that the one? She had seemed so grown up, so alive. What should I say? But Ann was talking, 'Here, give me that can. Come in out of the cold, you shouldn't be standing about. You are only just out of bed.' And, as she bustled Juno indoors, she said, 'I bet the old devil never thanked you.'

Juno said, 'But he did, he trusted me with the can,' and the opportunity to say something about the girl was missed. What in any case could she have said? She had not spoken to her and hardly at all to Evelyn.

Ann was still talking. 'Are you really going on with the milking? Helping Bert?'

'Yes, if it's of help, I'd like to, I enjoy it, he takes my mind off things.'

'Does he indeed? Here we have a new role for Bert.' Ann spoke dryly.

Diffidently Juno said, 'Mr Copplestone said that Bert is your husband.' She had no wish to be reminded of the things Bert and the cows' company had made her forget.

'Oh, did he!' Ann sniffed as she led the way to the kitchen and sniffed again as she filled a kettle and set it to boil. 'Ah well,' she said, 'in a manner of speaking, he's right.'

Juno sneezed and sneezed again, blew her nose and heard Ann say, 'We went through the formalities, but I didn't take to what goes with them. I left Bert on the farm and came back to the house. Bert and I cleave in different ways. Cleave is one of the words in the marriage ceremony,

84

"cleave unto", that's what it says, but if you add a letter you get "cleaver", a thing which splits. That's what happened to us, we split.'

Juno said, 'Oh,' assimilating this information.

Ann said, 'He will be eating out of your hand if you go back and go on helping, he will be cleaving to you.' She sounded amused.

Not particularly enjoying the prospect, Juno said nothing.

Ann said, 'You've still got a nasty cold. I wonder where you caught it?'

Juno said, 'I've no idea,' but she knew quite well where she had caught it, in Evelyn Copplestone's kitchen, from the man who had said, 'I've got the most God-awful cold.' Was he too among those killed in the Café de Paris? Not wanting to think of it, she said, 'Is Mr Copplestone married? Is there a Mrs Copplestone?'

'Didn't Evelyn tell you? No,' Ann answered herself, 'he wouldn't. His mother died when he was tiny, he never knew her.' She was spooning tea into the pot. 'They were so young,' she said. 'Like it strong?'

'Yes, please. Who were so young?'

Ann reached for cups hanging on the dresser. 'Evelyn's parents. It's history now. It caused surprise at the time, there are still people who talk of shotguns, but it wasn't like that.'

Juno remained mute. Ann poured tea. 'Sit down, you must be tired.' Juno sat, waited. Ann passed her her cup. Juno sipped. Ann said, 'In that Shakespeare play they were even younger.'

Juno said, 'Twelve?'

'That so? I'd forgotten. Been told, never read it. These two were seventeen. Of course in those days, in nineteen hundred, girls who got pregnant married, unless the fellow deserted them. Not many wanted to stand by, but he did, gladly.'

'Mr Copplestone?'

'Yes. Both of them seventeen. How old are you?'

85

'Seventeen.'

Ann said, 'More tea? Do your cold good. No need to go back and milk if you are feeling rough.'

'But I am going back.'

Ann refilled her own cup and drank, glancing sidelong at Juno, sizing her up.

Juno said, 'What did their families think?'

'Said they were too young, of course, but they were glad to see them happy. I don't remember any great fuss.'

'Perhaps Evelyn's mother was a suitable girl.'

Ann grinned. 'I've heard it said the marriage was what both families wanted, though not so soon. She was to have had a season, and he was to go to university.'

'So on the whole they were pleased?' (How unlike the Johnsons and Murrays.) 'I suppose she was rich?'

'No, no, no. Money had no bearing.'

'Oh.'

'No bearing at all.' Ann sounded censorious. 'Her family were Fabians, whatever that means, high-minded, some-thing to do with not being in a hurry, but the young ones were.' Ann put her cup down. 'More tea?'

'No, thank you.' Juno watched the older woman. 'How old were you when you came here?'

'Sixteen. My father was gamekeeper to her, to Evelyn's mother's father. I started in the kitchen.'

'Then Mr Copplestone can't be more than eighteen years older than Evelyn—'

'Good with figures! Less. He boasts the child was conceived on his seventeenth birthday.'

Juno visualized Robert Copplestone at seventeen, comparing him with Francis and Jonty at the same age, noisy, high-spirited, godlike figures to a child of ten. In a similar situation would the Johnsons and Murrays have been 'high-minded' and 'pleased'? She thought not. She could see the scenario, could see her mother standing with the Johnsons and Murrays, could see Aunt Violet and her lodgers, could see Jack Sonntag. There would be no listening to her father, tainted by prison, no advice sought

86

from disreputable Lord Russell, no raised voices or light remarks, but a stiffening of lips, a closing of ranks, a calm and sensible solution to an awkward aberration, a ripple in otherwise well-ordered lives. She said, 'Gosh, he was lucky.'

Ann got up and carried her cup to the sink. 'Sometimes you'd think he never grew up, but that's men.'

'Were they happy?'

'They certainly were. A joyful pair.'

Juno murmured, 'And then she died.'

'Yes.' Ann dried her cup and saucer and, abruptly changing tone, asked, 'Have you brought your ration book? If you're staying, I shall need it.'

Startled, Juno said, 'Yes, it's in my bag.'

'And clothes coupons? You don't seem to have much in the way of clothes. Those boots of mine are too big for you—'

With her heart sinking into metaphorical footware, Juno said, 'But perhaps I should move on – I –'

The older woman, standing with her back to Juno, said matter-of-factly, 'You promised him you'd stay and help,' and then, as Jessie came pattering into the room, 'and for starters you can mix the dog's dinner. We can't keep that one waiting, she has a family to feed.'

FIFTEEN

*D*riving slowly up the hill so as not to overtax her old Morris, Priscilla Villiers noted a female figure crossing Robert Copplestone's farmyard. 'Who's that?' she called over her shoulder to a young man on the back seat. 'You never told me Robert had got himself another landgirl.'

The young man, whose name was Anthony Smith, said, 'I didn't know he had,' his tone indicating that neither did he care.

'I bet she's another of Evelyn's girls,' said Priscilla Villiers, craning her neck to catch a last glimpse into the yard. 'What an amazing coat, she looks like a Cossack. I wouldn't call that suitable for a farm.'

'Looks elegant.' Anthony also noted the coat. 'Did Evelyn have a lot of girls? Why didn't he marry?'

'He did not think it would be fair, his health being what it was, and now he's dead he is proved right.'

'But while alive there was a brisk turnover?'

'Not as brisk as all that, but there were girls – of course there were.'

'And his father, Robert, why didn't he marry again? I know he was widowed at eighteen or something, but you'd think he'd have another bash. Why didn't you marry him?' Priscilla laughed. 'Did you want to? Did you ask him?' Anthony persisted. 'He must have been jolly attractive.'

'Still is,' said Priscilla. 'In my day girls waited to be asked, and anyway I married John and I do not think it would have worked with Robert.'

'So you *did* want to marry him,' Anthony persisted. 'Why wouldn't it have worked?'

'I have always supposed that at the time Robert found me too bossy.' Priscilla crunched the gears as the hill grew steeper.

'As you still are,' – Anthony was jerked backwards as the car accelerated – 'Mrs Villiers.'

'You are not still resenting sitting in the back?' Aware of her passenger's mood, Priscilla noted with amusement that he did not call her Priss as he occasionally had during the past two weeks. 'You know,' she said as she changed gear again, 'that if you sat in the front with me Mosley would howl all the way and slobber down the back of your neck. Wouldn't you, my lovely boy?' She reached to stroke the head of a cross-bred dog perched on the seat beside her. The young man on the back seat grunted. 'On the way home I shall freewheel downhill to save petrol, and Mosley can run behind. Uphill he might strain his dear heart.'

'Really?' Anthony's tone indicated that this might not be a bad thing. But because they were nearly at their destination and he had no wish to be on bad terms, he asked, 'Why did you call him Mosley?'

'That was my late husband's joke; because he is black and because he has always been game when he met a bitch.'

'Ah.'

'But he is not the father of Robert's Jessie's puppies. I gather from Ann that they were born on the sofa in the spare room. Some people spoil their dogs.'

'Some people do.'

'Now then, Anthony, do not mock.'

'Certainly not, Mrs Villiers.'

'I bet that was one of Evelyn's girls.' Priscilla craned her neck to get a last look downhill. 'What an extraordinary get-up, she looked like a Cossack. I wouldn't call that suitable.'

'. . . to work on a farm. You are repeating yourself, Priss.'

'You mean I am growing old.'

'No, no, no.' Anthony was pained to have hurt. 'I do not.' But he had thought her old; in his twenties, fifty was a lifetime ahead.

Priscilla drove the last stretch of road in silence, and brought the car to a stop outside the house, saying, 'Well, here we are. I'll just turn the car round so that when we leave a push will start us downhill.'

'And that way you will save at least a teaspoonful of precious petrol,' murmured Anthony.

'Now you are making fun of me.'

'And freewheeling is illegal, Priss.'

'What a stickler you are.' Priscilla turned the car to face downhill. 'A stickler and a gossip, but, Anthony, I really am hugely grateful for your work in the garden. I can't thank you enough.'

'But I have enjoyed it.' Anthony got out of the car. 'Loved it, fresh air, country, kind company. Have you put the brakes on?'

'Yes, Anthony, I have.'

'Just checking.' Anthony walked ahead to push open the front door and shout, 'Ann?'

Hurrying across the hall, Ann called out, 'Sorry, Mrs Villiers, but you'd better not bring your dog in. Jessie might go for him, she's got her pups.'

'I know, Ann.' Priscilla closed her car door. 'Poor fellow, wait, I shan't be long,' she addressed the dog. To Anthony she said, 'Could you bring in the vegetables?'

Anthony said, 'Righty-ho.'

'I've brought you some broccoli, Ann.' Priscilla's voice rang loud in the hall. 'And some artichokes. Thought you might like them for soup.'

'Very windy things, but thank you.' Ann took the basket of vegetables from Anthony. 'You staying the night?' she asked.

'Can't,' said Anthony. 'I have to catch the night train. I'm due at the Ministry of Fear in the morning, cutting things fine as it is. My leave's over, the war goes on.'

'But you have time for some tea?'

'Just, and I've left some clutter. I'll go and collect it.' Anthony leapt up the stairs two at a time.

'You don't mind the kitchen, do you?' Ann led the way. 'It's the only warm room. We are all frightened, aren't we?'

'Ann, who is that girl I saw as we came up the hill? Has Robert got another landgirl? She was wearing the most unsuitable clothes, looked like fancy dress.'

'Friend of Evelyn's, arrived with a letter.'

'Oooh! What's her name? Would I know her?'

'Juno Marlowe.'

'Really? Never heard of her. No, wait a minute, wasn't there a girl called Marlowe at school with me?'

'I was not at Cheltenham Ladies' College.' Ann filled the kettle at the sink, her back to Priscilla.

'I remember now. Violet Marlowe, a very bossy type, good at games. That's the one.'

'She's helping Bert. She can milk.'

'What a godsend.'

'Hope so. Arrived in the snowstorm with flu, but she's all right now, a bit on the quiet side.'

'I can't stand noisy girls,' said Priscilla. 'It's awful to say, but that poor girl who was killed in the raid was noisy, the one whose funeral Robert has rushed off to. She brayed when she laughed.'

'Tsk.' Ann rattled the kettle onto the hotplate. 'Did Anthony do a good job?'

'Wonderful. He has got the garden in better trim than I've seen it since the war. Pity he can't stay longer. He is good company and an amusing gossip. He is lucky not to have passed his medical; I can't see much wrong with him, though he says he has a "chest".' Priscilla paused, then, lowering her voice, said, 'Do you think he is—'

Ann said, 'What?' and poured boiling water into the teapot.

Priscilla said, 'You know what I mean, Ann. Does he like boys?' She lowered her voice to a whisper. 'Is he queer?'

Ann said, 'All I'm concerned with is the work he's done in the garden. You don't take sugar, do you?'

91

'Not since the war.' Priscilla took the cup Ann proffered. 'Thanks, Ann.'

Pouring a cup for herself, Ann remembered that, before setting off to help Priscilla with her garden, Anthony had said, 'If I can come again I will bring a friend and we will get twice as much done. I know he would love it,' but she measured a meagre half-spoonful of sugar into her cup and kept her counsel.

'I don't suppose you have any eggs you can spare, Ann? My hens are all broody.' Priscilla cast her eye over a bowl on the dresser where reposed some dozen eggs. 'I will pay you, of course.'

Ann said, 'Sorry, Mrs Villiers, I haven't. Six of those eggs I am giving to Anthony to take to London, the rest we need ourselves.'

Priscilla said, 'It's all right, I only asked. I thought perhaps in exchange for the artichokes—'

Ann said, 'Artichokes! We have lots. Once you have artichokes in a garden you have them for ever. I don't want to sound ungrateful, Mrs Villiers, but I am going to ask John to try and get rid of them.' She wished Anthony would hurry up; she had had enough of Priscilla. She began to wrap some of the eggs in newspaper and put them in a box.

Priscilla said, 'John?' And again, 'John?'

Ann said, 'He has got himself exempted, he is the only son of a widowed mother.'

'So Robert is getting his gardener back! Some people have all the luck! Oh, Ann, I did not mean it like that! Oh, Ann—' Remembering Evelyn, Priscilla's eyes moistened. 'How could I be so tactless?'

With her back to Priscilla Ann did not reply, but she wrapped the last egg with vicious precision and fitted the lid onto the egg-box, giving it an unfriendly pat.

'Was this girl who can milk a particular friend of Evelyn's?' Priscilla enquired. 'Or just someone like Anthony, sent to help his father? Where did Evelyn find these useful people?'

Ann said, 'I have not asked.'

Priscilla said, 'I take it she was a girlfriend. When will she finish milking? I long to meet her. Is she very pretty?'

'Doesn't Anthony have to catch his train?' Ann wound string around the box of eggs.

'Yes, of course he does. Well, another time. I hope she stays; that other girl was gone in a flash.'

'Joined the Wrens.'

'Was that what happened? Wasn't she, too, one of Evelyn's discoveries?'

'Came through the Ministry.'

'Well, I hope this one suits Robert. How does she get on with Bert?'

'He likes her.' Ann was conscious of exaggeration.

'My word, she must be quite something. Goodness! Isn't Robert lucky! Oh, God! There I go again.'

'Ready?' Anthony came into the kitchen. 'I don't want to miss my—'

'I know, your train. I'm coming. What an old woman you are, we've plenty of time.' Priscilla put down her cup. 'Got everything?'

'Yes.' Anthony gulped the tea Ann handed him. 'Oh, bliss! Eggs!' He kissed her. 'Could you give us a push, Ann? Mrs Villiers makes me sit in the back and I can't leap from the back seat onto the road to open the moor gate without risking Mosley biting the seat of my trousers. Will you say goodbye and thank you to Mr Copplestone? Tell him I'll write.'

The two women watched Anthony swing his bag onto the back seat and get in. Priscilla got into the driving seat, released the brake and shouted, 'All right, Ann, push!'

Ann pushed, the car began to roll and, as it gathered speed, Mosley barked to be let out. Priscilla slowed the car and opened the car door.

Taking a short cut up the hill from the farm, Juno watched the Morris freewheel down to the moor road with the dog galloping behind. At the moor gate the car stopped, a young man leapt out, let the car through, shut the gate and leapt back in, leaving the dog to follow as the car continued downhill in ghostly silence. Juno resumed her climb.

At the back door she kicked off Ann's boots and removed a pair of extra socks she had taken to wearing to keep the boots on. Ann called, 'You have just missed Mrs Villiers and Anthony.'

'Oh?'

'Anthony spent part of his holiday working in her garden. He was sent by Evelyn to get ours in order, then went on to do hers. She's a widow and has trouble getting help, an old friend of Mr Robert's.'

'Why do you sometimes call him Mr Robert and at others Mr Copplestone? And sometimes sir?'

'Sometimes I forget he is grown-up.'

'Grown-up?'

'He was only a boy when I first came here, and was plain Robert to us all.'

'Oh.'

'And Mrs Villiers was a girl. She seemed to think she knew your family but couldn't quite place you.'

'I don't want to be placed.'

'No. Well. She's a gossip. Wanted to know whether you were a girlfriend of Evelyn's, she's that sort.'

'Nosey?'

'A bit. She was a bit miffed when I told her John is coming back.' Ann grinned.

'Who is John?'

'Didn't Evelyn tell you anything?'

'Not much.' Juno shrank.

'John is our gardener; he was called up but is now exempt. He will be pleased that Anthony has been here. Pity you didn't meet Anthony, you would like him, but he may come again. He works in the same Ministry as Evelyn – as Evelyn did, I should say. Oh my! It's so hard to realize he is dead and won't come walking in—'

Juno thought, and neither will Francis or Jonty come walking in, but she said, 'I'll mix Jessie's dinner, shall I?'

*   *   *

94

Priscilla Villiers allowed her car to slow almost to a stop, pushed the gear lever and restarted the engine. 'I hope he hasn't strained his heart.' She peered into the driving mirror.

'Taking his time, stopped for a pee, seems a trifle puffed.' Anthony craned back. 'I don't want to miss my train.'

'You won't, there is plenty of time. Here he comes. Get in, old boy.' Priscilla opened the car door, Mosley clambered in, Priscilla slammed it shut and drove on. 'That girl was not dressed like a landgirl,' she said. 'The other one wore breeches and a green jersey. Bert couldn't stand her.'

Anthony said, 'Ann does not seem averse.'

Priscilla said, 'She doesn't, does she? And for Robert's sake one can only hope it works out.'

Anthony, already dreading his return to the air raids and being back in his office, said, 'Yes.'

Priscilla said, 'If she's one of the Marlowes I think she is, it's quite a good family, but there is no money.'

Anthony said, 'Ah!'

'I seem to remember there was something funny about the father. It will come back to me presently.'

Anthony said, 'I bet it will. You have the memory of an elephant if it's anything to do with family trees.'

Priscilla said, 'I shall take that as a compliment. Whatever one thought of Evelyn he had good taste and was kind.'

Anthony pondered, 'In what respect do you mean?'

'Sending the girl to work for Robert. He was always very kind, even if the "turnover", as you call it, was rapid. They all remained on good terms. There was even . . .' Priscilla paused.

'Even what?' It was maddening when Priscilla remembered discretion. 'Even what?' Anthony niggled.

'I don't suppose it matters now. I was going to say, even one occasion when he went to Munich – prior to Hitler – just to keep the woman company when it was nothing to do with him or her husband, of course.'

95

'Munich? You've lost me. Am I being obtuse?'

Priscilla said, 'That clinic, you must have heard about it.'

Anthony said, 'No.' Guessing, he asked, 'Oh, for abortions?'

Priscilla said, 'Yes.'

Anthony said, 'That was big of him.' He gave thanks that he was not likely to have such an embarrassment.

Priscilla said, 'At the time I suspected Evelyn even paid the bill, her husband was badly off.'

'But of good family,' Anthony teased.

Hurt, Priscilla exclaimed, 'Do I sound as awful as that?'

Anthony assured her that he was only joking, while he memorized the conversation to regale to Hugh. It would gladden their day in the office. 'When next I come,' he said, 'I will try and bring a friend, we will get more done. He is called Hugh Turner.'

Priscilla said, 'What a very good idea.'

And Anthony said, 'His family is "quite good", too, and they are rich.'

Then they both laughed and presently Priscilla said, 'Here is the station, you need not have fussed. We are in good time for your train. Any friend of yours, my dear, will be welcome.'

Settling back in his seat after waving goodbye, Anthony exhaled. What an old gossip, he thought, what an old snob, relishing his late hostess.

96

SIXTEEN

*S*tanding bareheaded in the drizzling rain, Robert Copplestone observed his old friends watching their only daughter being lowered into her grave. Their faces were bleak. The girl's brothers stood on either side of their parents, both in RAF uniform, both distressed and uneasy. They probably felt guilty, Robert surmised; it was not for girls to get killed in a war, that was a male prerogative. 'Not any more,' Robert muttered as he put on his hat and turned to go. The service was over; if he said goodbye now he could just catch the last train.

'I say, just a minute, could you help us?' The man was a stranger.

Courteously Robert said, 'Of course, if I can.'

'We motored over, there was no other way to get here, but we got lost, kept taking the wrong road, the wrong turning. No signposts, you see.'

Popping up beside him, the man's woman companion repeated as though explaining to an imbecile, 'No signposts. It's the war. We got lost. Such a worry, we have to be careful of our petrol ration.'

'Don't we all,' said the man. 'Do you know this part of the world?'

Robert said, 'Where are you trying to get to?', cutting them short, mindful of the train timetable.

They told him.

Pointing, Robert said, 'Go down that road, turn right at the first crossroads, turn left, then second right and you are on the main road. Go straight ahead.'

Brightly they said, 'Crossroads, right, then left, then —
Oh, could you write it down? Got a piece of paper? Sorry
to be such a nuisance. Could you draw us a map?' The man
fumbled in his breast pocket for a pencil; the woman
opened and closed her bag in exasperation. 'Can't find any
paper, sorry.'

Quickly Robert drew a map on the back of an envelope.
The rain was turning to sleet. The bereft father was miming
to him to catch up, come to the house for a drink, give
some comfort. 'Don't go yet, don't leave us alone.'

He said, 'There you are, follow that, go that way and
you'll be all right,' and, thrusting the map at them, 'Curse
it, I shall miss that train.' He broke into a run to catch up
with his old friend. 'Who are those boring people?'

'No idea, come into the house. Press, I dare say, ghouls
of some sort. Say something to Lizzie, something to the
boys. We are all numb. You'll know what to say. Oh God,
isn't this awful?'

Robert said, 'Yes. Thank you.' He could not refuse. He
would miss his train; he must swallow his impatience.

His old friend said, 'The vicar tried to help, said we are
all in God's hands—'

Robert said, 'Terrible butter-fingers.' His old friend
yelped with laughter. Hysteria not far off, they went into
the house.

The next day, at last on the station platform waiting for his
train, Robert wondered what comfort he had been able to
give and what he had received? He had drunk too much,
talked about the war, wondered with the bereaved what was
going on over there, across the Channel, in the rest of
Europe? Agreed with Lizzie, the dead girl's mother, that
Lord Haw-Haw was tremendously funny, had quite the
opposite effect of that intended, said that at home Ann was
really annoyed if she missed hearing him, that Lord Haw-
Haw and I.T.M.A. were the highlights of her day.

'Don't cry, Lizzie,' he had said, 'try to remember her
happy. She had a great sense of humour, Evelyn always said

so, a lovely, lovely girl.' What lies one told in one's cups; he had no recollection of Evelyn ever saying anything of the sort.

Then, lying awake in his friends' spare room he had heard Lizzie break down and howl and his old friend, attempting to still her, say, 'But darling, he understands, of course he understands. Hasn't he just lost Evelyn? He knows what we feel.'

And Lizzie's bitter reply, 'It's not the same thing. Evelyn's been dying on and off for years. He could be spared, he wasn't an only daughter.' He hoped that the girl's brothers, stumbling late up the stairs to their beds, did not hear their mother.

Poor fellows, Robert thought next morning waiting for his train, stamping his feet to keep warm, both in the RAF, both likely to get killed; would they want to spend their leaves with such miserable parents or would they go somewhere jollier, more cheerful, where there would be someone they could look forward to meeting? Someone to fall in love with between battles?

Then, as his train came hissing and trumpeting to a stop, Robert remembered that at home, when he reached it, as well as Ann and Jessie and her pups, there would be the strange girl Evelyn had sent him. He at least had something to look forward to.

And now, he thought, climbing into the train and settling into a corner seat, he really must see what, apart from the suggestion that she might be 'rewarding', Evelyn had had to say about the girl. He reached into his coat pocket and, finding it empty, cursed out loud, remembering the tedious couple who had asked the way, made him draw a map on the back of an envelope, the envelope which held Evelyn's letter.

SEVENTEEN

*I*t had been all right helping Bert milk the cows on that first day, but not any more. There was now no ease as she sat on her stool, cheek brushing the beast's soft flank, ear tuned to its rumbling stomach, the swish as it snatched hay from the rack, the odd scratch of hoof on concrete and the munching of cud.

Juno was conscious that behind her, astride his stool, Bert swore at the cow he was milking, exclaimed, 'Stand still, you bugger,' when it had not moved, scraped his stool along the concrete floor to bang it abruptly down by the next animal in line, that he muttered aloud as he tramped to the dairy with a full pail of milk, banged against the door of the box which held the cow with the calf so that the beast inside shuffled in apprehension. She guessed the man was waiting for her to empty her last pail in the dairy, shrug into her coat and leave him to finish the work he had grumbled was too much for one man. She was aware and tensely irritated.

'Let me help.' Juno took the broom before he had time to resist. 'I am quite capable of sweeping out the cowshed.'

Bert exclaimed, 'Nah!', but she had the broom and had begun to sweep. He watched, aghast.

'*And* give the cows their nuts *and* fill the hayracks.'

Had she not learned these things long ago on the Murray/Johnson farm, as the child who had hung about filling in time waiting for Jonty and Francis to come back from hunting or fishing or playing tennis? (Hanging about like an unwanted puppy.)

100

'Mind your *feet*.' She was shaking with sudden inexplicable fury.

Bert raised his voice in high-tenored surprise above the swooshing broom, 'I can't be having it, it ain't fitty.'

Sweeping, Juno shouted, 'You complained that eight cows were too much for you, I heard you.' Briskly she swept cowpats and shovelled them onto a barrow. 'And now, when you get help, you resent it.' She wheeled the barrow to the dung heap and tipped it. Returning, she turned on the tap and began hosing the concrete between the cowstalls. Bert stood nonplussed and staring. She swooshed the water towards the drain. 'There.' She wound the hose and put the broom in its place. 'There,' she said viciously. 'Done.'

Bleakly Bert repeated, 'It ain't fitty.'

'What?' Juno faced him. 'What isn't fitty?'

Searching for a suitable reply, Bert glared.

Juno said, 'Look. I offered to help because it happens I can milk and you are short-handed. I like cows and I like milking. I promised Mr Copplestone I would stay until he gets back and that is what I am doing, filling in time while he is away. But while I am milking, you shout at your cows – "A-r-r-r".' Juno mimicked Bert's voice and from its stall the cow with the calf mooed in protest. 'You resent me but you take it out on your cows. And,' Juno narrowed her eyes, 'I don't mind betting that as you make them nervous they are not letting their milk down as easily as they should. Right? You are not stupid, you must have noticed.'

Bert said, 'I never,' voice rising higher but eyes full of doubt.

'So what is it?' Juno asked. 'What, apart from my being a girl, is making you so pestilential?' She was angry with a consuming pent-up rage. The accumulation of her fear and emotion in London, the interminable wait at Reading, the desolate surreptitious visit to her old home. She could not stop herself; she shook with a terrible frightening fury. 'What is it?' she hissed, staring closely at the man's bristly chin. 'Tell me.'

101

Bert stepped backwards. 'Gawd,' he said later to Ann, 'that little maid did frighten me. Her face was chalk white and she did not know she was crying.' But he must not show his fear, he must make an effort, try. ''Tis your coat,' he exclaimed, his voice cracking. 'You come poncing into my farmyard in that – that thing – that coat, that's what ain't fitty. This 'tis a farm, 'tisn't Piccadilly,' he shouted, and in the corner of the shed, so old he was hardly noticeable, his old sheepdog yelped in sympathy, roused from its sleep.

Juno faced Bert for long seconds, then she said, 'But it's all I have.' Her rage drained away, leaving her spent. 'Perhaps I should have nicked mink? Would you have preferred that? Or sable?' she suggested sweetly. Then she turned away and raced up the hill. She did not look back.

He hurried to the dairy, caught up the sheepskin coat and brought it up the hill and into the house to give to Ann. His dog, who usually rested his old bones in retirement, bestirred himself and tried to follow.

'So we had explanations,' Ann said on Robert's return while he stretched his legs in front of the library fire, rubbed tired eyes and gratefully accepted whisky. 'She said she was sorry, something had snapped; she was very rude to Bert. She has no other coat, no clothes other than the few in her case—'

'What's this got to do with coats? Clothes?' Robert interrupted. 'Sorry, go on.'

'They are in Canada by now, there was a houndstooth tweed Bert might have approved of and, oh God, she would apologize.'

'A great mistake. Go on—'

'And be on her way as soon as possible. Those were her words, if you can make sense of them.'

'On her way? Where to? Where is she now?' Robert straightened up.

'In the bath.'

'I must talk to her, get to the bottom of this.' Hastily Robert swallowed his whisky. 'Damnation!'

102

Ann said, 'I should leave her alone, if I was you. She was in a state, been crying, Bert said. She—'

'But I am not you.' Robert heaved his length out of the armchair. 'Evelyn sent her to me. I've lost the bloody letter and now this happens! Explanations! I don't notice much in the way of explanations,' he was shouting as he made for the door.

'Please, sir, take it easy.' Ann watched him take the stairs two at a time. 'She's—'

'Bugger easy!' He had reached the landing and was heading towards Juno's room.

'Now look what you've done!' Ann addressed the husband she had already sent back to the farm with a flea in his ear. 'Stupid tactless old fool,' she muttered. 'If that poor child noticed you upset the cows so that they won't let down their milk easy, what have you done to upset her?' She had mocked him standing there hangdog and embarrassed, clutching the sheepskin coat. Now, in spite of herself, Ann experienced a spasm of amusement, remembering her husband's description of the scene in the cowshed. 'That girl struck home,' she said out loud, savouring Bert's indignation.

'So this Juno knows one end of a cow from the other,' she had teased, taking Juno's coat from him, giving it a shake and hanging it carefully up. 'And you are jealous, you silly old fool.'

Now she stood in the hall at the foot of the stairs half on tiptoe to hear better. Along the upstairs corridor she heard Robert knock and again, louder. There was apparently no response.

She heard him open the door and call, 'Juno, Juno? It's me, Robert. May I come in?' Then a scuffle and, 'Oh, Jessie, Jessie, yes, yes, I'm back, good girl, good dog. Go on now, down to Ann, go and get your dinner,' and Jessie came hurrying and wriggling down the stairs, her toenails clattering on the polished treads, blocking out all other sound, her wagging tail banging against the banisters.

Straining her ears as the dog came to rest on rugs, Ann

103

heard Robert's raised voice, 'I have to talk to you. Yes, now. Can you come down? Please.'

And Juno faintly, 'I'm just out of the bath, I haven't any clothes on—'

And Robert, 'Then put on a dressing-gown.'

And Juno, 'I have been appallingly rude to Bert. I can't, I—' And then faintly, 'I have no dressing-gown.'

And Robert loud again, 'Don't prevaricate. Evelyn's dressing-gown is hanging on the bathroom door. Put that on and buck up.'

Ann put her hand to her mouth. 'Oh!' she said as Robert shouted again, 'Buck up, put it on. I am waiting. Hurry up.'

There was no answer from Juno, but hearing footsteps Ann retreated to the kitchen from where she was able to call, 'Yes, sir, of course,' when Robert called from the hall, 'Ann, could you be kind and bring Juno a hot drink? I think she could do with one.'

Putting Jessie's dinner down on the floor, Ann remarked out loud, 'Better be giving her some soup and him, too. They both look clemmed.'

In the library Robert, standing with his back to the fire, looking down at Juno sitting upright in an armchair, small in Evelyn's dressing-gown, pale, her hair damp, pushed back from her face, said, 'Idiot that I am, I have lost Evelyn's letter, the one you brought with you, so you will have to tell me what was in it. Tell me about yourself. All I can remember, I was distracted when I read it, I had just come from London, from his funeral, I was not thinking straight; the little I remember is that he said I would find you rewarding. So it's up to you to tell me what he said, what was in the letter. Oh! Here comes Ann with soup. Oh, Ann, for me too? Oh God, I am talking too much. Eat your soup first.'

Juno said, 'I didn't read the letter. He wrote it and licked the envelope and handed it to me. Sorry.'

She sat up in the chair and took the bowl of soup Ann was handing her. 'Oh, thank you, thank you very much.'

104

Robert said, 'Oh,' nonplussed. 'Thanks, Ann,' he said, taking the bowl she handed him.

Juno swallowed some soup and said, 'I was so rude to Bert. I am so sorry and it wasn't really anything to do with him. It was dreadful of me.'

Robert said, 'He has a thick skin. It will not have hurt him, will it?' addressing Ann, who was on her way to the door.

Ann said, 'Hide of a rhinoceros. Will there be anything else?'

Robert said, 'No, thank you, Ann.'

Ann said, 'Mrs Villiers brought Anthony back for his things and took him to his train, and John will be back at work tomorrow.'

Robert said, 'Did she want anything?'

Ann snorted, 'Nothing new! If you need me, I'll be in the kitchen.' She left, closing the door.

Robert spooned soup into his mouth, his eyes on Juno. 'Could you for instance tell me how – um – Evelyn seemed when you saw him last?' He put the half-eaten soup on the table beside him.

Dead. He had been dead. She couldn't possibly tell this man, Evelyn's father, that she had not even paused to close his son's eyes. She looked wildly at Robert and, in almost a whisper, said, 'He was drinking whisky. He was wheezy, very wheezy, seemed exhausted—'

'And?'

'He gave me some because I was frightened. There was a big raid going on. I didn't like it, but he said to drink it. I had never tasted it before.' Juno began to shake, her voice tailing off. 'Oh God, I am spilling the soup.'

Robert sprang forward and took the bowl from her. 'I am being selfish, please forgive me. Sit quiet for a little and we will talk about you. Take your time—'

Juno said, 'But I have to go,' half rising from her chair.

Robert said, 'Sit down, you are not going anywhere,' and sat down himself.

EIGHTEEN

*B*ut Robert could not sit. He got up and, standing with his back to the fire, looked down at Juno sitting, knees drawn up, clasped hands close to her chin. She looked small in the armchair, her frame almost lost in Evelyn's cashmere dressing-gown, an extravagant garment bought on a whim 'because I like the colour'. Robert remembered his son's voice and, too, the conversation that had followed, tracing men's fashions back a century or more to the time when men did not only wear drab greys, blacks and restrained check tweeds, but peacocked shamelessly in bright colours. The dressing-gown was a rich raspberry pink; the shop man, Evelyn told him, had eyed him with caution, mistakenly suspecting him perhaps of belonging to the persuasion of Oscar Wilde.

'Do you suppose if we live long enough we shall see the return of bright colours for men?' Evelyn had queried. 'Bright colours would be nice.'

And he, laughing, had said, 'For you perhaps, for your generation or your children's, but I shall be long gone.'

And Evelyn, putting on the dressing-gown, had said, 'Then in my small way I shall start the ball rolling with this.'

And now the girl was wearing it and Evelyn was dead.

Robert cleared his throat. 'Are you warm enough?'

'Oh yes, thank you.' Juno jerked upright. 'This is lovely and beautifully warm.'

'Finish your soup, to please Ann.' Robert handed her the bowl. 'It's still hot.'

106

'Thanks.' Juno took the bowl, finished the soup, hesitated, said, 'I—'

'Yes?' Robert took the empty bowl from her, put it aside. 'Yes?'

'Nothing. There is nothing.' She stared at the fire.

Robert said, 'I spoke abruptly just now. I would love you to stay – um – stay, but if you are not happy? I could, we could, work something out. Where would you like to go? What do you want to do? I will help if I can. Why else did Evelyn send you here?' When Juno found no answer, did not look up, he said, 'To begin with, should we not tell your family where you are? Or perhaps you have done that? Written or telephoned while I was away. They must be anxious.'

Shrinking back in the armchair, Juno said, 'I have not written or telephoned.'

'Your father?' Robert persisted. 'Surely he—'

'He's dead.'

'Oh. I'm sorry.'

'He went to prison.' Juno sat up straight. 'He was a conscientious objector in 1914.'

'Bully for him,' Robert exclaimed. 'And your mother? Is she dead, too?' He lowered his voice.

'Canada, she's gone to Canada, and she's taken all my clothes with her.'

'That sounds a bit extreme.'

'That is why I was so offensive, so rude to Bert. I only have the coat he sneers at – objects to. I asked him whether he would rather I wore mink or sable. I was surprised at myself, I am not usually like that. I raged at him.' (It had not been Bert, it was quite another pain, loss, fear. She had snapped.) 'I snapped,' Juno admitted. 'I am sorry.'

'I don't suppose Bert knows what sable is.' Robert grinned.

Juno said, 'I am not sure myself.'

'A sort of pine marten, the fur worn by the very rich.'

'Thank you. And I think I shouted that I had stolen it, stolen the coat.'

107

'And did you?' Robert was interested; this girl of Evelyn's was not at all like the others.

'Yes, I did.' Juno looked Robert in the eye. 'I had spent my last coupons on a splendid houndstooth tweed, but my mother packed it with my other clothes and took it to Canada. She—'

Robert guessed, 'Where you are supposed to join her?'

'Where I do not want to join her. I can't, anyway. I got the money back on my ticket and I just do not want to go, and then my Aunt Violet—' Juno stopped abruptly.

'So you have some family?' Robert pounced. 'An aunt at least.' When Juno said nothing, he said, 'But perhaps you do not like this aunt?'

'I don't. I should, but I don't. She is bossy, and insulting about my father; she is ashamed of him. She tried to push me into one of the services to "do my bit", "fight for my country".' Robert was laughing. 'It's no laughing matter. She also insinuates the man my mother is going to marry is German.'

'And is he?' Robert grinned.

'He is Dutch or Nordic, something like that, but really Canadian. The name just sounds German.' Juno flushed. 'My mother hasn't had much fun and he is safe, even if —'

'Dull?'

'You guess a lot.'

'Your tone of voice.'

Juno breathed in. 'Aren't you shocked that I stole the coat?' she enquired.

'It shows enterprise. I suppose you were cold.'

'I was, very cold. But the cap, I didn't steal that. A sailor left it on his chair in the station buffet, so I—'

'Appropriated it?'

'Yes.'

'That makes sense.'

'I feel somewhat bereft of that commodity.' Which of them had said that? 'I am somewhat bereft.' She tried to remember, could not, wracked her brain. Thinking back, which of them had said, 'I am bereft'? She strained to hear

108

their voices. Was it Francis? It might have been either of them.

Watching her, Robert thought, she is far away. Jerk her back, catch her attention, pin her down.

'Why not,' he said rather loudly, 'stay here with Ann and me? Ann can fix you up with clothes. It is what Evelyn wanted, isn't it? What he suggested in his letter? The letter you brought with you.'

'But you have lost it.'

'Yes, but I *know* what it said.' Robert visualized the letter, the stiff white paper folded square, the square envelope addressed to himself: Robert Copplestone, Copplestone, Catchfrench, Cornwall, its message as always brief, for Evelyn was ever succinct. He could hear his son's voice, 'Someone you will like, who will help on the farm, who will love the place as we do, not a regulation landgirl like the one you tried, who stuck to the rule-book and didn't know a thing anyway.'

Out loud he said, 'Evelyn wrote he would find some-one, man or woman, to help me now I am short-handed. He has already sent Anthony Smith to work in the kitchen garden. Did you meet him? He has been working, too, for Priscilla Villiers? No? He left today, you must have missed him. Jolly good worker, he will come again when he gets leave. He works, as you know, in the same Ministry as Evelyn, but perhaps Evelyn did not tell you about him. No reason he should.' Juno shook her head. 'Then, as I say, having found Anthony, he finds you at a loose end and dispatches you at once with the letter which you brought with you, and—'

Juno interrupted, 'He can't have said all that. I was with him; I saw him write it. It did not take long.'

Robert said, 'Of course not, the bits about Anthony were months ago. I am running the two, the several letters into one for your convenience.' Robert wondered whether what he was telling Juno was strictly true or merely careless. 'What I am getting at,' he said, 'is this. Will you do what Evelyn suggested, what Evelyn wanted for you, what I would

109

of course very much like, stay and help on the farm? You have already shown you can milk a cow and demolish Bert. You can pick up the rest as you go along, and if you are happy I can get you registered as my landgirl, or whatever. That should satisfy your aunt and your mother. You had better write and tell them pretty soon, to relieve their anxiety—'

Juno said, 'I don't think—'

And Robert said, 'Oh, but you must. I always worry if I don't know where Evelyn is. Oh my God, what am I saying! Oh my God, death is so bloody hard to accept,' and burst into tears.

Juno watched him weep and, remembering his son, said nothing, for there was nothing consoling to say. Then, finding herself close to weeping too, she got up from the chair and stood beside him, waiting for the storm to subside. When Robert blew his nose and wiped his eyes, she still said nothing but was partially consoled when he said, 'Evelyn said in his letter that I would find you rewarding, and I do.'

Perhaps this was the moment to tell this man, Robert Copplestone, how little she had known his son?

A matter of minutes? Hours, if you counted the time she had slept while, lying on his side, his arm across her body, he had wheezed out of life? Or tell him how she had freed herself from that chill embrace, tiptoed to the lavatory, slid down the banisters? Juno moved back into the armchair to stare miserably into the fire and chivvy her brain for suitable words, succinct phrases.

Robert blew his nose again and, bending, replenished the fire with logs, then sat too, quiet now, afraid he had rushed the girl, said too much. (Evelyn would have been more subtle, known what to say.) Deliberately Robert relaxed his legs, stretching them towards the fire, stifled a sigh and closed his eyes to blot out visual memory, uselessly of course.

Sneaking a glance at him, Juno thought, they are uncannily alike, but this one is taller, stronger, more alive, his

110

hair thicker. He breathes easily, does not wheeze. I must speak. She opened her mouth.

'You are not likely to keep body and soul together surviving on bowls of soup.' Ann bustled into the room. 'You must be starving, so please, sir, both of you, come along and eat the supper which is spoiling in the kitchen. I can't be doing with all this waiting about and, by the way, I have brought those puppies down,' she said bossily to Juno. 'They will soon be crawling and I can't have them messing the carpets upstairs. The kitchen is the place for them now.'

Obediently Robert rose to his feet and, holding out a hand to Juno, pulled her up from her chair. 'Here we come.' As they followed Ann towards the kitchen, he said, 'Juno tells me all her clothes have gone astray, Ann, and that she has no clothes coupons. What miracle can you come up with?'

With her back to Robert, Ann said, 'I can lend her enough coupons for working clothes, gumboots and overalls, and cut down Evelyn's clothes to fit.'

In the semi-darkness of the hall Robert drew in his breath, winced.

Still with her back to him, Ann said, 'What is the difference? She is wearing his dressing-gown. I can cut down shirts and trousers, can't I? What is the use of having learned tailoring if I don't use it? Tell her, sir, how I came to learn tailoring.' She chuckled.

'What a realist you are.' Robert recovered himself and then, observing Juno bewildered and embarrassed, he told, as they sat at supper, of how when Ann married Bert many years ago she had discovered that she did not care for the rumpy-pumpy that went with that state, and removed herself to Bradford. There she studied tailoring for a year until, overcome by homesickness, she had come back to Copplestone House. This all came with many embellishments to the tale, which had Juno laughing by the time he finished and laughing even more when Ann added a full stop, 'I came back on my own terms.'

111

Thus was Juno's moment to speak put aside as they ate Ann's steak and kidney pudding, parsnips, cabbage and jacket potatoes, restoring their physical and emotional energies. And Juno, munching, wondered what good it would do if she did speak. She weighed the pros and cons of her awkward situation and thought perhaps that it would be best to say nothing, for she hardly knew either the father or the son.

It was as they finished the meal that they became aware of the growling flight of German bombers, and almost simultaneously the thud of bombs falling in the valley.

Robert exclaimed, 'The farm, they may hit the farm, scare the animals,' and was out of the front door and running before either Ann or Juno got out of the kitchen.

Ann, moving fast, shouted at Juno, 'Put some clothes on, don't show a light or let the dogs out.' Pulling on a coat as she ran, she slammed out of the door after Robert and thudded across the yard.

Juno nipped up the stairs to dress in trousers and sweater, lace-up shoes over thick socks, then she too ran outside but, running, heard the telephone peal and doubled back to answer it.

A voice was shouting, 'This be Fred Pearse from ARP. Tell Mr Copplestone the bombs missed the village, but they was coming out your way, tell 'im that.' Juno said she would and the caller rang off.

Outside in the yard she had to accustom herself to the dark. The horses in the stables were whinnying, agitated. She picked her way across to their boxes and said, 'It's all right, it's all right, nothing to worry about,' stroked silky noses and patted necks. Then, leaving the yard, she strained her eyes downhill to the farm. A bomber was circling the valley, flying low. She watched its shadow cross the moon, then lost its silhouette against dark clouds as its engine growled and groaned, reminding her of London. From the farm she thought she heard voices and cows lowing, but could not be certain. Taking the short cut she

112

began to run downhill, but tripping over a tussock fell headlong, winding herself and wrenching an ankle. Getting up, she trotted on in the direction of the farm, unaware that, favouring the hurt ankle, she was bearing away from the farm towards the wood. As she ran she was afraid and found herself muttering, 'If there's a raid take cover, take a taxi or better still the tube, you'll be all right in the tube,' and fumbling in her pocket for the ten-shilling notes. When the whistle and shriek of a descending bomb halted her in her tracks, she cowered down, hands over her ears as it crashed into the wood a hundred feet away.

When the rustle, pattering and creak of broken branches stopped she got to her feet to listen, and hearing panting and whining nearby, made out, as the quarter moon shone through the clouds, the shape of dogs knitted together on the grass ride. Curiosity overcoming fear, she approached the entangled animals and recognized Bert's old and decrepit sheepdog with its penis trapped in the aftermath of mating inside a collie bitch. As she approached they came apart; the bitch shied away to bolt through the trees, while Bert's ancient animal slumped exhausted, apparently dying.

As Juno crouched by the dog she realized that the bomb had crashed but there had been no explosion. 'If there had been an explosion, I would have been blown away and so would you,' she said to the dog lying gasping on his side. 'Come along, it may go off yet.' She tried to recollect what she had heard of unexploded bombs. 'I don't like it here. Get up, boy, come along.' But the dog was spent and could not move.

Juno was carrying the dog when Robert and Bert met her limping into the farmyard.

'Where have you been? You are hurt,' Robert exclaimed, but Bert was shouting, 'What are you doing with old Nipper? Was he hit? Was he killed? What was you doing with the poor old bugger and enemy planes?' His voice rose to a shriek.

Robert said, 'Don't be a fool, Bert. Nipper's half-dead at the best of times. He looks no different from usual.'

Juno said, 'I tripped and twisted my ankle, it's nothing.'

Bert shouted, 'You fell over old Nipper, you've done him in.' He was beside himself.

Juno raised her voice. 'No. I found him by the wood, he was with a collie, they were sort of stuck together. I've never seen—'

'They was *mating*?' Bert let out a whoop. 'What sort of collie was it?' He peered into Juno's eyes.

'Very pretty, black and white.' Juno, not liking Bert so close, stepped back. 'She made off through the wood. She seemed all right but Nipper collapsed, so I carried—'

But Bert no longer listened, he was crowing. 'Oh, the good dog. That 'ud be Tom French's bitch, too good for old Nip, Tom said. Tom said my Nipper's too old for his bitch. We'll show 'um, won't us, boy? When she whelps with Nip's pups, he'll owe us the best of the litter. You'm a great dog, Nipper.' Bert leaned down to caress the aged Romeo, who lay where Juno had laid him, just managing a faint wave of his tail.

Robert said, 'A spoonful of brandy might help. Lust is extremely debilitating at his age.' He was laughing as he, too, bent to stroke the dog.

From outside the group Ann asked in a voice which indicated that there had been quite enough about the dog, 'What about the bomb, Juno? You might have been killed. Where did it fall?'

Juno said, 'I don't know exactly, but I was quite frightened. The farm, is that all right? As I was leaving the house the ARP post telephoned Robert.' She had not called him by his Christian name before. 'They wanted to warn you, said the bombs had missed the village.'

Robert said, 'Two bombs fell wide, one fell in the stream and the blast from another has damaged a wall, but the stock are safe.' Then, looking closely at Juno, 'I am thankful you are not badly hurt. We must get Ann to strap up that ankle.' Then he laughed some more. 'I've heard

114

air raids make people randy, but I didn't know it applied to dogs.'

Bert, pressing close to Juno, asked, 'You sure now what you saw? Sure the old dog was—'

Juno, backing away assured him, 'Yes, yes, I am certain.'

Bert, all smiles, assured her, 'Then you's welcome to come milking and I'll teach 'ee dairywork.'

Robert remarked *sotto voce*, 'The raid's made you a friend, Evelyn would love this.'

NINETEEN

*V*iolet Marlowe read her sister-in-law's letter with rising eyebrows, put the letter back in its envelope and laid it aside. 'Some people!'

'Trouble?' John Baines looked up from his newspaper; breakfast on Saturdays when they were in London was a leisurely affair; Bill Bailey was likely to sleep till noon.

Violet said, 'It's my sister-in-law.'

'Who was married to your conchie brother?'

'That's the one.'

'Mother of the niece who was scared in an air raid?' John liked to get things straight.

'Yes, John.'

'And?'

'My sister-in-law writes that she has married that Sonntag man and that from now on she will have Canadian nationality.'

'No harm in that.'

'Changing nationality in time of war when you are British seems—'

'Like jumping ship?'

John had got it in one. Violet said, 'Of course, and that's not all; she writes that Juno has not arrived, and do I know where she is?'

'She jumped ship too?'

'Don't be frivolous, John.'

'Wasn't she sailing to join her mother?'

'That was the plan, though, come to think of it, she did

116

not seem keen, but when I suggested various jobs she was not keen on those either. I thought perhaps she didn't look forward to the life her mother had planned for her in Canada. I know she told me Juno would have opportunities she would never have in England, they were very badly off. But oh my God, John,' Violet exclaimed, 'think of all the ships which have been sunk.'

John said, 'Don't be ridiculous, Violet, you would have heard. Were you next of kin?'

'Juno's mother would be next of kin. Oh, John, how ghastly, she was barely seventeen. Think of it!'

'I am thinking. If your sister-in-law met the ship, it can't have been sunk; it sounds as though the ship arrived minus your niece. When she came to see you, where did she say she was going next?'

'I gathered she was going home to collect a case of clothes. I supposed she would then go up to Liverpool to join the ship. Oh, John, she could have been transferred onto another ship! I wasn't kind enough to the girl, and if she's been torpedoed I shall never forgive myself,' Violet agitated. 'My brother may have been a conchie, but blood is thicker—'

'And water drowns. Violet, keep calm, don't jump to conclusions. Where was home? Your sister-in-law's and Juno's home, where she was to collect a case?'

'A cottage in Berkshire; they rented it from friends called Murray or Johnson. They've lived there for years.'

'Got the number?'

'Of course I have.'

'Then telephone these Murrays or Johnsons, they will have seen Juno when she fetched her case and know where she went. She is probably still there. You know what girls are like.'

'You may know, I don't. Shouldn't I phone the shipping company to check the passenger list?'

'Try the Murray Johnson people first. Then, if you get no joy, I'll deal with the shipping company.'

'Dear man, what a help you are.' Violet went to the

telephone and presently got through to Susan Johnson, catching her when she was just leaving the house to keep a dentist's appointment. She explained her dilemma, and asked whether Susan had knowledge of Juno's whereabouts.

Susan's voice on the line was clear. 'Of course I have. She went to join her mother in Canada.'

'Are you sure?' Violet gripped the instrument.

'Of course I am sure. Mrs Marlowe gave up the lease of the cottage and moved out; it's let to some other friends now. She's gone to Canada, and Juno's gone too.'

Violet said, 'But I hear from my sister-in-law that she hasn't arrived.'

'Hasn't arrived? What do you mean, hasn't arrived?'

'Hasn't arrived wherever you arrive in Canada. There must be a port.'

'There must be a port,' Susan Johnson echoed.

Violet tried again. 'When I last saw my niece, she said she was going home to collect a case. I wondered whether she might still be with you?'

Susan said, 'Well, she isn't.' Realizing that she sounded abrupt, she added, 'And I am afraid I know nothing about a case or your niece, and she certainly isn't here.'

Violet persisted, 'I am sorry to be such a bore, but I have to try and find her. I am so afraid she may have been torpedoed. Could you tell me when you saw her last?'

Susan said, 'That's easy. My son and his cousin let her travel as far as London with them when they went to join their unit. She was going on to Liverpool. Why don't you try there?'

Violet said, 'But if she had stayed in England and hasn't been torpedoed, would your son or his cousin know where she would be?'

Susan said, 'Why on earth should they?' Her tone was abrasive.

'I thought as her friends—'

'Not friends, the girl was just a child who was about the place. What are you suggesting?'

Irritated, Violet snapped, 'I am not suggesting anything. I am trying to find my niece who seems to have disappeared. I am worried and her mother will be frantic.'

Susan Johnson, irritated in turn, said, 'Well, I am sorry I can't help.' Her tone indicated clearly that Juno's whereabouts were not her concern.

Violet put down the receiver. 'Bloody woman! She doesn't care, and doesn't seem to like Juno.'

John, thinking, And nor did you much, suggested ringing the shipping company, but it was Saturday and the office was closed. Having failed, he murmured, 'I had no idea you were fond of her.'

Violet said, 'I am not, but she's my niece. I owe it to my brother.'

'Nor were you fond of him,' said John astutely, feeling bored with Juno for spoiling a peaceful Saturday morning. 'Hearing you speak of him has never given me that impression.'

Violet said, 'I dare say not, but I am dealing with family. Juno is a blood relation.'

'What is she like? Apart from the fact that she was caught in a raid, shot in here for a bath, was wearing unsuitable shoes for the snow and was gone when you got back from work, we don't know much.' John, hoping to alleviate Violet's fuss, adopted a teasing note. 'Is she for instance pretty?'

'Oh yes, she's pretty. Thin like my brother, dark hair, but rather—'

'Rather what?'

'She left the bathroom door unlocked and lay in the bath with her clothes scattered on the floor. She did not seem to mind my coming in. It was rather—' Violet paused, unwilling to tell John that she had thought Juno indecent.

John said, 'I wouldn't mind that. My girls scream if I try the door.'

Violet said, 'Your girls know how to behave.'

'Are you implying that your niece is a bit on the wild side? What used to be called loose?'

Violet said, 'I don't know her well enough to judge, but if she is anything like her father she would be difficult.'

'Who were her friends? Would she be likely to light off? Elope?'

'Heavens, John, no. Would one of yours?'

'I wouldn't be surprised by anything my girls did.'

'Well, Juno wouldn't. She's a shy and timid little thing, never had friends. My sister-in-law hoped Canada would help there, draw her out, that sort of thing.'

'Ah.'

'And now you're suggesting that she is wandering loose like some common tart! Oh God, John, I am so worried. The losses in the Atlantic are so frightening.'

John said, 'Come on, Violet, don't start that again. Don't work yourself into a state.'

'But what am I to tell her mother?'

John said, 'Try and keep calm. Wait a day or two and you'll get another letter to say she's arrived safe and well, your sister-in-law made some silly mistake. It happens all the time, there's a war on.'

Violet said, 'I could hit you, John.' And when, two days later, Juno, persuaded by Robert, telephoned her aunt to apprise her of her whereabouts, she flew into a rage. 'I could strike that girl. She rings up, cool as you please, as though I was not worried sick by her being sunk in the Atlantic.'

'And if not sunk,' Bill Bailey, who had joined his fellow lodger in the job of assuaging Violet's agony of mind, now asked, 'where might this volatile drownee be?'

'She's working on a farm in the West Country, milking cows, feeding hens and pigs—'

'Did she give you the address?'

'I was too angry to ask.'

'So what will you tell your sister-in-law?'

'I told the little fool to tell her herself. She is just like my useless brother.'

John Baines raised his eyes towards the ceiling and said, 'Family, Violet, family.'

TWENTY

'*K*eep still while I measure you. Stand on that stool so that I don't have to bend.' Ann held a tape-measure. 'Bending gips my back.'

Obediently Juno mounted the stool while Ann ran the tape from neck to bottom, armpit to wrist, looped it round her chest. 'Keep still a minute while I write it down.' She wrote Juno's measurements on the back of an envelope. 'When I have you measured, we'll go upstairs and see what we find in those cupboards and drawers.'

'What cupboards? Can I get down now?'

'Not yet! Evelyn's cupboards, haven't you looked? You are a funny one.'

'It seemed like prying. Was the room always his?'

'Yes. I put you there as it was the one room ready. He'd come at short notice when he managed a day or two off; I kept it ready with the fire laid.'

'It's a lovely room. Watching the firelight on the ceiling at night is marvellous.'

'He was born in it,' Ann said.

'Oh.'

'It was his mother's and father's when the young things married. They turned the room next door into a bathroom, used to have a fire in there, too. There had only been the one bath on the top floor. Sir put in the one he uses later, but Evelyn was born in your bed.'

'Goodness.'

'Sir moved to the other end of the house when she died,

and since then it's been Evelyn's.' Ann wound up the tape-measure.

'Did she die in it?'

'No, love, that room has nothing but happy memories.' Ann licked the stump of pencil and wrote, Hips – 35. 'There will be shirts I can cut down and cord trousers, linen, too, and a tweed suit. He kept his country clothes here. We'll soon get you kitted out.'

Juno said, 'You are very kind to me.'

'I'm enjoying myself. Don't move, I haven't measured your waist.'

'It's twenty inches.'

'You sure? I make it twenty-one.' Ann circled Juno with the tape.

'Positive. We once had a competition for the smallest waist and I won.'

'It's twenty-one now, and you can get down.' Ann led the way upstairs to open cupboards and drawers, pull out Evelyn's clothes, saying, 'We can use this,' and, 'That will cut down,' and, 'I can unpick these and knit them again,' as she handled socks and, 'I can reduce these so that you'll never know,' holding Evelyn's trousers against Juno's slight frame.

Juno said, 'It will be weird wearing his things.'

Ann said briskly, 'You'll soon forget.'

Juno, wondering whether one ever forgot, next concluded that she had known Evelyn so slightly that his trousers would not have much influence; and that, thinking of him now, she could barely visualize him. She remembered his voice better than his face, which blurred into Robert's, now seeming so unlike his son's. Evelyn had had a sad expression, as though he had grown out of happy endings. She said, 'What was Evelyn's mother like?'

'You must have seen the photo Evelyn had, she was lovely, about your size, fair, blue eyes. Evelyn liked blondes, but he took after Sir.'

Juno did not admit that she had not noticed the photo-graph. 'Were they happy? Did you know her well?'

'What they had was short, but as good as you'll ever get. They were the happiest of young creatures—'

'But she died when Evelyn was born—'

'Soon after. They had a lot of love and a lot of laughter. She was old for her age.'

'Perhaps being in love is ageing?'

Ann said, 'I wouldn't know. They were only seventeen.'

Juno said, 'I am seventeen.'

'And Evelyn was seventeen when he lied about his age to get into the war. Sir was already in it. Evelyn did not want to be left out – such a bitter waste.'

And it's happening again, Juno thought, and as bitter as ever. 'Did Bert go to the war, too?'

'He got no further than Catterick, never was anywhere dangerous. It was Evelyn who was gassed, the filthy stuff, shredded his lungs. Bert came back healthier than when he left, and Sir wasn't wounded.'

'Poor Evelyn.' Ann had loved him, known him from little baby to wheezy man. 'I did not know him well,' Juno said cautiously, 'not really.'

'Few people did, love. Now try this on, I didn't know it was still here. Look, it will fit you, a bit loose but it's a good fisherman's jersey. They never wear out. It will be useful for work.' Ann popped the jersey over Juno's head, saying, 'Good, it fits.'

Juno adjusted the jersey, watching herself in the glass. It was baggy but comfortable. 'Did Sir, did Robert not want to marry again?'

Ann laughed. 'Not so you'd notice, though there's a few who tried to catch him.'

'And Evelyn?'

'Said it wouldn't be fair on any girl to marry a man with rotting lungs. Did he not tell you?' Ann looked sharply at Juno. 'Still worried about your waist?' For Juno was checking her waist with the tape, holding it up under the jersey. 'It's twenty-one, as I told you, must be our country air.'

But Juno was not listening. They had all been in the

123

Murray's house playing ridiculous games. It had been Christmas; there had been a prize for the smallest waist. Her mother's had been twenty-four. She must write to her mother, get that letter off, explain that she was doing war work on a farm, give her the address, tell her not to worry, not to be anxious, explain why she would not come to Canada, how she wanted to stay in England. She would make it clear that it did not mean lack of love, impress that she was old enough to make up her own mind, quote Aunt Violet on war work – her mother disliked Aunt Violet – hope that she would be happy with Mr Sonntag, happy in Canada. Mr Sonntag's waist had been huge, and so had Jonty's and Francis's fathers'. Juno remembered the laughter. Jonty and Francis had held their breath, tucked in their stomachs, pulled the tape tight; they were slender young men but neither could compare with hers. Their mothers, Susan and Margery, had declined to compete; their waists had thickened as her mother's had not. Remembering their voices, Juno was suddenly consumed with rage. 'She is only a child, she is not yet grown, she doesn't count.' Juno tasted bile. She had never counted, they were determined she should not; to them she was an incubus.

Ann said, 'What's the matter? Did I say something?'

Juno, recovering herself, said, 'No, no, of course not, it's nothing, I just thought, I just remembered something.'

Ann, looking quizzical, said they had done enough for the moment, and to come down to the kitchen for tea, then would Juno feed the hens and shut them in for the night against the foxes? And to keep the jersey on. And Juno said of course, and that she was happy that Bert was now teaching her how to separate cream and make butter and that while she was out she would fill the horses' hay-bags and that the jersey was lovely and splendidly warm, while inside she was screaming, I am sick of being reminded. When shall I stop remembering? When shall I forget?

TWENTY-ONE

'*C*ome up the hill with me,' Robert called, 'we can see what's going on from the top.' He stood in the hall, humping himself into a coat. 'Put your coat on, it will be bitter up there.' He helped Juno into her coat, watched her pull on the woollen cap, then led the way out of the house and headed up the hill. 'Even though there is nothing we can do—' Robert left his sentence unfinished, then went on. 'It's impossible to sleep if one goes to bed with the war so near.'

For nights after the bombs had dropped near the farm, the raids on Plymouth had raged relentlessly.

In the kitchen Ann listened to the news on the wireless, turned the sound up for Lord Haw-Haw and jeered. From the hilltop Robert and Juno would see the sky glow red from the burning city, hear the anti-aircraft guns, watch the searchlights finger the sky.

Juno walked behind Robert up the steep path. He, knowing the way in the dark, zigzagged through the trees, ducking instinctively to avoid the hanging branches he had known all his life, and Juno aped his movements.

'This hill was Emma's and mine.' Robert's voice was angry. 'Our sky was full of stars. Look at it now, streaked with death.' His thoughts reverted to that magical summer when he and Emma shed their childhood, learned to kiss, to touch, make love.

Juno said, 'Tell me about Emma.' She hurried behind Robert, ducking when he ducked. 'Tell me,' she said, keeping pace.

125

The texture of Emma's skin, the taste of her spit, the flavour of sex; Robert thought back to a period of such transcendent happiness that every joy and sorrow that came later was paid for in advance. Could he possibly tell this strange girl? Perhaps, if he tried, she would speak of Evelyn?

'We were happy,' he said. 'We were in love. We made Evelyn.' He had his back to the girl; what he said sounded inadequate. She did not respond.

They reached the top and stood above the tree line; there was a view for miles. Robert thought, she is so young, but we were too. How can I tell what she has learned? How can I get her to speak? Should I even try? He noticed that she was out of breath. He had walked fast. He looked east towards Plymouth. At the foot of the cliff the sea heaved and sighed against the rocks; there was no wind.

Robert said, 'Look at it, Juno,' and pointed towards the city many miles away. 'Even destruction is beautiful in its way. Isn't the sky a formidable colour?' He remembered that Evelyn had written, 'There was a strangely beautiful glow over dockland.' What else had his son written? He said, 'Did you, too, see beauty in the raids in London? Tell me what you saw.'

Juno said, 'I saw the moon, the cracks in the pavement, a streak of light from an opening door.' She forebore to mention that she had been consumed with love and grief, for Robert could not know love as she knew love. He could remember his Emma, but would he sniff the air as she did, half-hoping to catch a remembered whiff of Francis's hair or Jonty's sweat as they kissed and petted her after that unheeding violence, or hear their voices exclaiming that they had not meant to hurt? Had Robert, she wondered, hurt Emma? And what had Emma had to say?

As she stared horrified at the distant city being destroyed, she was in half a mind to ask Robert about this, but he had grabbed her arm and was shouting, 'Here's another lot, here they come again. Look, Juno, you can see the black cross.'

Indeed she could see the cross as a German bomber, divagating from its course over Plymouth, or more likely on its way back to base having dropped its load, zoomed low down the valley chased by a Beaufighter with its guns spitting fire.

Robert was shouting, 'My God, my God,' and Juno heard herself yell, 'Look out! Look out! Oh God, it's *hit*!' as the plane lurched sideways, appeared to pause, then slid sideways into the sea. Then she was on her knees, vomiting, with Robert holding her head, his arm round her waist, saying, 'What a fantastic sight, the poor devil looked like a mallard shot over the marsh,' while the Beaufighter circled in triumph before flying off. Robert pulled Juno to her feet and she leaned against his chest, hearing the thump of his heart and his rumbling voice, 'Poor devils, poor devils, there will be no survivors. I must get back and telephone, but there will be no-one to save.'

As they ran downhill Robert held her hand and Juno cried out, 'What if we had known someone in that plane?'

Robert answered, 'I know, I know.'

She shouted, 'And you find the sky beautiful.'

He answered, 'But it is, it is beautiful.'

As they trotted down the path through the trees, she was again minded to ask whether he had hurt Emma when they made Evelyn, but it was hardly the right moment when his mind was full of the shot-down bomber and its crew, burning Plymouth and the horror of war. But as they got close to the house, she blurted, 'What did you do when Emma died?'

Robert answered simply, 'I went to university and tried to grow up, tried to forget.'

She said, 'And did you?'

Robert, opening the door, standing aside to let her go in first, answered, 'Of course not.' Then, as they reached the kitchen, he began telling Ann about the German plane and that Juno had been sick and would she mind her while he went to telephone, report the crash?

Ann, drawing Juno close to the fire, helping her off with

her coat, said, 'Well, that's one good job done by our lot which Lord Haw-Haw won't be boasting about, something cheering to put in your letter to your mother,' and was quite huffed when Juno shouted, 'It was a terrible thing, it was in no way good. I agree with my father.'

TWENTY-TWO

*R*iding down the hill to the village on errands for Ann, Juno considered the letter so long overdue which she must write to her mother. It would not be enough to say that she had a job on a farm, that she was living in a house called Copplestone, working for a man of the same name who owned the farm and the land roundabout. Her mother would want to know how this situation had come about and why she had not boarded the ship as her parent had planned. It belatedly struck Juno that her mother, meeting the ship and discovering her missing, would be alarmed, to say the least. She groaned. 'Oh my God, why have I not thought of this before?' She kicked the pony into a trot as she racked her brain for some cogent reason for the change of plan and, too, for not having had the courage to make it clear that she had never wanted to go to Canada and a new life with Mr Sonntag. That she needed to stay in England, desperately needed to stay where her heart lay.

'I should have been a more rebellious child,' Juno said to the pony. 'Get on with it, Millicent.' She kicked the animal, who had halted to snuffle over a gate at a carthorse, 'That's no suitable friend for you.' She shook the reins and Millicent broke into a reluctant trot, while the carthorse kicked up its heels and galloped clumsily, keeping parallel on its side of the fence. 'You should set your sights higher,' she told the pony. 'An Arabian barb would suit you,' she said and her mind reverted to her mother's aspirations for herself, clean-cut Canadians with prospects and private means magically produced by Mr Sonntag. She began to laugh out loud, for she was enjoying the ride and it was a beautiful day.

Trotting into the village, she was met by a procession of army lorries loaded with soldiers in commando uniform who, seeing Juno, whistled and waved, in high spirits returning to camp after an arduous day. Reining Millicent to the side of the road, Juno waved back. Her eyes searched the faces driving by and her heart beat in spite of common sense which told her that what she hoped to see was not there, that she was a fool to pin hopes on such slight resemblances as the set of an ear, the colour of an eye, that she did not know whether Jonty and Francis were in the commandos, for they had never told her what element of the amorphous mass engaged in the war was theirs. Had she not, a few nights earlier, imagined them in the plane which had shot down the bomber?

Dismounting at the Post Office and tying the pony to a rail, she found that the woman she had seen driving her car down the hill from Copplestone with a large dog running behind was standing beside her, holding out a hand, saying, 'I am Priscilla Villiers, a friend of Robert's, and you are Juno Marlowe.'

Juno shook hands, said, 'That's right. Stand still, Millicent.' She soothed the pony.

'Such an absurd name for a pony.' Priscilla patted the animal's neck. 'But that's Robert. He named a goose after another girl he had an affair with, whoever heard of a goose called Barbara? And Millicent's father so disapproved of Robert.'

Juno said, 'Oh,' digesting this titbit, wondering too whether there might possibly be a hen or turkey called Priscilla?

Priscilla, grinning, said, 'No, there are no Priscillas in Robert's farmyard,' and when Juno flushed, added, 'no such luck, but you may have noticed a sow called Eleanor, and that a lot of the cows have names.' Then she said, 'I

130

gather from the grapevine that you were with him when he saw the bomber shot down?'

Juno said, 'It was horrible. I was sick.'

Priscilla persisted, 'The coastguards say there was nothing next day but a patch of oil.'

Juno repeated, 'Horrible.'

Priscilla said, 'I know. It doesn't bear thinking of, but at least it was quick and they had been bombing Plymouth.'

Juno said, 'That makes it no better.'

And Priscilla said gently, 'So you take after your father, a brave fellow, I've always thought. I know who you are. I knew your family. I was at school with your Aunt Violet. How is she?'

Juno said, 'Belligerent, working for the Red Cross.'

Priscilla said, 'But presumably approves of what you are doing? I suppose she got you the job with Robert as a friend of Evelyn's. Evelyn knew all sorts, didn't he? I bet he found Violet rather comical, at least I would imagine so. I hope you don't mind my saying this—'

Juno said, 'Oh. I—' At a loss as assumptions were made, she said, 'She wanted, she tried to get me to—'

'Join up? Fight for your country? That's Violet all over. She should have been the man in your family. Your father, by all accounts, was a gentle fellow. I hardly knew him but know of him, courageous, stuck to his convictions. I dare say Violet is ashamed of him.'

Juno said, 'She is.'

'Silly old thing. He was quite a friend of my husband's at one time, that's the connection. Nice man.'

Juno said, 'Oh,' feeling pleased.

'And what does your mother think?' Priscilla was smiling, friendly.

Juno said, 'I haven't told her, she doesn't know. I was supposed to join her in Canada and I don't want to, and now it's quite awful. It's all so difficult!' Her voice rose. 'Oh God!' she exclaimed, 'I don't know why I am telling you all this. I am worried stiff!'

Priscilla said, 'No doubt your mother is, too.'

131

Juno, almost shouting, cried, 'Of *course*!' She was on the verge of tears. 'I don't know what or how to tell her.'

Priscilla said, 'My dear girl, don't tell me you are incapable of concocting a lie?'

Shocked, Juno said, 'What?'

Priscilla said, 'Send her a cable. Here is the Post Office, come along, I will help you. There is an art in this sort of thing. One has to remember later what one said.'

Juno said, 'Gosh.'

Riding back to Copplestone, she marvelled at Priscilla's competence, for it was Priscilla who composed the message which apprised her mother of her whereabouts and occupation, and stated in essence that the situation had come about via an introduction from her aunt. Only twice did Priscilla ask a question, first, for her mother's address and secondly, murmuring, how had it come about that Evelyn knew Violet? And before Juno could voice a yea or nay, said, 'Not that it matters, for Evelyn knew everybody, didn't he?'

And Juno had humbly agreed to yet another of the many half-truths assumed since her arrival.

So that night when she wrote, as Priscilla said she must, a long letter to her mother; she described the house, the farm, the countryside, her work with the cows, pigs, horses, chickens and geese. She told her mother that she could make butter, was helping to produce food, would further the outcome of the war. She wrote that she was happy, that she hoped her mother would understand. She wondered whether there was any possibility of her sending back her clothes, but please not to worry as Ann was being so incredibly kind. She wrote that she liked working for Mr Copplestone, who let her ride the pony and his horse, that a friend of Aunt Violet's who had been at school with her lived not far away, and please not to worry as she was busy and well. She was fortunate to have found such a useful job. Then she sent her love and best wishes to Mr Sonntag.

When she had signed the letter and sealed it in its envelope, she wondered whether, when she mentioned Ann in the letter, it was by mistake or on purpose that she had not made it clear that Ann was the housekeeper and not, as her mother would infer, Robert's wife? For a brief moment she eyed the closed envelope before deciding that her mother would be less happy if she knew that Robert was a widower who named his farm animals after a string of mistresses. The letter must go to the post as it was.

It would be all right, Juno told herself, riding back to Copplestone. Mrs Villiers had been right to concoct the half-truth which was cabling its way to Canada; her mother could not expect intimacy, must be used to silence and evasion. Riding up into the hills, Juno considered her parent with dispassion; they had never been close, had lived without demonstrations of affection. She had no recollection of being petted. There had been no hand-holding, for instance, unless it was necessary and kisses had been sparse. She would never have been able to speak with her mother as she had a few minutes before with Mrs Villiers who, loquacious and loose-tongued, had elicited in a few brief minutes a précis of her life.

If her mother had resembled Mrs Villiers, would she herself have taken a more sympathetic interest in her parent? Would she have discussed Mr Sonntag? Would her mother have listened? Would she have asked whether she, Juno, was happy to go to Canada, instead of taking it for granted? Almost certainly not, unless she had miraculously become another person. Riding up the hill, Juno laughed out loud and the pony twitched her ears back and forth.

With a mother of Mrs Villiers's calibre there would have been consultation and argument, laughter and probably tears, never those dreary meals and long evenings with hardly a word spoken, each wrapped in her own thoughts. And yet, Juno thought, I love her as far as she allows. I know that until she met her Mr Sonntag she was dutiful, not happy. Some of this had come bubbling out while speaking with Mrs Villiers, who assumed without being told that her mother had married the wrong man and did not love

133

her father. She had, though, been fiercely loyal, Juno remembered, standing up for him when he was criticized, even though she had found his political opinions irritating and embarrassing long after his death.

What her mother had wanted was to be like her neighbours, Mrs Murray and Mrs Johnson. Thinking of this, Juno snorted with laughter; her mother, Juno knew, and this she had not let on to Mrs Villiers, had never wanted to have a child, but if she had to have one would have wanted a son. Once, in a moment of unguarded irritation, she had told Juno this and Juno had not felt hurt but sympathetic, for it was clear her mother was an unhappy person who hated being poor, who would never be like Mrs Johnson or Mrs Murray, neither of whom had married the wrong man and had the wrong child.

'I hope and pray,' Juno said out loud, 'that she will be happy with her Mr Sonntag. Surely I am right to spare her embarrassment. After all,' she consoled herself, 'my mother did not confide in me, so why should I risk confiding in her? She has escaped, but I wish she had not taken all my clothes with her.'

TWENTY-THREE

*R*obert watched Juno jogging ahead on the pony and was glad he had asked her to come on his pre-breakfast tour. Normally he relished his solitude, viewing his land and stock, planning the day's work. But it was nice, he thought, to have company for once, all the more so since Juno did not chatter; when spoken to, she answered intelligently but most of the time was agreeably mute.

The landgirl who had stayed so briefly and got on so badly with Bert and Ann had been a chatterer and a know-all, airing her bits of agricultural lore, bending the ear of anyone who would listen. No wonder the man had taken against her.

It was a relief, he thought, watching Juno's back, that since her brief spat with Bert – what had that really been about? – she was as welcome in the farmyard and dairy as she was in the house. This morning his ride was as pleasurable as it had been when Evelyn was home to keep him company, as he had done regularly as a child. Juno rode well, with a straight back and long stirrups. Had she too ridden with her father, or had the man died too soon to teach her? Information Juno transmitted was remarkably sparse. The landgirl had barely lasted a week, but by halfway through she had apprised all who would listen of her every intimate family detail with elaboration and repetition. Her voice, too, had been an irritant, high and piercing. Juno's was low.

'Who taught you to ride?' Robert addressed Juno's back.

'A neighbour's groom.'

'Oh?'

'I helped exercise the horses.'

'Our fathers say we may have horses and hunt, provided they are properly exercised and cared for in term-time. We have thought it out. Jennings shall teach you, then you can ride while we are at school,' Francis had said.

'And help in the stables. It's a known fact,' Jonty had added, 'that little girls love hanging around stables and are horse-mad.' And so it had been that she had learnt to ride, groom, muck out and fill hay-bags. 'It did not last long,' she said.

'What didn't?'

'The riding.'

'Why not?'

'They sold their horses when they were old enough to drive a car.'

'They?'

'Erm – the – er – neighbours. Their family owned the farm where I learned to milk.'

She did not want to relive the disappointment, the sight of the empty stable when the horses were sold in favour of an MG. Jennings had not been happy, either.

'Which fields do you use for hay?' she asked.

Robert reined in his horse. 'Those two on this side of the brook, and the one across there where the cows are grazing. It's very old pasture,' Robert told Juno, since she seemed interested. 'It's never been ploughed; it's full of wild flowers and herbs. The cattle love it.'

So she did not want to talk about learning to ride, but as he enjoyed talking about the land he loved he went on to tell her of the three kinds of orchid which grew in the meadows, and of how he dated the hedges by their variety of trees and shrubs. He enjoyed her reticence but to test her, a slight tease, he asked, 'Did the horses you learned to ride have names?' She should know that he noticed she had deflected his attention.

Juno said, 'I expect so, I don't remember,' which was

136

untrue, for Jonty had named the horses Auden and Isherwood after a pair of writers he and Francis were interested in at the time and there had been an innuendo she had not understood. 'It was a long time ago.' Aware of sounding rude, she said, 'When I met Mrs Villiers she told me you named all your animals after friends. Is that true?'

Robert laughed, 'Yes. Girls.'

'Is Jessie named after someone special?'

'Not Jessie; there has been a long line of Jessies going back to my childhood, all canine. Come on, shall we ride to the top through the wood?' Robert kicked his horse into a canter and Juno followed. At the top, Robert reined in to gaze at the familiar view, west towards the Lizard and Land's End and east towards Plymouth. 'All quiet today,' he said, 'no bombers. Look, quick, there's a peregrine! See, it's after a pigeon. My God, those birds are wonderful. Look, Juno, see it jink. Look, do you see it?

She must share his delight, but Juno was sliding off the pony, handing him the reins, doubling over to be sick.

Robert got off his horse and watched Juno heave. Then she wiped her pale face with her handkerchief, gulped for breath and said, 'Sorry about that, I must have picked up some bug which is making me queasy. I felt sick yesterday morning when I was milking; it was the smell of warm milk.'

Robert asked, 'And the morning before?'

Juno said, 'Come to think of it, yes, how funny.' Her colour was returning. 'Where's the peregrine? I don't believe I've ever seen one.'

Robert said, 'It's gone now. I don't think you have a bug.'

Juno said, 'No. I don't suppose so, it's nothing.' She reached to take the pony's reins.

Robert said, 'Not nothing, it's a baby.'

Juno said, 'What?' Her hand was still reaching for the reins.

'Juno, you are pregnant.' He let her take the reins.

'I am what?' She stared at him.

'Going to have a baby.'

'Going to have a baby?' She jerked the pony's head up; it was munching grass.

'Yes, Juno.'

'But I don't like babies. I know nothing about babies. What on earth makes you think I am – what did you say?'

'Pregnant.' He watched her pull grass from the pony's mouth, it was frothy and staining the bit. 'You have morning sickness,' he said.

'Some bug called morning sickness?'

'No. A baby. A child.'

Juno said, 'How on earth would you know?'

'My wife and I had a baby.'

'Oh yes, of course, Evelyn, but that was ages ago.'

'The symptoms remain the same.'

'She threw up?'

'Yes. It doesn't last long, a few weeks—'

'But I'm not—'

Robert said, 'It's all right, don't worry. I will—'

'But how can I? I don't know anything. I don't like—'

Robert said, 'Hasn't your mother told you anything?' The pony was munching grass again.

'My mother,' Juno said, 'never even told me about the curse. She didn't even—'

They had been on a picnic. There had been other people. Jonty's and Francis's friends, another boy, several girls. She had said, 'I have cut myself. Anyone got a plaster?' Mrs Murray, a fussy mother, often put plasters in the picnic basket, someone usually managed to get a cut or a scratch. 'Give us the box of plasters,' she had said.

'Where's the cut?' one of them said. 'Let's have a dekko.'

Then they had laughed, a great yell of laughter. 'Our Juno's on heat,' they had cried for all to hear. 'Here's a turn-up for the book, you're on heat, luvvy, no plaster can help that,' and between giggles they had given her a rundown on the facts of life, information which when checked turned out to be garbled. Her mother when she got home had been annoyed, 'I wasn't expecting it for you for another couple of years.'

Juno said, 'She should not be eating this stuff,' and pulled the pony's head up. 'Oh, Robert!'

Robert said, 'Having a baby can be fun.'

And Juno said, 'Who for?' She glanced into his friendly eyes, then looked away.

Robert murmured, 'There hasn't been a baby at Copplestone for forty years,' but Juno was staring at the sea and did not hear him. She had turned away from him and the horses. 'It's all right, you can't conceive the first time,' one of them had said. Had she made some feeble protest? Then the other had said, 'I believe that's an old wives' tale.' Give him credit. They believed what happened to suit, and she had gone along with it, for her mother, when tackled, had backed away from discovering life for her daughter. She was embarrassed by bodily functions. Goodness! What was her mother up to now? Was it possible that with Jack Sonntag she was indulging, if that was the correct term, in what the dictionary called copulation? An activity which, according to the same dictionary, was similar to if not the same as fornication, changing its name with marriage as did the bride. The sea was very blue out there, the seagulls white. Millicent was cropping grass again and Robert, standing beside her, said nothing. My goodness, had he not said enough?

Juno said, 'Perhaps you could tell me a bit more. Tell me, for instance, what happened to your wife, Emma.'

'Ah.'

'I am ignorant,' Juno thought she had better not say desperate.

Robert said, 'Let's sit down, it's warm out of the wind. Sit with your back to that rock. I will tether the horses.'

Juno sat, watched him tie the horses, come back and sit beside her. He leant back against the rock and said, 'How much do you know? How much has your mother told you?'

'Precious little. As I said, she never even told me about the curse and it took me ages to find out that all women have it and what it's for.'

Robert said, 'That's unbelievable.'

'Believe it.'

'I'll begin at the beginning, then.'

'Please.'

Robert coughed, 'Emma and I discovered how to make love. You with me?'

'So far.'

How lovely Emma had been when they made love that first time on a rainy day, tumbling and rolling in the bed which Juno slept in now, and all the other times that magical summer, indoors and out, up here on the cliff to the sound of the sea and cry of gull. But one must skip that, stick to the essence. 'So we made love and after a month, six weeks perhaps, Emma started to feel sick in the morning, like you just now.'

'And?' For Robert in turn was staring out to sea, silent, remembering. Was he remembering that Emma had enjoyed it? Lucky Emma. 'Go on, what happened next?'

'Oh! Yes. Well, after a while, not long at all, she stopped feeling sick and felt very well.'

'Good. And?'

'And the baby grew inside her, as yours will in you, and after nine months Evelyn was born.'

'Was she pleased?'

'We were both tremendously pleased.' (Ecstatic would be the right word.)

'There must be more to it than that.'

'Oh, there is. There is the moment when the baby first moves, that's magical.'

'Moves? Where? Inside the body?'

'Yes.'

'Good Lord!'

'And I remember she wanted to pee pretty often, she found that a bit of a bore. It's pressure on the bladder. And she got pretty big, enormous, actually.'

'And?'

'That's about it. The baby grows into a tiny human being.'

'But you were in love?'

140

'Tremendously so, yes.'

'So she put up with bits of boredom?'

'Of course.'

'Does it hurt when the baby is born?'

'I am afraid it does.'

'I don't like the idea of that.'

'Nor did Emma.'

'But she managed to bear it and had a lovely baby and you married and lived happily ever after,' Juno was shouting. She had angry tears spurting, felt herself shaking. 'But I – I am not – I do not – I do not know what to do or where to go or anything – I –'

Her shouting alarmed Millicent, who tossed her head, neighed and jerked the rein tying her to the tree. Robert's horse, uneasy too, shuffled and shifted his feet. Robert thought, ever after was pretty marvellous. I was lucky to have even those few months, I know that, and I must try to hang on now Evelyn has died, but blast the girl, why is she shouting so?

He was suddenly angry and snapped, 'You stay here, you little fool, that's what you do. There is no need for you to go anywhere.'

Juno said, 'What?'

Robert said, 'Ann and I can look after you.' He stood up, furious. 'Unless you want to be shipped off to Canada to join your mother, though the shipping lines probably draw the line at pregnant girls in wartime. Anyway, is that what you want? Canada?'

Juno exclaimed, 'I couldn't possibly. No!'

'Well, then.' Robert sat down again, his anger diminishing.

Juno said, 'What will your neighbours say?'

Robert said, 'Fuck my neighbours.' And, observing Juno's startled expression, 'They are rarely surprised by anything at Copplestone.'

Juno said, 'I believe you mean it, mean I can stay.'

'I do.'

'I am not married,' she prevaricated.

141

'I know that.'

'Or likely to be.'

'So?'

'I shall be a nuisance, a burden, a bore.'

'A nuisance and a burden probably, but not a bore. Look! There goes the peregrine, see it?'

'Yes! He is beautiful. Oh, Robert, thank you.'

Robert said, 'Time enough when we've had the baby.'

'We?'

Robert said, 'I intend to enjoy it and I propose that you do, too. Come on, there is nothing to cry about.'

'Your kindness, I am crying about that.'

Robert said, 'Don't embarrass me. You'll upset the horses.' For Millicent, annoyed at being tied and lusting after the forbidden grass, was jerking at the restraining rein. He said, 'Sit down a minute, Juno.' Her tears were gushing again and her nose running. Obediently she sat with her back to the rock, blew her nose and stared at the sea.

Robert thought, I should not have been so cavalier, I should have left this to a woman. How is it possible for the girl to be so ignorant? 'How is it possible,' he heard himself say, 'for you to be so ill-informed?'

Juno snapped, 'I seem to have managed. As I said, my mother never told me anything. I gleaned hints from girls at school but they knew nothing, either. I did not want to embarrass my mother, so I didn't ask. She seemed to assume that I would be informed by divine intervention—'

Robert said, 'I always told Evelyn everything.'

Juno said, 'Gosh.' Then hesitantly she said, 'Might I ask you?'

'Ask away.' Robert stretched his legs.

Looking away from him, Juno said, 'You say it grows inside and moves about?'

'Yes.'

'But how does it get out?'

Flabbergasted, Robert asked, 'Have you never seen an animal born? Puppies? Kittens? A foal?'

142

'Never.'

Robert swallowed. 'Juno,' he said gently, 'the baby gets out where it went in when you made love. It comes out head first between your legs.'

'But how could it? Babies are huge! D'you mean to say? My God, you must be joking!'

'I'm not.'

'Is it possible?' Now she turned to look at him. 'Are you seriously telling me—'

'Yes.'

'No wonder it hurts.'

'Yes.'

'You are telling me the truth?'

'Yes.'

'What a performance!'

Robert said, 'You could call it that.'

Juno groaned, 'What a fix I'm in.'

'It's not a fix. It's a child, not an illness. It's something to be happy about.'

'Happy?'

'Yes.'

'I am not happy.' She had stopped crying. 'I am angry.'

'Ah.'

'For being such a stupid gullible fool.' She had raised her voice to a shout and the horses jingled their bits, laid back nervous ears.

Robert said, 'Well,' and crossed his legs while they sat on with their backs to the rock and Juno, nursing her anger, tried to arrange her thoughts.

Presently she said, half to Robert, half to herself, 'My mother is forty, she has gone to Canada. She is going to marry again. I couldn't believe it at first, at her age.' Robert smiled and Juno went on, 'She is marrying this man even older than her. He's conventional as hell, but she seems happy.' Robert raised his eyebrows and Juno went on, 'I believe now that she was never really happy. My father shamed her by voting Labour, being a conscientious objector, going to prison, all that, but she made a good

143

widow. Then along comes rich Mr Sonntag. Heaven opens and she plans for it to open for me, sees a vista of wealthy young Canadians to make me happy ever after—'

'She packs your houndstooth overcoat—'

'You remember that?'

'And?'

'And what on earth will she think now?' Juno shouted. She was shaking with rage. 'It will wreck her life,' she cried, 'shatter her conventions.'

Placidly Robert said, 'There's the Atlantic Ocean between you.'

'So?'

'So why tell her? Why spoil her happiness? Why not just shut up?'

Juno said, 'Could I do that?'

Robert said, 'I don't see why not.'

'But that would be lying to her.'

'Not exactly, and surely you've lied to her before?'

'Well, yes.' (Of course I have, often, often.) Then Juno said, 'I get the impression you quite want me to have this baby!'

Robert murmured, 'It will give us all something other than the war to think about.' And Juno thought, other than Evelyn, but did not voice it.

TWENTY-FOUR

'*I* can't just sit here.' Juno sprang to her feet. 'I shall be late for milking and Bert will revert to being testy.'

Robert watched her unhitch Millicent, swing into the saddle and clatter off down the hill. Slowly he got up, untied his horse and followed at a sedate pace, pausing now and again to listen to the pony's diminishing hoofbeats.

What had possessed him to be so abrupt? Surely he could have found a more gentle approach? He was appalled by his bluntness and lack of tact, not used to encountering such complete ignorance, and yet – there by the path was a primrose in flower. Spring was on the way. He dismounted and, picking the flower, sniffed its wet and hopeful scent and threaded it through his buttonhole as Emma had once done. Had he ever managed to tell Evelyn what his mother was really like? A girl as delighted by the first primrose as by the discovery of something rare, a girl who had said, 'Each time is the best,' as she lay sated in his arms? Was it possible or was it essential for each to discover love for himself? What had Juno discovered? Impossible to ask. He had told her more in those few minutes than he could have told Evelyn. It was probable Evelyn had judged him by the sophisticated and knowledgeable females he had consorted with over the years. With none of them had he been in love. Had not Evelyn taken a leaf from his book and acted in much the same way, played the field, remained uncommitted, excusing his lack of commitment by his ill health?

'But none of my girls or his were ignorant,' Robert muttered as he remounted his horse. What was he to think now? 'Juno must have known something,' he said out loud. Was this sneaking feeling of hope mere wishful thinking? His horse, alert to the pain in his voice, twitched its ears back and forth as it picked its way down the stony track.

At the house the dog Jessie greeted him, her puppies tumbling clumsily after her. Soon she would leave them and be back to keeping him company. The pony Millicent was in her box and poking her nose out to whicker a greeting. There was no sign of Juno. Robert slid off his horse, took off its saddle and bridle and let it into the stable. Then he crossed the yard and went into the house, calling, 'Ann?' Ann should have been the person to tell Juno she was pregnant; it was a woman's job. Anxiously he raised his voice, shouting, 'Ann.'

'I am here.' Ann's reply came from the depths of a cupboard. He could see her tweeded beam as she stacked plates onto a low shelf. 'What is it? No need to shout.'

'Have you seen Juno?'

'She clattered into the yard a while ago, put Millicent in her box, went upstairs for a few minutes, then out again. Gone down to milk the cows. What's the matter?'

'Did she say anything?'

'As I say, she came in and went out. What's up?'

'Oh God!' Robert was hurrying out to where they could see Juno loping down the hill to the farm, not using the path but short-cutting down the slope, running sideways to keep her balance, her arms swinging in rhythm with her feet. 'I can't think what possessed me, what I have said may be irreparable. I am an idiot, I should have left it to you. It would have come so much better from you.'

'What would? What's going on? What's all this about?' Ann was irritated and showed it.

'I made her weep. Her tears gushed. Oh, dear God!'

Ann said, 'She isn't weeping now.'

146

Juno had reached the bottom of the slope where the ground levelled out and was turning cartwheels, once, twice, three times, legs flailing the air, long hair brushing the grass. Upright again, she straightened the fisherman's jersey and walked into the farmyard to vanish into the cowshed.

Ann said, 'Whatever have you done to her? Ah, here comes the Army. They rang up after you went out. It's about the bomb in the wood, it's unexploded.'

Robert said, 'Oh, bloody hell.' With hand politely outstretched, he went to greet his visitor who, stepping out of his car followed by his sergeant, was introducing himself. 'Captain Lazenby, sir, bomb disposal. Your ARP reported your bomb and I have come to have a dekko. It's pretty dangerous if it's live.'

Robert said, 'Oh, ah, yes. It fell in my wood over there. My er – our – landgirl was collecting my cowman's dog, who was mating with a neighbour's bitch. Though what am I drivelling on about? It has no connection—'

'Not the cartwheeler we saw just now as we drove up?'

'Yes.'

'Expressing a certain lightness of heart, joys of spring, that sort of thing? *Joie de vivre*?'

Robert said, 'Complete change of climate.'

'Not quite with you, sir.' Captain Lazenby was puzzled.

Robert said, 'Mood. I'm not quite with me, but let me show you where the thing fell.' Pulling himself together, gathering his wits, frustrated, unable to wait to tackle Juno and shout, 'What the hell's going on? First it's tears, now it's cartwheels?' But quietly he said, 'It's about fifty yards into the wood, it damaged a beech. No, it did not explode, the ARP's report is correct.'

'You say that girl was near when it fell?'

'Yes.'

'Then she had a lucky escape; if it had exploded, she would not be here to do cartwheels.' Robert winced and the captain went on, 'We will have to blow it up, sir. Defusing's dodgy. I hope there won't be too much

147

mess. If you can show me where it is, we will get the job done.'

But Robert's mind was elsewhere; had not Ann told him that Juno came into the house and went upstairs before running down to the farm? Of course! She was upstairs for a few minutes, discovered she had the curse and was not pregnant. This would account for the cartwheels. Relief, it was bloody relief made her cartwheel! Out loud Robert said, 'Bloody fool!'

Captain Lazenby said, 'Sir?'

'Oh, not you, no, no. I just realized something, my mind was miles away. I beg your pardon. Oh dear, what a disappointing surprise!' And again Captain Lazenby explained that he was at a loss, which irritated Robert into paying some attention. Striding ahead into the wood, he said, 'Along here, follow me, my pigs roam here after acorns – Eleanor's particularly keen – I let them roam in the autumn.'

'Eleanor, sir?'

'Prize sow. Her namesake had a sashaying walk, very much the same. She wore a black and white bathing dress. She was snub-nosed, too. I'll show her to you presently. Here, it's about here.' Robert stamped the ground and poked with his stick, wishing this interfering young officer would go away so that he could get at Juno and – and what exactly? What was there for him to say? Was he supposed to be overjoyed? Turn a few cartwheels? Be enchanted that it was a false alarm? 'There, the bloody thing's there.' He stamped his foot and drove his stick into the ground.

'For God's sake, sir, don't do that!' Captain Lazenby and his sergeant sprang back. 'We must rope it off. Do for God's sake tread carefully.'

Robert laughed and said, 'Haven't you heard of the unexploded bomb in Knightsbridge? The buses rumbled over it for six whole weeks before someone got around to defusing it. These things don't go off that easily.'

But later, when Captain Lazenby and his party had set their fuse and exploded the bomb, the procedure dis-

148

rupted the working day, for cows, horses, sheep and pigs had to be moved away from the farm, the windows of the farm and cottage opened in case of blast and the whole area roped off for the explosion. This in itself was anticlimactic, only really upsetting the rooks, who continued to circle long after all was over, caw-cawing in turbulent unease.

Robert, in nervous anxiety to speed his parting guests, found himself inviting them in for a stiff tot of his precious whisky and even asking them to stay for supper, which fortunately they were unable to do, as there were errant bombs on other people's land which demanded their attention. When they had driven away Robert was left with Ann and Juno and a dampening sense of loss which he knew he had little right to. But Juno, watching the departing car, secretly hugged herself, for that morning, on first sighting the Army car, she had not been constrained to scrutinize its occupants for someone familiar but, buoyed by the burst of joy which had struck her as she ran down the hill and caused her to turn cartwheels, she had been happy to work all day with Bert, herding recalcitrant animals to safety and, when the bomb was exploded, bringing them back to their rightful places.

'You picked the first primrose.' Juno pointed at Robert's buttonhole. 'I saw it this morning as I rode down the hill.'

'It's dead.' Robert removed the faded flower, handing it to Juno. Should he speak now? Repair the morning's damage? Congratulate her, perhaps? Or behave as though nothing had been said? The day had been long, he had found it tiresome. Juno took the flower from him. 'Poor little thing.'

Ann called, 'Supper is ready.'

In silence they sat at the table, all of them tired. Robert said, 'So that was all very exciting,' not enjoying the silence.

Tartly Ann said, 'It would have been exciting in another way if Juno had been blown up.' Forking food into her mouth, she munched and remarked, 'We should be grateful for bad German craftsmanship. There might have been no Juno.'

149

Juno sipped water, swallowed and, glancing sidelong at Robert, murmured, 'And no baby.'

Sleep was evasive. Juno lay listening to the stillness of the house. The ankle which she had not spared working with Bert was hot and painful; the sprain, which she had hardly noticed when the bomb fell nor during its aftermath, was making itself felt. Turning cartwheels from joy, now she had time to consider, was an action which had done nothing to improve it.

Ann had strapped the ankle but it was bound too tight; she unwound the bandage and felt the muscles throb as her blood flowed freely, almost as freely as the blood which had suffused Robert's face when she had mentioned the baby. He had flushed dark red and his eyes, glancing at her, had appeared very blue. Quickly he had looked away and his face faded to its normal tan as he said something to Ann, and Ann replied. Then he had risen from the table saying, 'Time for bed.' He had let the dogs out for their last run, as he usually did, packed up the library fire, covering the smouldering logs with ash, put the fireguard in place and gone up the stairs, calling, 'Goodnight, goodnight, it's been a long day.'

Had one of them answered, 'Eventful'?

'Thank you for all your hard work,' he had said. 'Sleep well, sleep well.'

But she could not sleep. She rolled up the bandage and tested her ankle, moving the joint. Ice would help. There was ice in the kitchen; she slid out of bed and reached for Evelyn's dressing-gown.

Walking barefoot, she made no sound except for the skirt of the dressing-gown whispering behind her on the stair. The house breathed and creaked as old houses do as they cool from the day. Only the long-case clock measured her passage and Robert's forebears watched from their frames inscrutably, each with the Copplestone look, strong nose, blue eyes, brown hair and the expression of amusement often present in Robert. It had been there

150

too in Evelyn, known so briefly, almost forgotten. She paused on the stair, remembering Evelyn. Had he been amused? Questioning, she looked at a portrait level with her shoulder, a man in a green coat, in the Copplestone eyes a cast which the artist had made no effort to hide. His expression was racy and *louche*, giving nothing away. She moved on to the kitchen. Here she filled a bowl with ice and cold water, sat by the Aga, plunged in her foot, gasped at the cold, bore it, stroked Ann's cats asleep against the stove with her other foot, feeling their warmth as they sleepily mewed.

As the pain eased, she considered the past day, beginning with Robert sighting the peregrine, being sick and Robert's voice, 'It's not nothing, it's a baby.' And, later, 'Having a baby can be fun,' his tone gentle and calm, absolutely certain. This remark, sinking in, had infected her with the spasm of delight which had led to the cartwheels, snuffing out her other feeling, which had been of acute and reminiscent embarrassment at once again displaying her ignorance of bodily functions.

As the pain left her ankle and it stopped throbbing Juno sat on by the stove, considered her ignorance and resolved to cure it. Could she question Ann, who would give matter-of-fact answers? To a degree, yes. She removed her foot from the bowl, dried it, emptied the bowl and, the ankle no longer hurting, left the kitchen. Crossing the hall she noticed that the library door was ajar and, looking in as a log slipped sideways in the grate and a flame flickered up, saw by its light the book-lined walls. She would explore those shelves for the knowledge she needed; there was bound to be a book. She would ask Robert. He would not mock, she need not fear. If he was amused it would not hurt. Climbing up the stairs past Robert's squinting ancestor she felt elated and secure, a condition of mind she was not used to.

TWENTY-FIVE

'So how was your leave?'
Francis leaned against the bar.

'All right. A beer, please, landlord.' Jonty stared at the rows of bottles behind the landlord's head.

'You don't sound enthusiastic.' Francis watched his cousin's beer froth into the glass.

'Actually I am quite glad to get back.' Jonty accepted the proffered tankard. 'Thanks.'

'What went wrong?' Francis quizzed.

'Nothing.' Jonty brooded.

'Come on, you were so keen to get home.'

Jonty let out an exasperated sigh. 'It's all changed, nothing is the same. Let's sit down.'

They carried their drinks to a table and sat. Francis said, 'Tell me.'

Jonty gulped beer, sighed, said, 'Father's wrapped up in village minutiae, ARP, war committees for this and that, Home Guard, Dig for Victory. He's taken the war into his soul and your father's no better; he's planning to dig up the croquet lawn and grow potatoes.'

'No!'

'He would do the same for the tennis court, if it were not macadam. I tell you, they are really enjoying themselves.'

Francis said, 'But they were like that before we left.'

'More so now, and Mother—'

'Oh, how is she? What's wrong there?'

'She'd invited Angela Addison to stay.'

Francis whistled. 'Angela? And were you supposed—'

152

'Yes, and she made it so obvious it was embarrassing.'
Francis laughed. 'Well may you laugh. Just wait till you get
the treatment. They have plans, my ma and yours. I think
they have gone off their collective rockers, they want us to
propagate the species. Your mother even went so far as to
hint at marriage.'

Francis, laughing, said, 'I thought the theory was that we
are too young and should concentrate on wild oats.'

'It was, but all that's changed. You can't sow wild oats
with Angela, she's not that sort.'

Francis grinned. 'I suppose not. I like Angela but I see
your point. I take it you held back?'

'Of course.'

'Not even a chaste kiss?'

'Not even that. We went for long walks in the rain, played
chess and went to bed early.' Jonty gulped his beer.

'You sound disgruntled.' Francis was amused.

Jonty said, 'I am, a perfectly good leave wasted.'

Francis said, 'Well, I haven't been letting the grass grow.
I've been mowing.'

Jonty whistled, 'Who with?'

'I am not sure I shall introduce you.'

'Is she pretty?'

'Not very, but she has good legs.'

'Mystery?'

'No mystery, no.'

'Pity.'

'Mystery wasn't much help to us that other time.' Francis
set his empty glass on the table. 'But perhaps you'd better
meet her. I think she's an amateur tart, very spritely, I
learned a lot.'

Jonty said, 'Oh. You make me envious, curious anyway.'

Francis said, 'Actually I've made a date, want to come?'
For Saturday if we can both get off.'

'Won't she mind?'

Francis said, 'Of course not, she'll bring a friend. It's all
right, I've met her, she has good legs too.'

Jonty said, 'Oh.'

They sat silent while Jonty finished his beer and Francis watched him, then Francis said, 'London is the place to spend our leave. A night at home to soothe parental feelings, then London.'

Jonty said, 'You may well be right. I had set my heart on getting home but it's not the same, everything's changed. It's not just the war, there is something missing.'

Francis said, 'Juno.'

'Juno?' Jonty glanced quickly at his cousin, then looked away.

Francis said, 'She was part of the furniture.'

Jonty raised his voice, 'What a horrible thing to say.'

Francis said, 'But it's true,' and presently, as they drove back to their billet, he said, 'Didn't she have an aunt in London? One could ask.'

And Jonty snapped, 'Ask what?'

Francis said, 'Ask how she is I suppose,' but he sounded uncertain.

Jonty said, 'And where does this aunt live?' When Francis admitted that he did not know, he remarked sourly that their mothers would not know either and enquired whether Francis knew the aunt's name, and when Francis admitted that he didn't, he shouted something to the effect that Canada was a large country, so what was the use?

TWENTY-SIX

*M*eeting Ann coming out of the village shop, Priscilla Villiers stood in her way. 'Oh, Ann, I am glad to see you. It will save me telephoning.'

Ann said, 'Good morning,' shifting her shopping from right arm to left, indicating that she had no time for chat.

'I've had a letter from Anthony,' Priscilla said. 'He is coming in two weeks' time to work my garden, and he is bringing a friend, Hugh Turner. I thought you would like to know. They could come on to you when they have finished with me.'

'We are not as short-handed as we were, now John is back for the garden. He gives Bert a hand on the farm and his wife Lily is helping me in the house.' Ann was aware, as was Priscilla, that Anthony had originally been sent by Evelyn to help his father. Priscilla was poaching.

Priscilla said, 'I thought Robert would appreciate help with the haymaking, all hands to the pump, that sort of thing.'

Ann said, 'Probably.'

'Of course he should have contacted Robert, but he seems rather to have adopted me,' Priscilla pressed on.

Ann said, 'So it seems.'

'And you have wonderful Juno, such a pretty girl. Is that arrangement working? Is Robert finding her useful?'

Ann said, 'Yes.'

'I have not seen her for months except in the distance. Has she heard from her mother? She was so bothered about not joining her in Canada. I helped her sort that one

155

out. She was determined not to go,' Priscilla said, 'and I do see her point; in Canada she would have been away from the war, missed all the action.'

Ann said, 'Copplestone is pretty isolated.'

'But you did have a bomb,' Priscilla exclaimed.

'Unexploded.'

'But excitement and drama after, I was quite envious, but where were we? Oh yes, Juno's mother. Has she heard from her? Was she upset by the change of plan?'

Ann said, 'Not so you'd notice.'

'Oh?'

'It appears she got married.'

('It slipped out,' Ann later told Juno, 'the woman's such a gossip it's infectious.' They were sitting at supper.)

Priscilla said, 'Goodness! Then there's hope for us all. What does Juno think about it?'

Ann said, 'It came as no surprise.'

Priscilla persisted, 'Really? And you say she is happy? That's good. As you say, Copplestone is terribly isolated for a young person. I expect Anthony and his friend will make a nice change.'

Ann said, 'I dare say. I must be getting on. I will give your message to Mr Copplestone.' She was disinclined to discuss Juno's happiness with Priscilla or, since it was not yet public property, its cause, but recollecting Juno's cartwheels she chuckled, surprising Priscilla and leaving her perplexed.

'Oh,' Priscilla said, following Ann from the shop, 'I see you have Millicent in harness, pulling a trap. What a good idea. I had forgotten there was a trap at Copplestone, we used to use it for picnics in our youth. Millicent looks splendid but is she safe in harness? She is such a frisky pony.'

Ann said, 'Perfectly,' and began stacking her shopping under the seat.

Enviously Priscilla said, 'I wish I had a pony trap, it would save so much petrol.'

Ann said, 'It does.'

'Let me help.' Priscilla came forward to snatch at Ann's parcels. 'Knitting wool, I see, what are you knitting?'

'Socks.'

'For Robert?'

'Yes.'

'But you have baby wool here.' Priscilla peered into the parcels. 'You can't knit socks from baby wool, Ann, it won't wear five minutes.'

Ann said, 'No.'

'So it's baby clothes, too. Is somebody having a baby?'

Ann said, 'Yes.'

'Anyone I know?' Priscilla pried. 'Not John's wife again? They have three, haven't they? Surely that's enough.'

'No.'

'Then who?' Priscilla persisted.

'I didn't answer that,' Ann told Robert and Juno. 'Millicent chose that moment to tread on her foot.'

'Which is what her namesake would have done, those two girls never got on.' Robert was amused. 'Poor Priss, she has always been a prier, she loves to know other people's business.'

Ann said, 'She certainly does.'

But Juno surprised them. 'I don't mind her prying. She helped me with the cable to my mother, and that's given me a happy breathing space.'

Robert said, 'Happy?'

Flushing, Juno answered, 'I don't believe I was ever so happy before,' but was unable to enlarge.

Possibly the day would come when she would be able to tell Robert how happy she was, but sitting at supper that evening she was unable to elaborate. Nimbly changing the subject from personal feelings to work on the farm, she asked Robert when he would be cutting the hay, so setting him off on a dissertation on the quality of the grass in the top and bottom meadows, his hopes for fair weather, the time the hay harvest would take if all went well, how large a haystack would be the end result, that if Anthony

157

and his friend came to help Bert and John, the whole enterprise would be accomplished within a week.

'What we need is hot sun and a stiff north breeze.' Robert let his eye rest for a moment on Juno, grateful that she was happy.

Juno met his eye. 'And the orchids?' she asked.

'Seeded by now. They will flower again next spring.'

Juno said, 'Good.'

Ann, getting up to gather the dishes and take them to the sink, said, 'I dearly love the smell of new-mown hay.'

Juno murmured, 'Smells,' aware that scent, beginning with the first primrose, had contributed much to her happiness in recent months – grass after rain, freshly tilled earth between rows of vegetables, the sharp tang of box, the stuffy smell of hen where an obstinate fowl laid a daily egg in Millicent's manger, horse shit, cowpats, the stink of fox in the wood, cows' breath, the warm smell of pig, the tang of sheep, the crazy mix of lilac, roses, honeysuckle and wisteria which drifted in at her window as the wall of the house cooled, the secret whiff of bluebells under the beeches in the wood, the sharp tang of freshly chopped logs and the salt breeze on the cliff where she had sat with Robert and, in the house itself, wood smoke, Ann's cooking, the reassuring comfort, if he was near, of Robert's shaving cream and Pears soap.

As she got up from the table to help with the dishes, Juno wondered what, when it was born, her child would smell like? For that evening when she had come up the hill from the farm, pausing to sit on the seat in the porch, pull off her boots and look at the view, she had felt the first quickening of her child, a secret intimation of life.

Juno put her arms round Ann's thick waist as she stood at the sink, her bare arms bubbled with suds. 'Did anybody ever call you a saint?' She squeezed the older woman's thick middle.

158

Ann said, 'Don't be daft, you nearly made me drop the pie dish.'

'And Robert? The seigneur of Copplestone?' Juno squeezed harder.

'Oh, that one needs his head examined. Now let me go, girl, get a drying cloth or we'll be here all night.'

TWENTY-SEVEN

'So who is the father?' Priscilla came up to Robert as he stood by the gate of the hayfield. The hay had been cut, raked in lines, heaped into haycocks, loaded onto wagons, tossed up to the rick which now stood at the side of the yard, the result of four days' hard work in blazing sun.

Bert and Juno had gone to their milking, John to the walled garden to water his vegetables; Anthony and Hugh mopped sweaty brows and stretched aching limbs as they watched the horses drink at the trough before letting them loose in their field; then they would trudge up to the house, hoping for a bath. It had been a good day. The harvest was excellent; all the workers weary, satisfied, content. Robert swung the gate towards him. A few days' rain and the grass would grow again but the rick must be thatched first.

'So who is the father?' Priscilla was at his elbow, her arms filled with baskets full of empty thermoses whose contents had soothed the thirsty workers.

'Gadfly.' Robert closed the gate.

'I asked.'

'I heard you.'

'I should say four or five months. It's no secret, is it, even under that loose shirt? Was it one of Evelyn's or one of yours, the shirt?'

'Evelyn's.'

'So who—'

'Observant.'

160

'It's obvious, Robert, one can't help but notice.'

'Yes.'

'So?'

'I don't know, Priscilla.'

'You don't *know*!'

'No.'

'Haven't you asked?'

'No.'

'Has Ann? Surely Ann . . .'

'No.'

'Honestly, Robert!'

'What?'

'Do you mean to tell me—'

'I wasn't telling you anything, Priscilla. Let me help you carry those baskets.' They had started the climb up to the house.

'No, no, it's all right, they are quite light. Robert?'

'Yes.'

'Is that girl, that pregnant girl, going to have a baby here at Copplestone?'

'Looks like it.'

'Robert, you are mad.'

Robert laughed.

'It's no laughing matter, Robert.'

'No.'

'So what are you going to do?'

'What would you advise?' Robert took the basket from Priscilla. 'Your young men have been a great help,' he said, 'buckled to, both of them. I fear their townees' hands will be blistered, poor fellows.'

'Don't change the subject, Robert.'

'Are you staying for supper?'

'If I am invited.'

'Could you call off your Mosley, he is rogering my bitch.'

'And you don't want unwanted puppies! Mosley! Come here, my lovely boy. Mosley, leave her alone!'

'Thanks, Priss. Perhaps you could leave him in your car while we eat?'

161

'All right, but he was only doing what comes naturally.'

'Yes.'

'And I take it—' Priscilla returned to the attack.

'Priscilla, you can take it whatever way you please, but I would be grateful if you would curb your curiosity and if necessary choke.'

'My goodness, Robert, you can be nasty! All right, I won't ask her.'

'Thanks.'

'It will be a severe test of our lifelong friendship.'

Robert said, 'If we have any energy left after supper we could all troop to the cove and go for a swim by the light of the moon, as we did in our youth.'

Priscilla said, 'Does she? Swim? The expectant mother?'

'Regularly.'

'Are you sure, Robert, that you are not losing your marbles?'

'No.'

'And you allow her to swim?'

'It's good for her. She also milks cows, feeds pigs, makes hay—'

'She has certainly done that!'

'One more snide cheep, Priscilla—'

'And I am out on my ear, lifelong friendship over. Sorry, Robert, sorry.'

'Then let's see whether I can find you a drink before supper,' Robert suggested more amiably. 'We have masses of rough cider if you can make do with that, but please shut your animal in your car. I don't want him in the house.'

Priscilla called, 'Come along, my lovely boy, get in,' and shut Mosley in her car.

Robert said, 'Leave a window open or we might have a happy event.'

'Such as?'

'Suffocation.'

Priscilla said, 'In all the years I've known you, I've never known you so touchy and disagreeable,' and quietly, as if to herself, 'I shall ask her if I get the opportunity.'

'I — do — not — think — you — will.'

'Do not frighten me, Robert.' But Priscilla was frightened, and choking back further questions, fell temporarily silent and accepted a tumbler of rough cider, a drink she abhorred. Presently, drinking some more, she joined loudly in the conversation at supper which, following a question from Hugh Turner, veered towards the namesakes of Robert's farm animals, the carthorses Horace and James, the pony Millicent, the sow Eleanor, and cows with rather grandiose names such as Constance, Victoria, Elizabeth, Penelope and Maud.

'Horace and James were Robert's uncles,' Priscilla informed Hugh. 'Horace was a director of the Bank of England and James made a fortune in jute, but it's the girls you should be interested in. They are much more amusing. Can I have a little more cider?' She pushed her empty glass towards the jug which Hugh, with a glance at his host, poured. 'Tell us about the girls, Mrs Villiers.'

'They were all Robert's girlfriends at one time or another. Am I not right, Robert?' Priscilla looked at Robert sitting at the head of the table. 'We thought for a while he was serious about Millicent, but in the end she married a merchant banker. Constance, Victoria, Elizabeth and Maud came and went after raising expectations; they married masters of hounds, people in the Foreign Office, gents in the city, didn't they, Robert? One still comes across them shopping in Fortnum's or Harrods. Then there was Eleanor, she seemed a serious proposition, not only sound but sexy. Back me up, Robert, she was very sexy, had lots of what our mothers called "it". I rather liked Eleanor, in fact I believe it was I who introduced you. I'd met her at a house party in Norfolk.'

'True.' Giving no change, Robert watched Priscilla drink her rough cider. 'You are going to have a terrible head in the morning,' he said amiably.

Priscilla cried, 'Oh, I know. God help me, I loathe this stuff, it's lethal,' and drained her glass. 'Makes me talk too much, say things I regret,' she exclaimed. 'But all those

163

girls, every which one, they fell in love with him, but oh dear me, he is not the marrying kind. He went to bed with them and that was it, their quota, their lot, and only their memory lives on in his farmyard. Oh gosh, I shall regret saying this, but they all said the same thing in later life; having an affair with Robert spoiled them for anyone else!'

Sitting at the end of the table, Ann said, 'You have forgotten the turkey called Priscilla, Mrs Villiers. We ate her.'

And Robert, laughing, said, 'Priss, I think I should drive you and Mosley home.'

'We should have swum, it's a lovely night.' Anthony came into Hugh's room; he was naked except for the towel turbanning his head, 'I've washed my hair, it was full of grass seed.'

'Here, let me rub it.' Hugh reached up to his friend. 'Sit down.' He took the towel and rubbed Anthony's hair. 'Such lovely hair.' He teased the hair with the towel, then combed it with his fingers. 'There, nearly dry.' He kissed his friend's neck. 'We can swim tomorrow if the weather's still good.' He leaned with his arms round Anthony's shoulders looking out into the dark garden. 'What an enchanted night. I am almost inclined to feel grateful to Hitler; if it were not for him I should never have developed such a liking for the country, certainly not for anywhere as isolated as this. Would you?'

'No, I should have stuck to the pavements and kept my hands soft. I have blisters from the pitchforks, look at them.'

'So have I,' said Anthony. 'They will heal. Which bed shall we sleep in tonight?' He rubbed his jaw against Hugh's cheek. 'I don't think for one minute Ann is deceived.'

'What about Lily?' Hugh returned the caress.

'She wasn't born yesterday. Every bed in the house is double. They know and we know we sleep in them turn-about. It's just happier all round if both are rumpled. But

164

since you are here, let's get into mine.' They got into the bed.

Presently Anthony said, 'There are not many hosts as tolerant as Robert.'

Hugh said, 'Or as discreet. Do you think he knows about Juno? It's interesting.'

'He must, it's obvious.' Anthony propped himself up on an elbow.

'So the baby is Evelyn's?' Hugh yawned.

'Has she said so? Has she talked to you?'

'No, nothing, just does not deny, and I haven't pried.'

Anthony said, 'One couldn't, there's a wall of silence, but *is* it Evelyn's? I get the feeling it might not be. Makes one think.'

Hugh said, 'Priscilla thinks it is, definitely. You've heard her hints. She was having a go at Robert.'

'Priscilla would,' said Anthony. 'Priscilla is so basic.'

'And Robert? What does Robert think?' Hugh questioned. 'You know him better than me. And Ann? What's her opinion?'

'Ann is a clam.' Anthony laughed. 'She would never let on. I have been assuming Robert thinks it is Evelyn's,' he said. 'Why else would he have taken her in, kept her here? Given her a job, looked after her. My God, they all cherish her. Even Bert would lick her boots if they needed it.' He yawned, lay back on the pillows.

'There *is* another possibility,' Hugh murmured.

'No!' Anthony stopped yawning. 'You don't mean—' He whistled.

'Why not? It's a thought. It's perfectly possible.'

'Oh my!' Anthony sat up. 'Oh Hugh! Oh, darling, do you really think?'

'Might be. Why not? There are any number of permutations once you start.' Hugh grinned mischievously.

Anthony said, 'I don't think we should laugh, it's a serious matter,' then burst into a crisis of giggles.

Hugh said, 'Don't make so much noise, somebody will come up to see what's the matter.' And he, too, began to

165

giggle. When at last their mirth had subsided, he said, 'Oh God, how tiring laughter can be, nearly as exhausting as an orgasm. Have we any energy left?' And when they had expended their energy and were almost falling asleep, he murmured, 'When it's born it will look like a Copplestone, then we shall know.'

Anthony replied, 'But we still won't know which.'

Hugh, drifting into sleep, questioned, 'Why doesn't one of us ask Juno?'

Anthony said, 'Don't be a cretin.'

TWENTY-EIGHT

*R*obert helped Priscilla out of her car and led her into her house with Mosley padding alongside. She had grown quiet, volubility spent. Pushing and pulling, he persuaded her up the stairs. 'Come on, old Priscilla, make an effort, nearly there.' She was a dead weight.

'Don't — call — me — old.'

'Affectionate terminology. Heave-ho, here we are. Now let's find you an aspirin.' They had reached her bedroom.

'Some in the bathroom.'

'All right. I'll find it, you get undressed.'

'Can't manage.'

'Try.' Robert explored the bathroom cupboard. 'Here we are.' He tipped two aspirin into his palm and filled a glass with water. 'Swallow these.'

'Don't want to.' She kicked off her shoes.

'Come on, old girl.'

'Do — not — call — me — old!'

'Oh, all right. Come on, let me help you get out of that. Hold your arms up.' Robert helped Priscilla out of her clothes, found her nightdress, lowered it over her head, held the glass, handed the aspirin, watched her swallow. 'Good girl, there we are, into bed with you.' He swung her legs up from the floor, arranged the pillows under her head, pulled up the covers, tucked her in. 'Comfy now?'

'Bye-bye romance.'

'Yes.'

'Leave the light on.' Priscilla lay with her eyes closed.

'All right now?'

'Where's Mosley? Mosley! Mosley!'

'He's here.'

'My treasure.' Mosley clambered onto the bed to rest his chin across Priscilla's ankles.

'How will you get home?' She opened an eye.

'I'll walk.' He stood looking down at her. 'I'll telephone tomorrow.'

'Anthony and Hugh – those boys –'

'Yes?'

'Would they have noticed I was tiddly?'

'No, Priss, of course not.'

'That's all right, then – goodnight.' She snuggled into the pillows, turned away.

Robert watched her fall asleep, then left the room, trotted down the stairs and let himself out into the moonlight. He would walk home by the cliff path, sniff the sea, remember walking it with Emma, with Evelyn, with Priss and Priss's husband, who had been a nice fellow but a bit of a boozer. Robert crossed Priscilla's garden and set off across the fields. When one was young and making love with Priscilla, one would not have imagined putting her to bed drunk and solo in middle age. Robert chuckled as he walked. He had had a long day, had been tired, but now, getting a second wind, he felt fresh, good for a swim in the cove before bed. He quickened his pace, striding across the fields towards the cliffs.

The night was still; it was hard to imagine war raging in Russia and the Middle East, submarines lurking in this exquisite sea, men and women dying over there out of sight. It was so beautiful here. He reached the cliff path and strode along its springy turf. If he was lucky he would see a fox going about its business, and, ah, an owl on silent patrol. How Evelyn had loved all this; one should be grateful to Priscilla for this excursion. Robert walked on, sniffing the salt air, listening to the suck and roll of the sea at the foot of the cliffs.

168

Reaching the cove, he paused to look down. The path could be tricky. There was someone down there, a figure walking by the stream as it fanned out across the little beach, a naked girl, Juno.

Robert squatted back on his haunches. What to do?

She looked white in the moonlight and her hair very dark, as was the pubic shadow between her legs. She walked across the sand to the sea, waded out, dived, swam slowly and luxuriously into the moon's path.

Robert watched. He could not join her; she was naked.

Was she safe? She was swimming far out. Should he stand up? Shout? 'Come back, do not swim so far, there is a current which is dangerous.' He had told her all that when he showed her the cove the day he told her she was pregnant. Had she taken it in? He watched the lazy movements of her legs and arms in the clear water, her hair trailing like seaweed. He had been aware that she bathed, but had not taken in that she bathed alone. Fool! He should have warned her. Ah, she was turning back, floating now on her back, looking up at the cliffs. If he moved she might see him, be startled. He froze.

Reaching the shallows she waded ashore, stood squeezing water out of her hair, brushing drops off her arms and legs, smoothing her curved stomach, walking slowly up the beach. He imagined her footprints. In the shade of the cliff, she pulled on knickers, trousers and shirt while he, letting breath out in a long sigh, watched.

He had feared for her swimming alone in the night. What if she had been attacked by cramp? Could he have reached her?

She had her clothes on and was unhitching Millicent. She had ridden here. She put her foot in the stirrup, swung onto Millicent's back, disappeared, the pony's hoofbeats diminishing.

Robert felt a fool; he could not tell her he had watched her swim naked. He could not warn her without giving himself away, a voyeur.

She had looked beautiful, and he had lost his wish to

swim. He felt very tired and in need of his bed. But reaching the sand after scrambling down the cliff he changed his mind. The line of Juno's footprints led to the water; soon they would be gone. Robert stripped off his clothes.

Juno's feet were narrow, he observed. The weight of the child made her heels imprint the sand firmly, the indentations from her toes were slight. Adjusting his stride, Robert paced towards the water and, reaching it, waded in as he had watched the girl do. Waist-deep he dived, as she had done, and swam out.

Floating on his back, he looked up at the cliff from which minutes before he had watched. Resting in the water, he tried to empty his mind of immediate thoughts and all memories past, to let the sea hold him, rock him, soothe him, while he persuaded himself to blank out. But his head was crowded by the minutiae of the day, farm noises, petty irritations, small pleasures, the mass of detail which composed the hay harvest. The day had gone smoothly. Each person had fulfilled his or her task, the young men from London had been willing and helpful; only Priscilla had struck a jarring note. He should not have plied her with rough cider and made her so drunk she had to be put to bed. Floating in the moonlight, Robert remembered there had been another occasion, a similar scene when, discovering her normally 'steady as a rock' husband had been unfaithful, she had come to him for consolation. He had plied her with whisky, taken her home and put her to bed, but on that occasion, rather drunk himself, he had joined her in the bed. There had been a brief sexual conjunction.

Out loud Robert said, 'Whew! Poor old Priss!' For Priscilla must, he hazily recollected the distant incident, have mentioned it to Ann. Why else would Ann recall a turkey eaten? In spite of himself, Robert chuckled. Juno had looked puzzled. One would not forget an encounter with Juno. This thought struck Robert a stunning blow. He felt suddenly cold and, needing to pee, emptied his

170

bladder, staining the sea, then swam violently out from the land, away from his thoughts until, exhausted, he paddled back to regain the beach where the tide had come up and obliterated all but the last of Juno's footprints. Robert trod on it hard and, pulling on his trousers and shirt, closed his mind with a resolute snap. But that night in his sleep he ground his teeth and woke, bathed in sweat and shouting for help, as he dreamed of drowning.

TWENTY-NINE

*J*uno leaned over the low wall and, reaching with a stick, scratched Eleanor's flank. The stick made a rustling noise as it travelled among the bristles. 'That's nice, that's luxury.'

Eleanor's amber eye glinted through stiff lashes. Ten piglets nestled along her flank, snouts pointing towards her teats, temporarily sated, asleep.

'She must like you to allow you to do that.' She had not heard Robert's soft-footed approach.

'I like her.' Juno continued the rhythmic scratching.

'You will send her into a trance.' The sow had closed her visible eye.

'I admire her.'

'She is indeed an admirable sow. This is her third litter.'

'I shall be content with one,' Juno murmured.

Robert cleared his throat. 'I wanted to talk to you about that.' Not since that morning on the cliff had they discussed Juno's child. 'If you will allow me,' he said.

'Oh?' Her glance was cautious.

'I would like you to see a specialist just to make sure that everything is all right with you and your baby. I would, of course, arrange it and pay.' Robert's embarrassment was obvious.

'But Ann, Ann has told me what to expect.' Juno stopped scratching. Eleanor opened an eye, jerked a trotter.

Ann, one could not leave all responsibility to Ann. Robert had leaned his elbows on the wall. He straightened up and looked down at the girl. 'I would be happier, it

172

would set my mind at rest,' he insisted more loudly than he intended.

Juno thought, what about my mind? She did not speak.

'I do not want you taking any risks.' Robert forced himself on.

'I should have thought they had already been taken.' Juno's tone was dry.

Robert said, 'I am thinking of future risks.'

'I bet she would make a good poker player.' Juno resumed scratching the pig. 'That eye gives nothing away.'

'Nor does yours.' Deflected, Robert grinned. 'So you play poker?'

'I learned.' (Funnily enough, she had always won; Jonty had complained, 'You deal her the best cards,' and Francis said, 'I believe she cheats.' They had lost interest, tried to teach her a complicated German game called Scat.)

'And now you should learn to look after yourself,' Robert laboured on.

'I do, I am healthy.'

'All the same, I would like you checked by a specialist,' Robert insisted.

'Ann has taken me to your doctor.'

'For the child's sake. I was thinking of a London man.'

'London?' Juno switched her eyes from Eleanor, looked at Robert. 'Why London?'

'As I say, to make absolutely sure all is well.'

'I would much rather not.'

'Tell me why.'

'I am happy as things are.'

Robert felt frustrated. 'There are things he would tell you.'

'Such as?'

'To ease up, for one thing. You are doing far too much, I know you are. I have asked John's wife, Lily, and she is going to help until you have had your child and are ready to work again.'

'You have planned this behind my back.'

'If that's how you want to put it, yes.'

173

'But I so love what I am doing.' Juno stopped scratching, Eleanor grunted.

'Lifting weights isn't good for you, nor is so much standing about. You can still come and scratch the pigs. I know what I am talking about.'

'The doctor says I am fine,' Juno protested.

'I dare say he does, but I am not having you carrying heavy buckets any more.' Robert was irritated. 'From now on you take a leaf from Eleanor's book, relax, rest.'

'I shall be bored stiff.' (And have too much time to think.)

'You won't. The house is full of books, you can read, lie in the sun, swim, build up your strength.'

'Hear that, Eleanor?' Juno poked the pig. Her grunt woke the piglets who, squealing, hustled towards her teats, scrambling over one another for the best position. 'I take your point; I am in for a busy time if Eleanor is anything to go by,' Juno said dryly.

'Juno.' He did not often use her name. 'Juno, listen, I would still like you to see a specialist. It would be sensible, this is a first baby. Be on the safe side.'

'Did Emma see a specialist?'

'Actually, no. Things were different then, she didn't.'

'So?'

'Juno, you could go to London. I would make you an appointment. Stay a couple of nights, more if you like, stay with your aunt.' He must persuade her.

'My aunt?' Juno flinched.

'It would be natural, but stay in an hotel if you'd rather. I only suggested your aunt because she is your family. You could see the specialist, do some shopping, buy things for the baby. You don't need coupons for baby clothes, Ann has told me—' Seeing Juno's expression, Robert paused. 'What have I said that's wrong?'

'The aunt.'

'Aunt?'

'She doesn't know I am pregnant.'

'Ah.'

174

'Nobody does.'

'Your mother?'

'Haven't told her either.'

'I see.' Robert assimilated. 'So they are in for a surprise?'
Juno said, 'I favour the *fait accompli.*'

'Yes,' Robert said, 'yes, I see your point. I had not realized, not quite, had not thought—' had been too shy, too
fearful of imposing on the girl's privacy to ask. Fearful, too.
'So,' he said, 'so there we are.'

Juno said, 'Yes,' and guided her stick to a point behind
Eleanor's ear. 'Only Copplestone is aware.' She traced a
circle among Eleanor's bristles. Robert was probably
smiling. She knew better than to ask why he was so kind;
he would answer, 'Because you were a friend of Evelyn's',
shrug his shoulders, and she would not have anything
adequate to say for it was too late now to confess how brief
the acquaintance had been.

THIRTY

*F*inding Violet was not difficult. The telephone directory yielded her address; she was the only Violet among the Marlowes. In London for a few days, Priscilla yielded to curiosity and listened to the telephone ring in Violet's house. It was answered abruptly, 'Violet Marlowe here, who is it?' The tone brooked no nonsense.

'This is Priscilla Villiers. You would perhaps remember me as Priss Lugard? I was briefly in your team when you were captain of hockey, but you may not remember.' Already Priscilla regretted her impulse; ringing Violet Marlowe would amount to prying in Robert's book. She could hear him, 'You've always been a Nosey Parker, what business is it of yours?'

'Hockey? Lugard? Knock knees, of course I remember you. What do you want?'

'It was a long time ago—'

'I seem to remember I dropped you.'

'It was a big disappointment—'

'I had to consider the team.'

'Of course you did.'

'Well, what can I do for you now? I hardly imagine you rang up to discuss hockey.' Violet chuckled.

'I rang up because – well, because your name came up when I was talking to your niece. I remembered you from school and wondered what had become of you—'

'Did you say niece?' Violet interrupted.

'Yes.'

'Juno Marlowe? You sure?'
'Yes.'
'And you've spoken to her?'
'Yes.'
'So you know where she is?'
'Of course.'
'No of course about it, all I know is that she is working on some farm in the West Country, or so she says.'
'She is working for a neighbour of mine, Robert Copplestone.'
'Never heard of him.'
'He farms.'
'Would she be working on a farm if he didn't?'
'I suppose not.'
'Do you have the address?'
'Of course, he is a neighbour. He's—'
'Because I haven't.'
'Oh!' (Why not?) Priscilla enjoyed this.
'Will you give it to me?'
'Of course I will.'
'Why not come to tea? I shall be in this afternoon, come at four-thirty.' Violet switched to affability. 'You can do me a good turn. I have a large parcel sitting here for Juno, didn't know where to send it. You will save me the postage. A friend of her mother's brought it from Canada, very good of him.'
'Canada?'
'That's where her mother is, hasn't she told you?'
'Oh yes, of course she has.'
'See you at four-thirty, then.' Violet rang off.
'She was abrupt at school,' Priscilla would tell Anthony, 'hasn't changed a bit.'

'So who is this man Copplestone?' Violet presently enquired as she handed Priscilla a cup of weak tea. 'And what's the place? Is he someone one should know? Have a biscuit. No scones, I'm afraid, it's the war.'
'A biscuit would be lovely.' Priscilla chose a ginger

177

biscuit from the proffered plate. 'The place,' she said, 'is Copplestone House, the farm is Copplestone Farm and the village is Copplestone, too. It's near Catchfrench in Cornwall.'

Violet said, 'A superfluity of Copplestones. I take it the farm is large?'

'Fair sized.' Priscilla bit the ginger biscuit; it had been too long in its packet and grown limp.

'And this Mr Copplestone would be—' Violet allowed her unvoiced question to hover. Had Robert been to a public school, was he county?

Priscilla swallowed a mouthful of biscuit. 'Copplestone's in the Doomsday Book, as is my husband's place.' If we are playing *that* game, she thought, I can play it better than hockey, and was amused to see Violet's expression of relief.

'And Juno, my niece, is working there?'

'Yes.'

'I did suggest the forces, but I suppose what she is doing contributes a little something towards the battlefront.'

Priscilla said, 'Of course it does, the country has to be fed.'

'And does my niece pull her weight?'

'I gather she works very hard.' Priscilla accepted another biscuit. 'Far too hard, if you ask me, for a girl in her condition. But I believe Robert is persuading her to ease up.'

'And what condition is that? She isn't ill, I hope? I was quite worried the last time I saw her, she looked dreadfully peaky.'

'She isn't peaky now, she looks radiant. It's the baby.' Priscilla smiled.

'The *what*?'

'Didn't you know?' Later Priscilla would tell Anthony that her feet had grown cold from the shock of her heart sinking into her court shoes as Violet said, 'Don't be ridiculous, how could I know? I haven't her address. This is absurd, Juno isn't married.'

Priscilla said, 'I believe not.'

'Then is this man, this Robert Copplestone, going to do

the right thing?' Violet snapped. 'We are no longer in the nineteenth century, young men rogering the maids and getting away with it.'

Priscilla gasped. 'Oh my goodness, the baby is nothing to do with Robert.'

'Then who?' Violet stared at her former schoolmate.

Priscilla said, 'Who indeed?'

Violet said, 'What on earth am I to tell her mother?' Her voice sagged.

Priscilla had nothing to suggest.

Violet said, 'Could the girl not have done something about it?'

'Such as an abortion?' Priscilla raised her eyebrows.

'Of course not, that would be illegal,' Violet sighed.

Priscilla, aware of having said too much, belatedly stayed mute.

Violet said, 'This is just the sort of thing her father would have done. He was a conchie, she must get it from him.' She repeated, 'What am I going to tell her poor mother?'

Priscilla said, 'I imagine that's up to Juno.'

'The poor woman has just got married – very suitably, I now hear, though I was unsure at first. She is happy. To be honest, my brother was not much of a husband. It will be such a shock. Not the sort of thing to tell your new husband, is it?'

Priscilla said, 'No.'

Violet said, 'What would you do in my shoes?' She sounded rather pathetic, as Priscilla would tell Anthony when they met for dinner, but now she said, 'In your shoes I wouldn't tell Juno's mother anything. I think I would just—'

Violet said, 'Just what? Just what would you do in my shoes?' She sounded as tough as when she had been captain of hockey.

Courageously Priscilla said, 'Send some money for the child, send your love?'

'But that would be condoning her behaviour and I don't love her, never have.'

179

Priscilla said, 'I see,' and laid the uneaten half of biscuit on her plate.

Speaking as though to herself, Violet said, 'She is of course "family", one can't escape that,' squaring shoulders which had bowed from shock.

Brightly Priscilla offered, 'All the best families have blots.'

Violet answered, 'That's the sort of comfort my lodgers dish out. I have friends who lodge with me, they have daughters and know what girls are like. I shall consult with them, though they are rather too soft-hearted.'

And bravely Priscilla ventured, 'I expect they would, in similar circumstances, send a cheque,' but this was venturing too far.

Violet snapped, 'I hope you are not suggesting my friends' girls would get themselves into such a pickle?'

Priscilla exclaimed, 'No, no of course I am not,' and then, 'I am sure you are busy, I must not take up so much of your time.'

Violet, pleased at signs of departure, said, 'I will get the parcel, and write down Juno's address. I should know it even if we are not in touch.'

Shaking hands on the doorstep, she said, 'Goodbye. I will think over your suggestion,' and as Priscilla set off along the pavement, she called after her, 'Sorry I dropped you from the team.'

THIRTY-ONE

*J*uno dragged herself up the hill from the river. She had grown too bulky to ride Millicent, and walking to the sea entailed effort. There was, however, a pool under a waterfall not far into the wood and in this she dipped on hot days, sunning herself afterwards on a rock, watching Jessie's puppies dip their noses, sneeze and pat the water after elusive trout while she listened to the sound of woodpigeons cooing in the branches above her head.

The puppies were now quite grown, one brindled and one black and white, their origin a mystery since no dog in the neighbourhood resembled them and Jessie, a dumb animal, was not informative.

'You and I, Jess, have much in common.' Juno fondled the dog's ears as she paused to look down at the farm. 'Whereas old Nipper,' she said, 'is a proud and legitimate pa.'

There had been quite a rumpus when Bert had claimed Nipper's puppy; Robert had been called in to arbitrate, smooth neighbourly awkwardness. Now the puppy was referred to as 'the unexploded bomb dog' but answered to Jupe or Jupiter, who Bert insisted must be a relative of Juno's, and Juno accepted the compliment. She could see the puppy now as it lurched about the farmyard inciting its aged parent to play, getting snapped at for its pains.

A car was grinding up the hill; Juno could hear the crash of gears. 'A visit from Mrs Villiers,' she exclaimed. 'Come on, dogs, up we go, heave-ho, hurry, she won't see us if we go in by the back door.' Quickening her pace, she lurched up the last of the hill to let herself in by the kitchen and climb up to her room where, out of breath, she lay on the bed to watch the sunlight play on the ceiling. She murmured, 'How much longer do I have to cart you around?' crossing her hands over her stomach, feeling the mysterious humping and bumping. 'Oh, you great little footballer.' Her hands fell away and she slid into sleep.

Downstairs Priscilla prowled the cool hall, looked in at the library, opened the doors of the drawing-room, so rarely used it smelled musty, inspected the dining-room, hardly used either, and made her way to the kitchen, which was empty too. 'Everybody out,' she said out loud and dumped the package she carried on the kitchen table. 'Anybody home?' she called and, receiving no answer, sat down to wait.

In the hall the long-case clock tick-tocked; in the sunlit yard a rooster crowed, hens clucked. Somewhere in Russia Germans and Russians were killing each other. Priscilla rendered thanks that she had no children; reading the papers and listening to the wireless was worrying enough. Time was, she thought, when I minded dreadfully, but not any more. Look at Robert, how he has endured Evelyn dying by slow degrees. 'Oh, poor Evelyn,' she exclaimed out loud, waking the cats by the Aga, who stretched like elastic, yawning, displaying needle teeth and sharp claws, fixing her with their green and yellow eyes, curling pink contemptuous tongues.

She remembered Robert, a widower at nineteen, father of a baby boy, a desirable young man who hardly noticed the child Priscilla growing up in the neighbourhood, to marry eventually one of his friends, a good man, a friendly man, but oh dear, so inclined to be boring and, come to think of it, his children might have been boring too. Boring, boring, Priscilla remembered, as she thought of her husband. I should miss him more than I do. Of course I miss him, but not as I would have missed Robert if I had had Robert. But then, she mused, if I had had Robert more

182

than just the once, would he still have had that succession of affairs? Would I have been able to endure that? All those flighty and amusing girls? Better to have things as they are, Priscilla concluded, Robert very much alive and a friend.

'Oh!' Priscilla exclaimed. 'I did not hear you, Ann. I have brought a package for Juno. I thought I would wait for somebody to come in.'

Ann said, 'I saw your car. Did you want to see Mr Copplestone? He said he was going to look at the corn and decide when to harvest.'

Priscilla said, 'Actually, I came to see Juno. I brought this package from her aunt – it's from her mother.'

Ann said, 'Fancy that. Well, well,' irritating Priscilla by her tone, and as Robert came in from the yard, 'Here is Mrs Villiers. She has brought a parcel for Juno from her aunt.'

Robert, deadpan, said, 'I take it you sleuthed in the telephone book? Could not resist?' He pecked Priscilla's cheek, not altogether friendly or welcoming, putting her on the defensive.

'I thought I would look her up.' Priscilla plucked up courage. 'We were at school together. I found myself passing her house. She lives in that nice square off the Brompton Road, so convenient for Harrods, the Oratory too, of course. I popped in, and wasn't it lucky? She had this package for Juno from her mother and no idea where to send it. So she was delighted to entrust it to me,' Priscilla babbled, 'to bring down to Juno. I told her I lived near you.' Priscilla paused to draw breath. Neither Ann nor Robert said anything. 'Can you believe this? When I was leaving she apologized for dropping me from the hockey team. Did I say she was captain of hockey? Much older than me, of course, one of the older girls, and she asked me to tea. We had a good old gossip.'

Robert said, 'I bet you did.'

Priscilla said, 'She is a big noise in the Red Cross. She made me feel inadequate with my tiny contribution to the WVS down here.'

Robert said, 'And the gossip was about?'

'Oh, you know the sort of thing, catching up with the years. She married young and her husband was killed in the war, same name, he was her cousin.'

Robert said, 'Absorbing.'

Priscilla flushed. 'It was absorbing to me.'

'And you told her her niece Juno is having a child.'

'Well yes, I suppose I did, *en passant* as it were.'

'And this Red Cross hockey queen was surprised?'

'Well, yes. Juno had not apparently told her.'

'And she expressed delight?'

Priscilla said, 'I can't say she did.'

Robert said, 'Can you never keep your great nose out of other people's business?' A query which Priscilla failed to answer, for at that moment Juno came into the kitchen with a rush of dogs and Priscilla was able to hand over the package and explain its provenance.

Juno exclaimed, 'How wonderful! I believe my mother has sent back my clothes. How absolutely super.' Looking very pleased, she tore open the package. 'Oh look, my houndstooth coat. Jerseys and shirts and a skirt, just what I need. What can these be? Nylons? Has anybody ever heard of nylons?'

Priscilla said, 'They are American, a kind of silk stocking, I have heard of them. Those are very pretty underclothes, what good taste your mother has.'

While Juno said, 'She must have bought them for me in Canada, how lovely. Oh look, I nearly missed this, a letter.' Slitting the envelope with her thumb, she began to read. 'I hope she is happy, I hope she is all right—'

Juno read the letter twice, then folded it and put it back in its envelope. Priscilla said, 'Good news, I hope, from across the Atlantic?' failing to read Juno's expression.

Juno said, 'Just – it's just rather difficult to take in. Across the Atlantic my mother is having a baby, "a little brother or sister for you," she says. I didn't know people that old could! Oh my, oh my! Robert, why are you laughing?' Raising an astonished voice, she said, 'She's practically forty! How on earth – Ann, you are laughing too. What's so hilarious?'

Ann remarked that life did not stop at forty in her experience, but she stifled her laughter, and they all watched anxiously as Juno bundled up the clothes, biting her lip, safety-pinning her mouth against any further naive remark.

Then, brightly, Priscilla said, 'Well, I must be off. I have left poor Mosley in the car.'

Robert said, 'I will see you out, Priss.'

Then Juno made a little speech of gratitude for her trouble and Priscilla said it was a pleasure, and kissed Juno's cheek before walking towards the hall followed by Robert.

As they left Juno called after her, 'I suppose you told my Aunt Violet about my baby?'

And Priscilla admitted, 'Actually, yes. I had taken it she knew.'

Rather stiffly Juno remarked, 'She will prefer the legit relation in Canada,' adding under her breath, 'to its nephew or niece.'

On the doorstep Robert said, 'You nosy tactless bitch.'

Priscilla said, 'How was I to know?' Getting into her car, she exclaimed with a bubble of laughter, 'I believe you are in love with the girl, Robert.'

As she started the engine, he said, 'A mismatch of generations, wouldn't you say?' slamming shut the car door, cutting off but still hearing her query, 'Discovered who the father is yet?' as she put the car in gear.

THIRTY-TWO

When Robert got back to the kitchen Juno had disappeared with her package and Ann was mixing something in a bowl, using unnecessary force. Belligerently she said, 'Decided when to harvest, have you?'

Mildly Robert answered, 'Yes, next week,' and sat down at the table. Presently he said, 'So Juno has her wardrobe back, I expect she is pleased.' When Ann did not answer, 'Isn't that the overcoat she suggested Bert might tolerate when he took exception to her sheepskin? I like the sheepskin, it has style.'

Ann grunted, 'I dare say it is.'

Robert grinned, 'So you are not interested?'

'Should I be?' Ann pounded the contents of the bowl.

Robert said, 'You are angry with Priscilla. She is a tactless busybody.'

'And not only that.'

'But she has a good heart, Ann, we shouldn't blame her for bringing that letter. We can't shoot the messenger.' When Ann did not reply, he said, 'You must admit it's quite funny about Juno's mother, a talking point for the next generation.' Ann grunted again.

Robert stretched his legs and stroked Jessie, who leaned her head on his knee. 'I want to discuss Juno with you, Ann. Stop that a minute and sit down.'

Reluctantly Ann said, 'Go ahead.'

Robert said, 'I wanted her to see a specialist but she

186

refuses. Do you think I should insist? I have left interfering rather late. Juno isn't easy to talk to.'

Ann said, 'You can say that again. Our doctor thinks she is fit, she's a strong girl.'

Robert said, 'I suggested a London man, but no, she says no.'

Ann said, 'What power have you?'

'You mean what rights?' Robert frowned. 'Rights?'

'That's what I mean.' Ann looked him in the eye.

Robert said, 'Ah. I stand corrected. None. I had not thought. I am nothing.' Looking into Ann's honest little eyes, he asked, 'You think I have imagined too much?'

Ann nodded, pursing her mouth.

'Then what do we do?'

'Book her in for the birth in the Cottage Hospital.'

Disconcerted, Robert protested, 'But I had imagined the child would be born in this house.'

'First babies are born in hospital these days.'

'But I – and Evelyn, we were born here.'

'That was then, that was you and Evelyn—'

'I will consult with the doctor.'

Ann said, 'You do that,' and tipped the contents of her bowl into a cake tin.

'And Ann, we must plan for later. She has her room and bathroom, what about a nursery? We have plenty of rooms—'

Ann said, 'You seem to assume—'

'What?' He tried to read the woman's expression but she had turned away and was putting the cake tin in the oven. 'I assume what, Ann?'

Ann said, 'That she will stay on.'

'Good God!' Robert shouted. 'Where else would she go? I can't see a welcome with either her mother or her aunt. She belongs here, for God's sake. I should have thought that was obvious.' When Ann did not reply, he said, 'We should have discussed all this sooner, but she is so hard to talk to, such a clam, she manages to make it difficult for me even to talk to you.'

187

Ann laughed, 'You are right there.'

'And what about cradles and things? We must be practical. What else does she need? I seem to remember a vast pile of nappies when Evelyn was a baby, great loads of laundry, constant incontinence.'

Ann said, 'There is no shortage of cradles. There are two in the attic, yours and Evelyn's. Oh,' she said as Juno came into the room, 'we were just speaking of you.'

'We were saying,' – Robert sprang forward and pulled out a chair – 'sit down, dear girl, we were saying that it's about time we made provision for your baby. Sit, please, we want to talk to you. No, don't run away. Put it this way, we have to make a nest and line it. I will start by buying nappies. No, don't shy away,' for Juno was on her feet, 'we have to talk.'

Juno said, 'Talk?' looking from Robert to Ann. 'Talk?'

'Yes. Break your habit of minimal communication. I don't want to bully, but we have to plan for the baby.'

Juno said, 'What I can't make out is why you are so wonderfully kind. It's unnatural. Nobody in my life has ever behaved like you. I am not in the habit, it shatters me.'

Robert said, 'Then stick to practicalities. Where can I buy nappies, Ann?'

Ann said, 'Almost anywhere.'

'Then what else? What do babies need?'

Ann said, 'Would you mind her using the shawls?'

'Shawls?'

'Cashmere. Your mother's, they are all there, they were used for you and Evelyn both. Would you mind?'

'Why should I? They are not sacred. What else does she need?'

Ann said, 'I have done a bit of knitting.'

'Show us.'

Ann opened a dresser drawer. 'These,' she laid sets of tiny jackets and leggings in front of Juno, 'might be useful.'

Juno put her arms round Ann and hugged her. 'How can I thank you?'

'No need. Your head seemed in the clouds so I made a start, hope you don't mind?'

Juno said, 'Mind? How could I possibly—'

Ann said, 'That's those, then, but—'

Robert said, 'What other miracle?'

'There are some things,' Ann's expression was curious, 'never been used, but as they are there, seems silly not to. They seemed all right when I looked at them, but then I thought—' She hesitated.

Robert said, 'Get on with it, Ann, come to the point.'

Ann said, 'All right, then. Will you hold the chair while I reach up?' Setting a chair against the dresser, she climbed up while Robert held it and reached for the top drawer from which she drew a brown paper parcel. 'It's some things I sewed once,' she said. 'Fashions change, but it's good flannel, never worn, but if you think not I shan't mind.' She opened the parcel and pushed it across the table to Juno, who lifted out six little nightdresses with silk ribbon fastenings beautifully feather-stitched.

Juno said, 'They are absolutely beautiful.'

'Then I'd like you to have them.'

Juno stiffened. 'I couldn't—'

Ann said, 'Please.' Recovering her usual tone, she said, 'They were meant to be used. They are not museum pieces. Before you know it the baby will have been sick on them. And now,' she said, 'if you've nothing better to do, Juno and Sir, will you stop cluttering my kitchen, I have work to do.'

Robert took Juno's arm, led her to the terrace and, indicating a seat, said, 'Sit down. Look at the view while I catch my breath.'

Juno did as he asked, looking across the garden to the stretch of moor, the farm and the ripe corn in the valley while the child inside her kicked against its confines. In her mind she dressed it in one of the little nightdresses and wondered what it would be like to hold in her arms, what would it smell like? Beside her Robert let out a long sigh. 'Oh, the poor woman. We never guessed.'

189

Juno looked at him, turning sideways to stare.

Robert said, 'We were so full of our own joy, Emma and I. Why Ann lit off to Bradford nobody really knew, she came back. She had married Bert and left almost immediately. She never spoke of her time away; she moved into the house to work. We got the impression she had not been happy, but we were absorbed in our own happiness; we did not question and, like you, she was no talker. But I see it all now.'

'She sewed these lovely clothes for her own baby?'

'Must have done.'

'Lost it? Miscarried? Born dead? It was Bert's?'

Robert said, 'I imagine so. One can't ask. Too late now. This is her way of telling.'

'She loved Evelyn,' Juno said.

'And she will love your child if you will let her.'

Juno exclaimed, 'My child will be grateful for every scrap of love that comes its way.' Then she said, 'I shall be so proud to dress it in those nightdresses.'

Robert said, 'You will make up to her for my and Emma's selfishness.'

'What could you have done?' Juno snapped. 'If she had wanted to talk, she would have. She did not waste her love, she spent it on Evelyn.'

'You are shrewd.'

Then Juno said, 'She can't have wanted Bert's baby, she doesn't like him.'

Robert said, 'True enough,' and sat on, looking at the land he loved, enjoying a silence that grew between them which he presently broke by asking, 'Have you a name for your child?'

Juno said, 'Inigo.'

'A very good name.'

'And since we are onto babies,' Juno surprised him, 'could you tell me what a newborn baby looks like? I have never seen one.'

And Robert, remembering Evelyn, thought it looks exactly as its father will when he is a very old man, but he

190

said, 'They look as though they had been soaking in the bath for ever. They look all crinkled. They look very red and very cross and awfully old. Their finger and toenails are as tender as the shells of baby shrimps.'

Juno said, 'That I shall like, thank you, Robert.'

THIRTY-THREE

*T*he horses plodded round the cornfield drawing the reaper, their heads nodding, harnesses creaking and jingling in the still air. Juno could smell their sweat as they went by. Each time they passed, the oblong of uncut wheat in the middle of the field grew smaller, the rabbits crouching in it more vulnerable.

Several bolder or sillier rabbits had already made a run for it and been snapped up by Jessie and a lurcher from the village. There had been shrill screams of 'rabbit pie' from watching children, a cheer when a brace of pheasants whirred up to wing into the wood, and Robert had shouted, 'Leave her,' when a hare broke racing, ears flattened along her back, to slip through the hedge, leaving Jessie and her pups frustrated. 'We have very few hares,' Robert called to Juno, 'but the rabbits are a pest.'

The children from the village were armed with sticks and men not otherwise busy were strategically positioned round the field; now and again Bert, driving the reaper, would let out a whoop and point out a victim. Juno had often witnessed the same scene on the Johnson/Murray farm, had eaten rabbit pie, rabbit stew, rabbit ragout. She had skinned rabbits and handled their slippery bodies, but today there was something about their furry despair which sickened. Even Bert's aged Nipper, rejuvenated by the tension, was lying in wait and, as she watched, stood up, head cocked, paw raised, to pounce on a harvest mouse. Then it was down his throat like an oyster, chumped, swallowed,

192

gone. Juno struggled to her feet to climb back to the house.

Priscilla was sitting on the terrace. 'Come and join me.' She patted the seat. 'Tired?' she asked. 'It's very hot.'

'So-so.' Juno sat, legs apart, easing her back, pushing her hair off her forehead, feeling sweat trickle between her breasts.

Priscilla said, 'Such a peaceful rural scene. You'd never think there was a war raging in Europe, would you? Lovely cornfields, aren't they?'

Juno said, 'They make me think of ghettos.'

'Oh?' Priscilla turned to look at her, 'How's that?'

Juno said, 'I have been reading an article about ghettos surrounded by troops and the Jews inside, that's what is happening to the rabbits in the corn.'

Priscilla said, 'But my dear! They are the most frightful pest!'

Juno said, 'I gather that's what the Germans say about the Jews.'

'I like your analogy.' Priscilla quizzed Juno's face. 'I hope you inspire your child with a similar philosophy,' she said. 'It or he/she won't be long now. Are you impatient? Are you nervous?'

Giving nothing away, Juno said, 'I am not impatient, I just feel ponderous,' but she thought, I am afraid, and I can't ask Mrs Villiers what having a baby is like, she is childless. And my mother, who is going through the same process, isn't here. I am glad of that. I am solo. 'I admit I am a bit daunted,' she said.

'Our old doctor is very competent,' Priscilla exclaimed. 'He will look after you and they are all perfect dears in the Cottage Hospital. I shall come and visit you there.'

Juno said, 'It defeats me. Why is everybody so kind?'

'Simple.' Priscilla smiled. 'You give Robert and all who care for him something to enjoy.'

'Something other than Evelyn?'

'That's about it.'

Juno said, 'I had not thought of myself as enjoyable.'

193

'Then it is time you did,' said Priscilla crisply. 'There, they have finished and here comes Robert. I expect he is in need of a drink. Hullo,' she said as Robert sat beside her. 'All over bar the threshing.'

'Yes.' Robert stretched his long legs. 'I have arranged for the threshing machine to come next week.'

'As soon as that?' Priscilla looked surprised.

Robert said, 'Might as well get tucked up for the winter.'

Juno said, 'I'll get you a drink,' and went into the house.

When Juno was out of earshot, Priscilla said, 'My word, Robert, that girl has imagination,' and repeated Juno's metaphor of the rabbits.

Robert said, 'Ah. Humbling. In these blissful surroundings we do not worry enough about what's going on.'

'And a fat lot of good it would do,' Priscilla answered. 'Let us worry about what is under our nose. Your little Juno is not feeling the joys of anticipation usually associated with girls in her condition.'

'Nor am I,' Robert said. 'And to be honest, Priss, I worry. That's why I hurry to get the threshing over. I don't want anything interfering with that event. I rather wish old Davey's partner had not gone off to the war, he was a lot more spry.'

'Dr Davey is experienced, don't fuss.'

'He is not all that agile, he's getting old.'

'When did agility matter in delivering a baby?'

Robert laughed, 'I don't know, Priss—'

Priscilla said, 'You have grown very fond of her, haven't you?'

Simply, Robert said, 'Yes.' As Juno came from the house with a glass of beer, he said, 'Thank you, Juno, that is just what I needed.'

Priscilla watched Robert drink and, while drinking, watch Juno, who had sat again to view the sun sliding behind the distant hills and the shadows lengthen over the cropped fields. Suddenly nervous, Priscilla said she must go, there was much to do at home, she had stayed too long and talked too much, but she talked to conceal the shock

194

of surprise she felt, reading the expression in Robert's eyes when he watched Juno over the rim of his glass.

'I wonder whether he is aware?' Priscilla said to Mosley as she let her car freewheel down the hill to save petrol. 'Thank heavens I have you to talk to,' she said to the dog. 'What a mercy the Almighty knew what he was up to when he made animals dumb.'

THIRTY-FOUR

'Comfortable?'

'Yes.'

Anthony and Hugh stood looking down at Juno where she lay sleepy in the late afternoon sun. 'Did we wake you?' Their smiles were affectionate.

'I was counting butterflies on the buddleias. Peacocks and Red Admirals. Have they finished with the threshing?'

'Yes.'

'I must have woken when the machine stopped; the noise lulled me to sleep. Did you enjoy yourselves?'

Anthony said, 'The drama's enjoyable. Golden grain pouring into sacks, muscly sunburned workmen stripped to the waist – I like those heavy belts they wear to hold up their trousers – the air full of chaff; there's an earthy satisfaction.'

'I got chaff in my eye, it hurt like hell.' Hugh sat by Juno on the grass. 'But it washed out. I have excellent tear-ducts. Yes,' he said, 'it was a job well done.'

'And tomorrow back to London?' Would she miss them?

'Poor us,' Hugh sighed. 'That's the shape of things, and it's so lovely here, but yes, we must go.'

'And your job still to do.' Anthony found it impossible to avert his eyes. Juno's arms and legs were long and slim, her neck fragile but her belly was outrageous, enormous, bulging, vast. 'Are you really comfortable?' he questioned as he folded his legs and subsided on the grass.

'I have a cushion under my head and another under my knees, so yes, I am comfortable, at the moment, prone.'

196

'But otherwise? Walking about?' Anthony was interested. How did she keep her balance? She looked grotesque. All that weight.

'Can't say I am. The question of balance is peculiar but it's not for ever, not like a fat man carrying a big stomach, paying in perpetuity for overeating and drinking.'

Hugh said, 'Gross, disgusting. Extremely unfetching.'

'And you are after all only paying for your pleasure,' said Anthony comfortingly.

Juno said, 'Is that what it was?' Her voice was almost inaudible. 'So that was pleasure.'

'Juno!' they exclaimed in distress. 'We had assumed – we imagined – well, we thought you had had a wonderful time – a marvellous experience – we certainly thought,' their voices were earnest, 'of pleasure of a subliminal sexual nature, that kind of pleasure.'

Juno said, 'I don't know anything about that, but then I know so little about anything. I have never learned.'

'Juno!' they said. 'You disappoint us. Are you sure? Not pulling our legs?'

'Sure of what?'

'That there was no pleasure?' They were frowning now, aghast, disappointed.

'I can't honestly say that there was.' Juno's tone was flat.

'How awful.' Hugh was shocked.

'You will simply have to learn.' Anthony was censorious.

'Who from?' Juno grinned. 'From whom?' she teased. Neither would volunteer.

'Robert, of course! Robert will know, Robert would teach you!' The young men collapsed into helpless laughter. 'For we can't, sweetie, we belong to another persuasion, as you must be aware.'

Juno, laughing too, said, 'I was too discreet to think about it, though the idea had occurred. Why suggest Robert?'

'Why?' cried Hugh. 'Silly girl, he is the most dishy man there has ever been. For one, you should hear Priscilla on

197

the subject. She is the neighbourhood expert on Robert in love.'

Anthony said, 'Be accurate, Hugh, you must have noted that she swears he has never been *in love* since Emma. Lover, maybe, bed, yes, great booster for a girl's morale, a great cheerer-upper, but never *in love*, absolutely not.'

'But she and he—'

'Yes, yes, but she knows and he knows it was to repair the old ego when her husband had strayed—'

'And the husband?'

'Oh, I expect he knew, they were all friends.'

Juno said, 'Wow.'

Anthony said, 'I expect our Juno thinks Robert is too old, or she is fixated on Evelyn.'

'No!' Juno protested. 'Robert appears much younger than Evelyn did.'

'And he is alive, which Evelyn is not,' said Hugh, dissolving into irrepressible giggles. 'Oh, we shouldn't laugh,' he yelped as Juno and Anthony, infected, joined in. 'Oh, Juno, look, your baby is laughing too, or it's protesting at the disturbance. It's dancing a tango in there. Isn't that dreadfully uncomfortable?' He stopped laughing and watched Juno's heaving stomach with fascination.

Juno said, 'Sometimes it is. Perhaps it's letting me know it wants to come out.'

Anthony said, 'I bet that's it. Now that is something you are going to learn, sweet girl; it's called the mystery of birth. It won't be long now, will it? You must promise to tell us all about it, every detail, when it's over.'

Juno said, 'I certainly will not,' and again the three of them laughed as they lay on the grass on an Indian summer afternoon with the warm sun slanting down on their youth and high spirits, the air still full of bees, butterflies sipping the buddleia.

'Oh!' Juno wiped her eyes. 'You silly fools, you make me laugh, you make me happy,' and she was happy lying on her back on the cool grass with cushions under her head and knees, the unknown character dancing in her womb,

Jessie coming out of the house to see what was going on, licking her ear, making a draught with her tail. She was happy hearing Robert calling, 'Ann asks whether you lot are going to loll there all evening or whether you want some supper?'

Juno shouted, 'Tell her we are coming,' and began to struggle up onto her feet.

Anthony, helping her, whispered, 'Promise you will ask Robert about sexual pleasure, promise us that.'

And Juno said she would think about it, laughing, for she was happy in the way that is remembered in old age for no discernible reason.

At some moment during that golden afternoon, in another part of the country where Jonty and Francis in their final week of training were practising with live ammunition, some of it exploded, blinding Francis and blowing him off his feet, so that in spite of massive injections of morphine he died in agony hours later, leaving Jonty to travel alone into the actuality of war.

THIRTY-FIVE

*H*aving reported Copplestone's faulty telephone from the Post Office, Robert hurried back to his car. The village was empty.

People were staying indoors; the storm was growing more violent with a rising wind and black rain clouds sweeping in from the west. As he drove out of the village the rain came in sheets and even between high hedges gusts of wind made the car swerve. The autumn gale had come early while the trees were still in leaf, roaring in from the Western Approaches, sweeping hungrily inland, ripping up the valley, crashing through resistant branches, whipping twigs and leaves onto the road and to clog his windscreen; twice he was forced to stop and clear the detritus by hand, his fingers clumsy and cold. He cursed the weather as he leaned against the wind, catching the eye of his dog on the back seat, soothing her as he got back into the car. 'It's all right, I'll have us home in no time.' He drove on between hedges chiselled by the wind to lean permanently east, but now they flicked back and forth, demented. He was reminded of his mother brushing his hair when he was a child, 'Your hair is thick as a hedge and more unruly.' A broken branch blocked the road; he stopped to drag it to one side, then squeezed past, barely clearing the ditch.

In the valley before the long climb up to the moor the wind was quieter; he made good progress and began to whistle. Normally he enjoyed a storm, found the roar of the wind exhilarating, loved the sound of rain, but today he was anxious. Juno was near her time and there was no telephone if he needed to send for the doctor. Too, the doctor might be unwilling to come in this weather and the drive to the Cottage Hospital was a long one.

At the foot of the hill a meagre little stream had been transformed into a raging torrent which came up to his hubcaps. He drove through in low gear and was congratulating himself when, fifty yards down the road, an ancient beech keeled over suddenly to crash across the lane, blocking his way. Feeling shaken, he stopped and got out. There was no way round; tangled branches, a great trunk and pathetic upturned roots made progress impossible. Robert cursed. The road would be blocked for days. A few seconds more and he might have been killed. With this sobering thought he tightened the scarf round his neck where rain trickled in and prepared to walk. Calling his dog, he pushed and scrambled past the fallen tree and then, leaning into the wind, began the climb up to Copplestone. As he climbed he mourned the tree, remembering its tender leaves in spring, the carpet of bluebells, the harvest of beechmast in autumn.

When he reached the farm he pushed the door open and shouted for Bert, but got no answer. There was no fire in the grate, no sign of Nipper or his pup; the only occupant of the house was a cat which hissed and spat at Jessie. Grateful to escape the elements for a moment, he stood and listened, hearing nothing but the wind. All the doors round the yard were firmly shut, cattle, pigs and horses under shelter. He turned back into the gale with Jessie following.

The moor gate, blown off its hinges, lay on its side; he left it, the effort of righting it too great. It took all his strength to fight his way up the last bit of hill, cross the yard, open the front door and stand panting, adjusting to the quiet after the turbulence outside. Relieved and exhausted, he sat to pull off his boots, watch Jessie vigorously shake, spray water from her coat, roll. He breathed in, filling his lungs with the warm air, sniffed wood smoke,

201

felt fatigue seep into his bones, looked forward to his armchair and a stiff drink. Then the silence was broken by a voice screaming, 'Ouch, oh, *oh bugger. Aah!*' and he took the stairs three at a time.

Ann said, 'Thank goodness you are back. Bert and Lily are boiling water in case you didn't – we should go at once, shouldn't waste time.'

Robert said, 'The road is blocked. I walked, there is no getting out, no car.'

'And the telephone?' Ann snapped.

'Lines down all over the place, they say we will be cut off for days. They said—'

'There's a war on,' Juno gasped. 'Oh, Robert.'

Robert took her hands.

'And the doctor,' Ann sounded almost pleased, 'is old, is lame and won't be able to get here. We will manage.'

Juno shouted, '*Oh! Ah! Oh bugger!*' gripping Robert's hands. 'Sorry to yell,' she said.

Robert said, 'Yell as loud as you please, it's supposed to help.'

Juno shouted, 'Oh God!'

Robert said, 'Sorry, darling, but you'll have to make do with us.'

Juno laughed at his slip of the tongue and said, 'You are sopping wet. I am so glad you are back.'

Robert said, 'How far have we got?'

'I am walking about, it seems to help. It comes in waves then there's a gap. I want to get in the bath but Ann won't let me.'

Ann said, 'An idiotic idea.'

Robert said, 'You're wrong, it should help. The water will support her and the warmth comfort. Go and run it.'

Ann said, 'Some people!', but went to run the bath.

Juno pleaded, 'Make it deep, please.' Gripping Robert's hands, she cried, '*Oh, oh, whoops*, oh gosh, Robert, this does hurt, o*uch*, oh, how right you were when you told me it hurts.' She was wearing a pyjama top he recognized as Evelyn's.

202

'Let's get you into the bath. Can you walk?'

'Of course I can, but help me climb in. I feel so clumsy and huge.'

Robert helped her into the water. 'How's that?'

'Oh, lovely. Oh.' She rested in the bath. 'Don't go away.'

'How's the pain?'

'Gone for the moment. Robert, those two, Anthony and Hugh, said I'd pay for my pleasure. This must be it. I told them I'd had none—'

'What?' What was she talking about?

'No pleasure, of course. Don't be stupid, that's my prerogative – *Oh, ouch,* off we go again.' She gripped the sides of the bath. '*Oh, what a mess!*'

Robert said, 'Don't fight it, don't resist. Try and push the little bugger out when the pain comes. That's what cows and sheep do.'

'And Eleanor?'

'Yes, Eleanor's a great pusher.'

'Okay, I'll push.' Juno relaxed. 'They said, those two jokers, that you could teach me about pleasure.'

'Did they indeed?'

'Yes. So will you?'

'What?'

'Teach me.'

'This is hardly the moment to discuss making love.'

'It seems a very good moment to me,' Juno shouted. '*Oh,*' she yelled, 'we are off again.'

'Then push, for God's sake.'

'And will you?'

'*All right,* but for God's sake concentrate, let's get on with this job.'

'I'll hold you to that! Oh gosh, I'm getting the hang of it, aren't I, pushing?'

'You are doing very well.'

'And to think Eleanor's litter was fourteen!' Juno leaned back to rest. 'Stay near, don't go away. Oh, Ann wants you—'

'Sir, you'll catch pneumonia, get out of those wet

clothes.' Ann held an armful of dry clothes.

'I'm all right, don't fuss.'

'Look sharp about it, sir, get into these dry things.'

'Do what she tells you, Robert. *Oh, ouch, oh!* Go on, Robert, don't be so modest, I won't look.' She lay back in the water, breathing hard. 'This is lovely, but do get changed.'

Obediently Robert got out of his wet clothes, put on dry trousers and pulled the sweater over his head.

'How long is this likely to go on?' She looked up.

He was touched by her trust. 'Not long. Let me rub your back, it's supposed to help.' He pressed his fingers down her spine, feeling the knobs. Her forehead was beaded with sweat.

'Lovely, thanks. How are the dry clothes?'

'Fine.' Oh God, he found himself praying.

'Do you do this to Eleanor?'

'She manages on her own.'

'I bit Ann. I am awfully sorry, Ann—'

Ann said, 'That's all right, you could do it again if it helps.' Ann was wonderfully calm.

'What charity! Ouch! Oh, I can hear Bert, what does he want?'

'What is it?' Ann went to the door.

'Was you wanting them kettles? Don't tell me Sir is in there!'

'Sir's in the bathroom helping her.'

'Should 'un be? T'aint fitty! What's going on?'

'What's going on is what would have gone on with me, you old goat, if I hadn't miscarried.' They heard Ann shut the door with a click.

'Robert, did you hear?' Juno was laughing. 'We shouldn't laugh.' Their eyes met. 'Whoops,' she exclaimed, 'we're off again.'

Robert said, 'I think you should get out of that now and onto the bed. Hang on to me, just—'

'I know, I know – push. Oh! Something*is* happening.'

Robert helped her onto the bed.

Ann said, 'Brave girl, nearly there. Wait, steady, oh, Juno, a little boy, your Inigo, he's lovely.'

'Oh but—'

'Look out, sir, hold this one, there's another, it's twins. Hey presto! Another lovely boy!'

'Give them to me, let me look.' Juno, white, sweating, exhausted, held out her arms. 'Oh, oh, poor, poor little things, don't scream.'

Ann exclaimed, 'Oh, dear God, one of them is blind.'

'Oh no, he isn't blind.' Juno looked into those reminiscent eyes. 'He just has very pale eyes.' She gazed at her sons, the one with black eyes, the other's pale as water.

Robert snorted and blew his nose, staring at the babies. Looking up at him, Juno said, 'Oh, Robert, you look awful. I think you should give yourself a very strong drink.'

Robert was muttering, 'I thought – oh, my God, I thought – yes, a stiff drink is a good idea.'

Presently, with a bundle on each arm, Juno said, 'You were right about shrimps, look at their fingers.'

Gently Robert let one of his fingers be grasped by each tiny fist. He felt terribly happy, almost hysterical. He said, 'I am so relieved.'

Juno said, 'You and Ann were marvellous. How can I thank you? We managed jolly well without the doctor, did we not?'

And Robert said, 'We did. I think I will get myself that drink now.' But downstairs in his library, pouring himself whisky, he had to pause and fumble for a handkerchief.

THIRTY-SIX

'What are their names?'
Priscilla peered into the cradles.

'The dark one is Inigo and the fair one Presto.'

'Presto? Is that a name?'

'It's what Ann exclaimed when she picked him up, "Hey Presto", so so far he is Presto.'

'It seems a frivolous name.' Priscilla looked surprised.

'He may be a frivolous person,' Juno suggested.

'They are not identical twins.' Priscilla examined Juno's infants. 'I must say, as babies go, they look splendid. I know one is supposed to ask what they weigh, but don't bother to tell me. I am sure they weigh enough.'

Juno said, 'They haven't been weighed, but it seemed a ton when they were inside me.'

Priscilla said, 'I bet it did, but you look wonderful now, radiant.'

'It was Ann who was wonderful, and Robert. I did not enjoy it one little bit – yelled my head off. I feel as though I'd been run over by a bus.'

'They say you forget about it.' Priscilla sat by the bed. 'Are you nursing them?'

'Yes.'

'That will keep you busy.'

'Yes.'

So many questions one would like to ask. Priscilla held her tongue; neither infant bore the slightest resemblance to anyone she had ever seen and the mother looked like a postcard Madonna, butter wouldn't melt. 'Has the doctor managed to reach you?'

'Not yet. How did you get here, Mrs Villiers?'

'By the cliff path, it's a bit of a scramble. I shall go back by the road. Ann tells me Robert and the men are chopping and sawing to get it clear.'

'Yes.' Juno wished Mrs Villiers would go away. Watching the strain of those pent-up questions made her tired; she had been dozing when the woman arrived, listening to the gasps and grunts of her infant sons, resting between feeds to snooze, relax, feel happy, wonderfully happy.

'Now you will be able to wear all those lovely clothes your mother sent you.' Priscilla was speaking again. 'Get your figure back.'

Juno said, 'Yes.'

'Has your mother had her baby yet?' One could surely enquire.

Juno said, 'I don't know.'

'Oh.' Priscilla was thoughtful. 'Does she know about these?' She gestured towards the cradles.

'No.'

'I see.' I see nothing, Priscilla thought. 'No business of mine,' she said.

Juno smiled.

'Their uncle or aunt may not even be born yet,' suggested Priscilla. 'It's an original situation.'

Juno laughed.

'And your aunt?'

Juno shook her head.

'I won't put my foot in it a second time,' Priscilla promised. 'I have often wondered what one is supposed to have trodden in.'

'Shit?' Juno suggested. Seeing Priscilla's eyebrows rise she said, 'Sorry, I found myself yelling words I hardly knew while they were being born. I can't have fully recovered. I should have said dog mess, shouldn't I?' And Robert had called her 'darling', deranged by the situation.

Priscilla said, 'It's in the dictionary. Speaking of which,

I ought to go. I have left my poor Mosley tied up in the porch. Now if there is anything I can do at any time,' she leaned down to kiss Juno's forehead, 'you know where to find me, please remember that.'

Juno said, 'Thank you, I will.'

Priscilla said, 'I admire your gumption,' and went, leaving Juno listening to her receding footsteps.

At the foot of the hill Robert and the men had finished clearing the road; he greeted Priscilla with a friendly kiss. He smelt of sawdust and sweat. 'Couldn't keep away, I see. Curiosity lent you wings.'

'I walked over by the cliff path to see whether there was anything I could do to help Ann, but she says no, everything is under control,' said Priscilla. 'And you seem to have managed the *accouchement* brilliantly. Congratulations.'

'It was uncomplicated.'

'Very lucky.'

'Yes.'

'Neither infant resembles anybody I have ever seen.' Priscilla eyed Robert closely.

Robert called, 'Bert, if you can clear my car of branches, I can drive us all home. You never give up, do you, Priscilla?'

Priscilla persisted, 'Do they look like anybody you know, Robert?'

Robert said, 'No.'

'No friend of Evelyn's, for instance?'

'No.'

'You know, Robert, I rather supposed, and I dare say you did too, that Evelyn was the father,' Priscilla ventured.

'Did you really?'

'Yes, really. I thought he might have slipped up. Come on, Robert, you must have thought so too.'

'No must about it.'

'And have you asked?'

'No.'

'Shall you?'

'No.'

'Shouldn't you?'

'No.'

Priscilla exclaimed, 'I don't know how you can bear not to.'

'Oh, Priss, you old sleuth.' Robert laughed outright. 'Do you want a lift home?'

'No thanks, dear Robert, I'll walk, but I shall see you very soon.'

'I am going to London.'

'Oh? For long?'

'I have to see to Evelyn's house. I have not been up since his funeral.'

'Oh.'

'Bert and Ann can see to things here. It's a good time to go away, nothing much to do on the farm.' Robert strolled towards his car, where Bert and John already sat on the back seat.

'Don't you think it peculiar, Robert, that one child is dark and the other fair?' She peered in at the car window.

Robert pressed the starter and the engine sprang to life. 'Mind your head.' Priscilla withdrew.

I have to get away, Robert thought, reorder my mind, go through Evelyn's things, get used to my new situation. Get used to this fresh pain. 'Goodbye, old girl,' he shouted and set the car at the hill; if he hurried, he could catch the night train.

THIRTY-SEVEN

*R*obert paid the taxi and watched it drive off. The steps of Evelyn's house were unswept. Fragments of paper and cigarette stubs had drifted into corners; the letterbox and door-knocker, unpolished for months, were almost black. Fumbling for the key, he noticed that the house across the street had had a direct hit. Had Evelyn told him? The windows of the ground floor were boarded up, but on the second floor he could see into what had been a bathroom. A lavatory bowl was suspended in space, a basin dangled at an angle; in an adjoining bedroom beautiful wallpaper hung in strips and what looked like a good flower print still hung on the wall. Had Evelyn known the occupants? Had the war made them friends? In the previous war he remembered the stink of the trenches, scuttling rats, parts of bodies to be collected for burial, the distended stomachs of dead horses, the disgust engendered by lice. Now one was treated to the intimacies of a neighbour's bathroom. He wondered why such a pretty print had not been salvaged, where the inhabitants of the house were now. He pushed Evelyn's latchkey into the lock and let himself in.

The hall was musty and dry. He switched on a light, laid his hat on a table, set his case on the floor, listened.

Time was when the house was full of sound. Evelyn had had many friends, loved music. Walking to the stairs his footsteps sounded loud. Somebody had rolled up the rugs. He climbed to the first floor, went into the drawing-room where Evelyn had died. There was no sign of him now. He sat at his son's desk and began pulling out drawers, sifting through papers. He had done this after the funeral, taken care of the few unanswered letters, paid the bills; there had been little of interest but he might have missed something. It was here that Evelyn had written that last letter.

Finding nothing, Robert picked up the blotter and took it to a mirror hanging on the wall, dusted the glass with his handkerchief, held the blotter up. Reflected in the glass he read in his son's writing: 'Dear Sarah', 'Dear Johnson', 'Yours sincerely, Evelyn Copplestone', 'Love, E', 'So sorry but', then, 'Dear Father, Juno', then a squiggle, a smudge, a note in pencil, 'Ring Sinclair Saturday'. He put the blotter back on the desk, said, 'Bugger Sinclair, whoever he may be,' and felt ashamed. On the desk the telephone rang; he picked up the receiver. 'Hullo?'

A woman said, 'I saw you arrive. I am the next door neighbour who—'

Who had found Evelyn, who had telephoned him at Copplestone, told him Evelyn was dead. Robert said, 'Of course, Mrs Hunt.'

'I wondered, can I help? Would you like a meal or a drink? Or am I intruding?'

'No, no. Would you come round? I would be delighted.' She had made soup, he remembered, came in every evening during the raids, was lonely, Evelyn had said. She might remember something. He could but ask.

She said, 'I'll come at once,' sounding pleased. He ran down to let her in, said it was kind of her to come. She said, 'I heard your taxi, thought it might be a visitor for me.' She was of indefinable age, past the middle years, not yet succumbing to age. 'You must think me very nosy.'

Robert said, 'Of course not, I am very glad to see you. I was going to call—' (Well, easily might have.) 'You were so kind when—'

'Evelyn died.'

'Yes.'

'I was fond of him, Mr Copplestone. The war brought

211

people together who were barely on nodding terms before. Your son's basement was open house. I used to bring soup for him and his friends.'

'He told me. Do call me Robert.'

'Oh, shall I? Very well. He had a lot of friends.'

'Please come up, we could light the fire. It's chilly.' Robert's eye roved over the desolation of the hall, furniture askew, rugs rolled up, his hat looking ridiculous. 'Let me lead the way.'

In the drawing-room he lit the fire, settled Mrs Hunt in an armchair. 'I wondered whether you could help me,' he said.

'Of course, Robert, but how?'

'I am looking to see whether there is anything I may have missed.'

'Oh?'

'About that last night.'

'Those poor young things! Surely I told you at the time? He warned them, you know, but they so wanted to dance and off they went—'

'Did you see the other girl?'

'What other girl?'

'A girl who did not go with the others?'

'Oh! Goodness me, there *was* another girl, I had clean forgotten. She came in with Evelyn, she refused soup, so did he. They came up here, I suppose. She can't have stayed long; he was alone when I found him.'

'Did you know who she was? Was she a friend?'

'Must have been.'

'Was she here often?'

Mrs Hunt frowned. 'No, I don't think I had seen her before. I knew all the others, of course. Why? Is it important?'

'Evelyn gave her a letter for me, suggested she should work—'

'Oh, the dear fellow! So he found you a girl! He said how difficult it was for you to find anyone suitable, that all he could send you were impermanent pederasts—'

212

Robert laughed, 'Anthony Smith?'

'That's the one, and he had a friend. But this girl, is she any good? Evelyn would be pleased.'

Robert said, 'A very hard worker.'

'Isn't that splendid? Evelyn was such a good judge.'

'I only wondered—' Robert hesitated. He had wondered so much it was hard to know where to start or even, he eyed Mrs Hunt, whether to do so. Awkwardly he said, 'I wondered how well he knew her?'

Mrs Hunt frowned. 'I wouldn't know that.'

'Or how long?' Robert forced himself on. This was worse than spying from the blotting paper.

'I wouldn't know that either. What does she say?'

'Not much. Very little, in fact. Hardly anything.'

Mrs Hunt regarded Robert. 'Are you wondering whether he was in love with her?'

'I—'

'And whether she was in love with him?'

'It—'

'Or whether they quarrelled and she walked out but, thinking better of it, came down to see you because she wanted the job? Or is my imagination taking a gallop?'

'Mrs Hunt.' Robert flushed.

Mrs Hunt chuckled, 'I can assure you he wasn't.'

'Ah.'

'Not in love, nor in the mood to take her to bed. I had learned to know your son, Robert.'

'You had?'

'He was very tired, dying as we now know. And, now I remember the girl, she looked knackered, too. She would be just someone he thought would suit you.'

'He wrote something rather odd in his letter.'

'What?'

'That I would find her rewarding.'

'Well, there you are,' said Mrs Hunt. 'What a good job you do.'

For a moment Robert felt like hitting her but resisted the temptation and, when she offered him a bed for the night, refused politely, saying that he had a bed waiting at his club and a dinner engagement with a friend.

From Evelyn's house he walked to Jermyn Street to have his hair cut at Penhaligons, then on impulse caught a bus which took him west to the Brompton Road. Walking down it, he came to the square where Priscilla had told him Juno's aunt lived.

Walking round the square, not even noting the numbers of the houses, he began to wonder whether he was quite right in the head. He had no wish to meet Juno's aunt, would not know what to say or what question to ask if he did.

What on earth, if she could see him now, would Juno think? Flushing with embarrassment he quickened his pace, hurried back into the Brompton Road and through the swing doors into Harrods where, in the perfumery department, he bought a large bottle of Guerlain before going up in the lift to the toy department, where he bought two teddy bears.

Back at his club, he had tea and a boring conversation with a man he barely knew. Then he had a bath and changed, before telephoning a woman he had known for a number of years to invite her out to dinner, arranging to meet her at a restaurant of her choice. After an amiable meal he went back to her flat and went to bed with her, a perfectly pleasant, therapeutic but fairly dull experience which, if nothing else, proved, if he had had any doubts, that he was still in excellent working order.

Back at his club he asked the night porter to wake him early so that he could catch the fast train home, then lay sleepless all night worrying as to whether the pattern of the wallpaper in the bedroom of the bombed house opposite Evelyn's was or was not a Morris print.

THIRTY-EIGHT

'*N*ot like that, darling, like this and this, then we are both comfortable.'

'I was not exactly considering comfort.' Jonty shifted his position. 'That better?' They were lying side by side on his parents' sofa.

'Much.' Sheena relaxed in his arms, pleased with him, pleased with herself, 'Love me?'

'Why do you keep asking?'

'A girl needs to be sure.'

'So does a man.'

'Well, then. But you are sure?'

'Of course I am sure. D'you mind moving? I am getting cramp in my arm.'

'Oh, Jonty.'

He rubbed his face against her cheek; she had lovely skin. Approvingly his mother had remarked, 'That girl Sheena has the most wonderful complexion, it makes such a difference.' He said, 'Everybody has gone to bed.'

She said, 'Goodness, you are scratchy. So they have.'

'So we could—'

'What?'

'Move up to my room or yours.'

She said, 'I don't think we should.'

'Are you not tempted?' They had had this conversational exchange on previous occasions.

'I want to discuss the best man.' Sheena veered to another subject. 'Who shall you have?'

'I don't know.'

215

'Darling, you must decide on somebody soon. The wedding is next week, after all.'

'Ten days.'

'Nearly next week. Choose somebody who looks nice. What about my brother?'

'I have told you I don't care.' Jonty felt a choking anger. Abruptly he sat up. Why must Sheena keep boring on? With Francis dead, what did it matter? If Francis had not got himself killed, he naturally would have been best man, there would be no question. Come to that, it might have been Francis marrying Sheena and himself being best man; that scenario was as probable as either of them marrying anybody. Jonty began to laugh.

'What's the joke?' She twined her arms round him; he could feel her breasts bubble against him.

He said, 'All right. If that's what you'd like, I'll ask your brother.' He chuckled again, and again she asked, 'What's the joke?'

'This whole charade, it's so improbable.'

'Falling in love is always improbable.' She laid her cheek against his, then risked sticking her tongue in his ear.

Jonty jumped. 'Christ! Who taught you to do that?'

'Just somebody—'

'Come upstairs.' Tiptoeing, they climbed the stairs to Sheena's room. He unzipped her dress, she his trousers. As he shrugged out of his shirt, he thought, if my mother heard us and came in now, she would save me. Then he thought, even if she hears us she won't come in, the wedding is in ten days.

As Sheena held back the bedclothes for him to join her in the bed, he said, 'My mother thinks you are a very nice girl.'

Sheena replied, 'I am.'

Had the somebody who had taught her to stick her tongue in his ear taught her all this? Did it matter? It was both exciting and agreeable. 'Oh! Ah! Yes!' he murmured, and, 'We used Juno as a short cut.'

Sheena, prick-eared, enquired, 'And who was Juno?'

216

He said vaguely, 'Oh, just somebody we knew when we were children,' then he said, 'Go on, go on, this is most agreeable.'

But less agreeable when she turned away to fall sound asleep. This, he had been led to believe, was the male prerogative. Lying wakeful, he thought, oh, God, next week I am marrying this girl called Sheena, a nice and suitable girl and talented, but she is not Juno. A little later he thought, when we were with Juno I felt infinitely tender, but now I just feel a void.

Then presently, while Sheena slept, he slipped from the bed, gathered up his clothes and tiptoed downstairs, where in the morning his mother found him snoring on the sofa, having emptied his father's whisky decanter.

THIRTY-NINE

*C*hanging his mind as he lay wakeful in the night, Robert stayed on in London. He should see his solicitor, make a decision about Evelyn's house; it was easier to sort things out while on the spot. He telephoned Ann telling her not to expect him, but eating a nauseating breakfast of dried scrambled egg in the club dining-room he regretted his decision and nearly changed his mind, for he was joined by an acquaintance who had been at school with him. The man was well known, he remembered, as the school bore, a reputation he proceeded to live up to by regaling Robert with a series of grouses: the state of London in the blackout, its dirty streets, messy bomb sites, broken glass, but worst of all the vandalous uprooting of the posts along Rotten Row; 'They were of historic interest, cast from the guns captured at Waterloo, irreplaceable.' He raised his voice. 'Can you see how it can possibly help defeat Hitler?'

Robert said, 'Not really,' and laughed.

His acquaintance exclaimed, 'It's no laughing matter. The idea was Beaverbrook's and he's a foreigner.'

'Canadian.'

'Same thing. London is full of foreigners, you must have noticed. Dreadful.'

Robert said, 'Oh, I enjoy them, and their jolly uniforms. I particularly like the French kepis, tremendously smart.'

'And what will you say when we are overrun by Americans?' The man leaned across the table. 'I hear Churchill is extremely thick with the Roosevelt fellow, they say he is persuading him to come in to the war. God Almighty! D'you remember them in the last lot?'

'Yes.'

'Well, then—' The man leaned back in his chair.

Robert said, 'It would certainly make a difference, alter the odds.'

'Good God! Have you thought? Have you any idea? What will your honest Cornish landlords say when they surge into their pubs, black, white and khaki, and drink all the locals' beer? Negroes! Red Indians too, I dare say.'

'They will say, "They are all foreigners to us," and joyfully relieve them of their dollars.' The man was even more boring than he remembered. Robert swallowed the last of his coffee, put his napkin down and rose to go. 'What brings you up to London?' he enquired as he turned away, anxious to escape.

'Our son is missing in the Western Desert, believed killed, but my wife insists that I come up and badger the War Office. What's the bloody use?' There was raw despair in the man's voice.

Ashamed, Robert said, 'Oh, Stephens, I am terribly sorry,' suddenly remembering Stephens's name and that he had been rather good at the long jump. 'Please,' he said, 'remember me to your wife.' (How could one be so crass?)

'And you?' Stephens was boring on. 'What brings you up from the sticks?'

Evasively Robert said, 'Oh, just some business I have to discuss with my lawyer.' Escaping, he went to telephone and make an appointment. Then, afraid of running into Stephens again, he walked in the park until it was time, turning his situation and Stephens's over in his mind.

Telling his solicitor, an old friend who had also been at school with Stephens, of this breakfast encounter, Robert said, 'I suppose I should count myself lucky; at least I know Evelyn is dead. I am not in limbo. I can come to you for advice as to what to do with his house and possessions.'

Eyeing Robert, his solicitor wondered whether to stick

219

strictly to business or whether to ask how he was bearing up. He had known Evelyn as a child and watched his slow inevitable dying. He said, 'Yes. Do sit down, Robert, try that chair.'

Robert said, 'I must not waste your time, Edwin. Here I come complaining about our school bore and his bother about the railings of Rotten Row, while I myself lay fussing all night as to what was the pattern on a bit of wallpaper I saw flapping in the bombed house opposite Evelyn's. We are two of a kind. Now come on. Let's to business, try a trace of sanity.'

Edwin said, 'Right. Very well.' He pulled a folder towards him. 'I suppose you know Evelyn's will? I wrote but you never answered.'

Robert said, 'Sorry about that. His leaving everything back to me was, still is, a shock.'

Edwin said, 'That's what he wanted.'

'I wonder why?'

'Back to his roots? Something of that sort. He did not explain. I did not ask.'

'You were ever discreet.' Robert smiled at Edwin, remembering a long thin boy who had grown into this long thin man married to a long thin woman. 'Alice well?'

'Busy with war work. Fed up that the war has put a stop to hunting, but otherwise fine.'

'I'd forgotten you hunted. Now, advice; what am I to do about Evelyn's house?'

'Hang on to it.' Edwin leaned back in his chair and made a steeple of his fingers. 'After the war houses will be at a premium; hang on to it now and sell it later. I take it you don't want to live in it?'

'God forbid.'

'Then let me find you a tenant. When the war is over you can sell and buy yourself a small flat.'

'I don't want a flat.'

'You come to London and dislike meeting Stephens at breakfast. A flat is a convenience.'

'I'll think about it.'

220

'There will be death duties. When you do sell, you can recoup and still get a flat.'

'Oh, Edwin, I hate all this.'

'Yes, I know, but there's another thing we should discuss. Your will.'

'I've thought of that. I need to make a new one, but I'm not sure of the names yet. I shall have to let you know.'

'Not sure of what names?' Edwin unsteepled his fingers and sat up. 'What names?' he repeated.

Robert said, 'The people in whose favour I am making a will have not been christened yet.'

FORTY

Violet Marlowe folded her sister-in-law's letter and replaced it in its envelope. 'What to do?'

'Trouble?' John Baines looked over the top of his newspaper, catching the eye of his fellow lodger. Their club had lately refused them breakfast on a regular basis, quoting the difficulties of wartime rationing. They now breakfasted with Violet, an arrangement which jarred on their nerves, for neither man cared for conversation before his bowels had worked, and Violet was given to chatting.

'My sister-in-law has had her baby.' Violet snorted and slapped the airmail envelope.

'Everything all right?' Bill Bailey spoke with his mouth full of toast.

'Oh yes, she is rapturous.'

'Boy or girl?'

'Girl. You'd think she'd be sorry, for there's already Juno, but no, she appears delighted, says her husband is totally enchanted. I quote. You'd think he'd want a son but he has bought her pearls and a bracelet.'

'I am happy with my girls.' Bill Bailey folded his napkin.

'And I with mine.' John Baines rose, intending to reach the downstairs lavatory before his friend and finish reading *The Times* in peace.

'Funny, she doesn't mention Juno.' Violet picked up the letter and began to reread it.

'Does she know about Juno?' Bill Bailey, seeing that John was one jump ahead, lingered. He would have to make do with the lavatory on the landing. 'Have you heard from your delinquent niece?' he asked. 'Isn't she about due to give birth to the Canadian infant's nephew or niece?' There had been jokes about the disparate Marlowe relationships when Violet had apprised them of Priscilla's news. 'Have you been in touch?'

'Actually, no.' Violet flushed. 'I haven't.'

'Why not, Violet?'

'It's embarrassing. The girl isn't married; the child will be illegitimate.'

'We are in the nineteen forties, Violet, not the last gasps of Queen Victoria,' Bill teased. 'She is your niece. It will be your great-niece or nephew, will it not?'

'Are you reproaching me?' One did not like being put in the wrong. Violet started as John, leaving his friend to the fray, shut the kitchen door with a snap. She looked at Bill. 'It's not your niece,' she said, 'not your family.'

'No telephoning? No letter? She thanked you for sending on her clothes, did she not? Minded her manners,' Bill persisted.

'I admit she did.'

'So why don't you have that little holiday you need so badly? Go and see her. You could visit your old friend who was so bad at hockey.' Bill was relentless.

Violet did not answer.

Presently, pedalling up the incline towards Hyde Park Corner, Bill Bailey said to John Baines, 'I have sown the seed.'

His friend replied, 'Well done. How glad I am that from here we can almost freewheel to Whitehall. If only manipulating Violet were as easy. Let's hope it works.'

But work it did, for Priscilla, caught off guard on the telephone, extended a pressing invitation and within ten days Violet found herself in the train heading towards the West Country.

Feeling apprehensive, Priscilla met Violet's train and seeing her step out of a third-class carriage hurried to greet her. I am on my own ground, she reminded herself, no need to be frightened. 'Violet,' she cried, 'how very nice this is.'

Violet, on best behaviour too, riposted, 'Delightful.' During the journey she had had second thoughts but, welcomed into Priscilla's house, which was both larger and warmer than she had expected, she concluded that she was doing the right thing and did not even take exception to Mosley when he slobbered over her skirt, exclaiming that she 'liked dogs' when Priscilla besought the creature, 'Get down, my precious.'

'I had not realized your house was so large,' she said, taking in the size of Priscilla's hall, hung about with portraits of gentlemen in uniform or hunting pink flanked by ladies with bedroom eyes and deep *décolletées*. (Nor that Priscilla, so colourless at school, was quite so county.)

Priscilla said, 'It's a lot to keep up. Let me show you your room and then we will have supper, you must be tired.' With any luck Violet would go to bed early, then she could get on with reading *The Power and the Glory*, which Anthony had just sent her from Hatchards. 'Here is your room,' she said, 'come down when you are ready. Robert Copplestone brought me a bottle of Tio Pepe, we will have a drink before we eat.'

Violet examined her room; Colefax and Fowler chintzes, monogrammed sheets and towels. She bounced on the bed; she would be comfortable.

In the drawing-room Priscilla poured sherry. 'I expect you are anxious to see your niece.' That she was aware of why Violet had invited herself to stay should be made clear.

Violet said, 'Oh. Yes, of course. I am anxious too to meet Mr Copplestone, see who she works for.'

Priscilla said, 'Robert's in London. I don't know when he will be back.' Violet could choke on her curiosity.

Violet said, 'Is Copplestone far? Shall I be able to get over? I can perhaps hire a taxi.'

Priscilla said, 'Don't be silly, I will drive you.' Not for anything would she miss Violet's meeting with Juno. 'They go by the names of Inigo and Presto,' she said.

224

'Who?'

'Your great-nephews, Juno's sons.' She watched Violet go red then white, then swallow some sherry. 'You did know, didn't you? That's why you are here, isn't it?' One had been dropped from the hockey team but here one was in one's own house. 'You did not expect me to be so uninhibited,' she said. 'Let me top you up, then let's have supper. Mrs Hodge's pie, she is my gardener's wife. He's away at the war but she, thank God, helps in the house and cooks too.'

Violet said, 'A treasure, you are lucky. My maids joined up in nineteen thirty-nine, but I bumble along. We eat in the kitchen.'

Priscilla said, 'And so do I, and they do at Copplestone too. Come and eat.'

At supper they discussed the progress of the war, Violet's work with the Red Cross and Priscilla's with the WVS. Violet praised the pie. It was too soon to discuss Juno. To both women's relief they went early to bed, Priscilla to lose herself in Greeneland, Violet to take refuge with Inspector Poirot.

'What an extraordinary garment.' Violet stood at the top of the hill, watching Juno walk up from the farm. She was wearing the sheepskin coat and the black wool cap she had worn on arrival at Copplestone. She carried a basket slung on each arm and her cheeks glowed pink from the frost.

Priscilla said, 'I am so envious, it's the warmest thing I've ever seen. She must have just finished milking, it hasn't taken her long to get back to work.'

Violet said, 'I'd call it unsuitable for farm work. I wonder what she has got in those baskets.' As Juno came within earshot, she waved and shouted, 'Hullo! Juno, hullo!' She was standing with her back to the sun.

Juno looked puzzled then, recognizing her aunt's voice, cried, 'Aunt Violet! What are you doing here?' stopping dead in her tracks.

'Tiny holiday – staying with my old school friend.' Violet advanced.

Priscilla watched.

Juno said, 'So you've come to snoop.' She came forward. 'Well, here's what you have come to see. Have a good look.' She deposited her baskets at Violet's feet. 'Your great-nephews,' she said with what Priscilla would later describe as perfect aplomb. Then, standing back from the baskets, she muttered to Priscilla, 'Your bright idea? A plot?'

Priscilla shook her head, whispering, 'No, no, no, hers.'

Juno, disbelieving, said, 'Ahem!' and, with her eyes on her aunt, 'I hope this won't cause a heart attack.'

Violet stared into the baskets; it was later said that their contents stared back. She said, 'No Marlowe ever had eyes that colour. Where on earth can those eyes come from? It might be blind.'

Juno said, 'He.'

Violet said, 'Sorry, he, of course. Should they be on cold ground?'

Juno said, 'They are well swaddled up,' but she picked up the baskets.

'You had them with you in the cowshed,' Violet stated.

'I park the baskets in a manger while I work. There is a precedent.' Juno grinned, and equably Violet replied. 'So there is. A peck of dirt never hurt anyone.'

Then Priscilla, scenting a truce, suggested, 'Why don't we all get into the house, where it's warm? Perhaps Ann will give us tea.' They trooped into the house, where Juno put the baskets on the hall table while they took off their coats.

Then Violet, surprising herself, said, 'You look marvellous, Juno. You've got your figure back. Your mother has put on two stone and is having trouble with her legs.'

Juno said, 'Oh! I had not heard.' She felt stricken and surprised.

Violet, her tone sharp, asked, 'Hasn't she written?'

And Juno said, 'No.'

'Not told you about your little sister? Not told you of the

pearls and the bracelet from your stepfather? Not told you that he is totally enchanted?'

'No.'

'Have you written to her?'

'Not yet.'

'Why not?' It was pretty obvious why not, but one asked all the same.

Juno said, 'It would be a pity to mar her happiness.'

Violet, surprised to find herself warming to Juno, said, 'Mar, such a good word.'

Juno said, 'I read a lot while I was waiting to explode. It enlarged my vocabulary.'

'While keeping your figure,' Violet approved, 'unlike your mother. One surmises that Mr Sonntag in his state of enchantment does not mind. Oh well,' she said, 'if I were you I'd be grateful to have the Atlantic between you. Twin sons, after all, trump one daughter, whichever side of the blanket. One can't help seeing the funny side,' a remark she would repeat ad nauseam to John Baines and Bill Bailey. Then she reached a tentative finger to touch each child, murmured, 'Not like any Marlowe,' looked up at the walls of the hall and stairs hung, as at Priscilla's house, with portraits, and scrutinizing Robert's mutton-chopped great-grandfather, an eighteenth-century lady in wig with lapdog, and a Copplestone in ruff with hand on swordhilt and *louche* expression, she repeated, 'not the remotest resemblance.'

Then Ann called from the kitchen, 'Tea', Inigo and Presto began to yell and the telephone to ring. The confrontation was over.

Driving presently back to Priscilla's house, Violet broke a ruminative silence. 'And what do you think?'

With her eye on the road, Priscilla asked, 'About what, Violet?'

'Will he make an honest woman of her?'

'Who are we talking about?' Priscilla hedged.

Violet snapped, 'The infants' father, of course.'

Priscilla said, 'And who would that be?'

227

'One surmises your Copplestone friend, I was sorry not to meet him – lurking in London.' She sniffed.

Priscilla said, 'Dear Violet, your imagination is bolting. Robert is not their father, nor, when you get around to thinking it, was his son Evelyn.'

'Then who is?'

'I too have asked that question.'

'Oh.'

'And as far as I can see it is to remain unanswered.'

'Does your friend Mr Copplestone not know?'

'My dear Violet, he has not asked either.'

Violet said, 'Then the man must be mad!' And although Priscilla was inclined to agree, she stayed loyally silent.

FORTY-ONE

*N*ovember turning into December found Robert still in London. The leaves floated off the plane trees in the parks and eddied about unswept; there were no children to rustle through them, no-one to sweep them up and burn their fragrant heaps. Remembering his pleasure in them as a child, and Evelyn running with the dog Jessie of his day, Robert visualized Juno's twins doing the same thing in five or six years' time. 'Inigo and Presto,' he said out loud and a man overtaking him glanced at him queerly, then quickened his pace as Robert, correcting himself, said, 'No, it's Inigo and Felix.'

Telephoning home two weeks before he had, after giving Ann instructions for Bert, asked whether Juno had yet found a name for the second twin.

Ann had told him, 'She's calling him Felix.'

Curious, he had said, 'D'you know why?'

Ann had replied, 'She says she is happy and Felix means happiness, but between you and me, Sir, she calls him Presto and I think it will stick and the Felix just be official.'

He had laughed and before they were cut off, their regulation three minutes being nearly up, he had asked, 'Anything else?'

Ann said, 'Oh yes, she says to ask you whether it's not time to let Eleanor free in the woods to eat acorns.'

He had said, 'Yes, tell her yes.'

So now, shuffling through the leaves, he was reminded of Juno and his thoughts were back to revolving as unhappily as had become their custom during the last month, as

229

he walked in the parks and visited what friends he had who were not too busy to see him, taking them out to dinner or to lunch-time concerts at the National Gallery, preferring the music to their frenzied talk of the war, the German army trapped in the snow in Russia, the American fleet bombed at Pearl Harbor, America's entry into the war, bringing hope of ultimate victory; stirring stuff, which should by rights override any other preoccupation, but did not.

When he went to Evelyn's house to finish dealing with what private effects he had left, he questioned the neighbour again and it became clear as clear that Mrs Hunt had not known Juno, and that for Evelyn she was the merest acquaintance, a girl he had helped get a job with a letter to his father, no more and no less. Juno herself had never hinted at anything else. Robert made a second appointment with his solicitor and instructed him as to his will.

Edwin looked at him over his half-moon spectacles. 'All right, Robert, that is quite clear, but out of interest who are these children, Inigo and Felix Marlowe? They do not seem to be family. Is there a connection I should know about?'

Robert said, 'I was present when they were born.'

'Yes?'

How strange it had been, helping Juno give birth. She had been so brave. Shouted so loud! Intelligent, too, to demand a bath. And between spasms of pain those odd disjointed queries about 'pleasure'; what was that about? He knew very well what that was about, it was sexual pleasure. What a time to ask! What possessed the girl? He remembered saying, 'This is hardly the moment,' pompously idiotic, for was her mind not obviously running on its consequences? And she had shouted, 'It seems a very good moment to me,' snubbing him at the full pitch of her lungs.

'No,' he said, meeting Edwin's eye, 'there is no family connection.' Had he not been certain of this at first sight of the infants? No Copplestone eyes had ever been black or of palest blue. 'None,' he said, smiling at Edwin, 'none at all,' remembering the euphoria that that first sighting had engendered, for these infants of Juno's were not, could not be his grandchildren, were not, as he had for months imagined, Evelyn's. Who had fathered them was immaterial. The euphoria had not of course lasted.

Doubtfully Edwin had said, 'I see. All right, I suppose. I take it you know what you are doing. I should be failing in my duty to you as a client as well as a friend, Robert, if I did not point out that this is rather irregular.'

He had snapped, 'No more irregular than an old lady leaving her money to a cats' home or a donkey sanctuary. I have no relations, Edwin, my will seems perfectly sensible to me and,' he added, 'my business.'

And Edwin had laughed and said, 'Very well, I will have it ready to sign in a couple of days. Send it round to your club, shall I?'

Robert had thanked him and, before parting, they had discussed the war – one of Edwin's sons was in the Far East, another in Cairo – and talked of the bomb site next to Edwin's office which had become a habitat for wild flowers; rosebay, buddleia and teazle, which attracted birds. A goldfinch had been sighted by one of Edwin's clerks.

Two days later Robert signed his will and now, kicking through the leaves in Green Park, he knew that there was nothing to keep him in London. He must go back to Copplestone, to his farm, and face up to being too old to make himself ridiculous, too old to be in love.

FORTY-TWO

*R*obert paused by the moor gate to look across to the farm and above it, nestling into the hill, his house, and felt the lift of spirit that he always felt on reaching home. It was stupid to have lingered so long in London. Here he belonged; there was nowhere else to go. It had been cowardly to delay his return.

The evening was still and frosty. Below him in the farmyard Bert came out of the cowshed, shut the door and stood looking up the hill. Robert followed his gaze.

Juno was standing in the dusk on the edge of the wood, wearing the sheepskin coat and woollen cap. She called, 'Eleanor? Time for tea. *Eleanor*—' Her voice carried across the valley.

Robert imagined the faint rustle of twigs in the top branches of the wood, heard the first screech of an owl, watched the girl wrap her coat tight against the cold. Would she call again? He imagined her filling her lungs but no, she had turned round, she was watching the wood. Had she heard a grunt? Eleanor would approach on delicate trotters, marshalling her litter home from their foraging, hopping and skipping, scuffling through the leaf-mould, emitting small squeaks as they quickened their pace, hurrying to keep up. Suddenly as if by magic the sow was brushing against Juno's legs; surrounded by piglets she was patting the sow. He heard her voice, 'All hams and sides of bacon present? Everybody there? One, two, three, four,' she counted, 'eleven, twelve? Right then, race you to your sty,' and she turned to run down the hill with the sow and litter streaming behind her.

Still Robert watched.

'You'll run all the fat off 'em.' Bert came to meet her. 'I've mixed their meal for you.'

'Oh, thank you, Bert, thank you. You should not have bothered.' Their voices carried in the frozen air.

'No bother.' (Robert raised his eyebrows. Well, well.)

'You need to get back to your own.'

'They are safe with Ann. In you go, Eleanor.' She held the sty door open; the sow pushed in, followed by the piglets.

'Maybe, but Ann can't feed 'em,' Bert nagged.

'They will still be asleep, they are always sleeping when I get in. We have this exchange every night, Bert,' she teased.

'Maybe so.' Bert watched her pour the pigswill into Eleanor's trough and shut the sty door.

Juno said, 'Anything else?' She looked round the yard.

'No, you get along up.'

'Goodnight then, Bert, thank you, goodnight.'

Bert watched her go. 'Goodnight, girl.' Then he shouted, 'Why don't you take the path?'

Juno's voice, diminishing as she climbed the hill, called back, 'I prefer my short cut.'

'You'll trip,' Bert called, 'fall, hurt yourself.'

'No, I won't.' She was laughing.

'Bert.' Robert came up beside the man.

'Sir? You're back? Didn't hear no car. No-one said you was coming. Made me jump.'

'The taxi was busy. I walked, glad to stretch my legs. Did I give you a shock?'

'Was just packing it in for the night, glad to see you. That Juno just called the pigs in from the wood; they are after the acorns.'

'I was watching.'

'Got a touch with animals, that one. Didn't allow so at first, but she has.'

233

'Good. Everything all right here?'

'Yes, sir, seems so, ticking over.'

'Good.'

'Very glad to see you back, sir.'

'Thank you, Bert. Eleanor's litter look fine.'

'See a difference in them babies, too, sir. Quite plumping out, two fine little babbies.'

'Oh yes, the babies, good.' Since when had Bert been interested in babies? 'You sound quite proprietorial,' Robert said.

'I sound what?'

'Interested, Bert, you were never a babies man.'

'Well, I am now, we all take a turn,' Bert snapped. ''Tis nice for a change to care for something you ain't going to eat.'

Robert said, 'I had not thought of it in that way. You have turned philosopher while I've been in London.'

Bert snorted.

Robert said goodnight. Turning to go he added, 'Where's this short cut?'

'You stick to the path, sir, or you'll fall.'

Robert said, 'I think I already have.'

FORTY-THREE

*R*eaching the house Robert let himself in, took off his coat and breathed the familiar smell of wood fires, furniture polish and something new. There was a bowl of hyacinths on the hall table. He stooped to sniff; not since he was a child and his mother planted them had there been hyacinths. The library door was ajar. He went to put a log on the fire. There was another bowl of bulbs on the table by the window. A patter of paws brought Jessie and her puppies to greet him and from the kitchen he heard voices and a gust of laughter. Caressing the dogs, he was glad to be home.

In the kitchen Ann exclaimed, 'Here's Sir! You did not say you were coming.' A baby lay across her knees; she was changing its nappy. Juno was in the rocking chair by the stove, nursing the other child. She said, 'Oh, Robert! How lovely. We did not hear you arrive.' The infant let go of her nipple then reached for it back, clutching her breast with its fist.

Robert said, 'I walked from the station. The taxi was busy, he will bring my bag later.' He returned her smile, amazed by her breasts. 'I am interrupting,' he said.

Juno said, 'Nonsense, how could you,' and moved the child to her other breast.

Ann said, 'Sit down, you must be tired, I'll make a pot of tea.' She pinned the nappy, laid the baby in its basket and went to fill the kettle. The baby made an indeterminate protest then lay quiet.

Robert said, 'And how are they?' He peered curiously into the basket. 'Which one is this?'

Juno said, 'Inigo. They are flourishing.'

'And grown a lot,' Robert said. 'I saw you calling the pigs in as I came up the hill.'

'Oh?'

'I was too far away to shout. I had a word with Bert,' he said.

Juno said, 'And?'

'He tells me everything is tickety-boo.'

'I bet he didn't say tickety-boo.' She grinned.

'No. And I don't think I have ever said it before, it's not a word I use.' (I am ridiculously nervous.)

'That's a very smart suit.' Juno appraised Robert's appearance.

'Evelyn suggested I have it made at the beginning of the war. He was percipient. He said clothes would be rationed and it would help my morale, if the Germans won, to meet them properly dressed, not shabby.'

'And now you only meet me!'

'It rarely gets an airing.' (Fuck my suit, I want to tell her how beautiful she is and I can't.)

Ann said, 'Strong or weak?' She had made the tea.

Robert said, 'Strong, you should know by now.'

'Thought a trip to the metropolis might have altered your tastes.' Ann poured tea into cups.

Robert said, 'I have something for your sons, Juno,' and went back into the hall to extract parcels from his overcoat pockets.

Watching him go, Juno said, 'But it is a beautiful suit,' meaning that she had not realized that Robert was so good-looking, and Ann, handing her a cup of tea said, 'Yes, and he's had his hair properly cut. They all had those long legs, the Copplestones. Evelyn was the same.'

Juno changed the baby's nappy and laid it in the basket beside its brother as Robert, returning from the hall with parcels, put two in her lap. 'If they have one already, chuck them away,' he said.

Juno undid the parcels, two teddy bears. 'Robert! Thank you. They will be so precious, their very first toys. Thank you.'

Robert said, 'Good,' taking the cup Ann held out to him. 'I hoped—' I hoped, he thought, that I would not be so pleased to see her, I hoped that she would have lost her looks, I hoped I would be sane again. 'I hoped you would be pleased,' he said.

Juno said, 'I am, I am very pleased.'

They sat drinking their tea and the silence full of the unsaid stretched until Juno broke it. 'And London? Tell us about London. Did you meet a lot of friends, interesting people?'

'A mixture. There's my generation, who think they know what's going on, opinionated bores, amazingly revengeful. Want to bomb Germany to pulp. They anger me. Your father's lot had the right ideas. There are not many like him, they come thin on the ground. The armchair lot would start a third war in time for those two.' Robert nodded towards the infants.

'God forbid! Who else?'

'Oh, Evelyn's generation, too old to be called up but could join up if they tried, but are cossetting their careers: writers, journalists—'

'They might be useless,' Juno suggested, 'but didn't Anthony say Graham Greene is in his Ministry? He would be useful, and there's Evelyn Waugh. I read something about him—'

'Oh, don't mind me. I make odious comparisons.' (I would rather like an argument. I'd like to shout, lose my temper, let off steam.)

'. . . asking where is Sassoon, Robert Graves, Wilfred Owen?'

'You've read them?' He had not somehow imagined her to be a reader.

'I have made use of your library. I hope you don't mind. I read when I can't sleep.'

'I am delighted.'

'Who is new?'

'There's Orwell, we shall hear more of him, Peter Quennell, Cyril Connolly, I suppose, and Henry Moore is making the most amazing drawings of people sleeping in the tube. I spent a lot of time walking about. I felt useless, though, I needed to get back here.'

'Tell me more.' She drew him out, making him describe what he had seen and who, until he protested, 'I did not know I had seen so much. You are an inquisitor. Now, tell me about you. What has been going on, apart from Bert's transformation into geniality?'

'Nothing much. The babies and the farm and oh! Bert allowed me to do the muck-spreading.' She could not tell him that recently she had woken with no thought of Jonty or Francis, that her days were no longer obsessed, that somehow they had evaporated, as bad dreams do. She was happy. She said, 'As you see, I am busy and happy, and fancy Bert allowing me to do that!'

'I'll have to have a word with Bert,' Robert said, 'but first this is for you, I thought it might complement the bears,' and he gave her his present.

Juno unwrapped the packet. 'Oh,' she said in awe, 'scent! I have never had proper scent. How wonderful, how delicious, now I won't stink of muck!'

And Robert, though pleased, thought, muck or Guerlain, it won't make a blind bit of difference to me.

238

FORTY-FOUR

*P*riscilla looked up to see Robert coming up her path. Mosley barked. She stopped weeding and got up from her knees. 'I am trying to get some sort of order in the garden before the weeds take hold; how are you, old friend?'

Robert kissed her cheek. 'Don't let me interrupt. I have brought you a joint of pork.'

'Oh, wonderful! Black market?'

'No, Priss, legit.'

'Juno will be sad.'

'Juno foresaw its fate, she is philosophical.'

Priscilla stuck her hand-fork in the earth. 'I have done enough for the day. Come indoors, it's been the most wonderful day but not warm enough yet to sit out.'

Robert said, 'No,' as if he had not noticed, and followed Priscilla into the house.

She said, 'Tea? Coffee? A drink, perhaps?'

'A drink, if you can spare one. I must not rob you.'

'Anthony and Hugh contrived to find a bottle, I can spare you a swig. Sit down, old friend, and tell me what's new. How are Juno's twins?'

'In rude health.'

'How old now? Three months?'

'Four.'

'Beginning to look human?'

Robert did not answer.

Priscilla said, 'Spring busting out all over quite cheers me up!'

Robert said, 'Good,' his tone glum.

Priscilla poured him a generous measure and, looking at him closely, handed him the glass. 'What's eating you, Robert?' She stood, bottle in hand. 'What's the matter?'

'Matter?' He took the glass from her.

'This is the fourth time in two weeks you have dropped in on me for no reason.'

'I brought you a joint of pork,' he protested.

'I am grateful for the excuse. You don't look yourself, Robert, what is it?' she persisted.

'I am all right, fine—'

'You have lost weight and you can't afford to do that.'

'Don't fuss, you are as bad as Ann.'

'I am stating a fact.'

Robert swallowed some of his drink. 'I am not sleeping very well,' he admitted grudgingly.

'It's the worry of the war.' Priscilla examined his face. 'You are mourning Evelyn, for one thing.'

'No, I am not.'

'You did not give yourself time to mourn him properly and now it hits you.'

'Priscilla, be your age. I mourned Evelyn from when he came back, lungs wrecked, in nineteen-eighteen, until he died. Don't talk rubbish.' Robert had raised his voice irritably, took a gulp from his glass.

Priscilla leaned forward and topped up his drink. 'Then what *is* the matter?'

Robert said, 'Nothing, as I said, nothing.'

Priscilla said, 'Oh, but there *is*, and it must be serious to bring you my way four times in two weeks!'

Robert burst out laughing. 'Is it so obvious?'

'So what *is* keeping you awake?'

Robert did not answer.

'It *is* to do with Evelyn, isn't it?' Priscilla pried.

'In a way.'

'So I am not barking up the wrong tree?'

'It was I who barked up the wrong bloody tree.' Robert set his glass down and stood up.

Suddenly enlightened, Priscilla whispered, 'Oh my God! Damascus! You thought what I thought, what we all thought.' She leaned forward with the bottle and poured again. 'What you pretended *not* to think? Oh, goodness, Robert. Oh my goodness me!' Reaching for his glass, she took a huge gulp from it. 'Goodness, I needed that.'

Soberly Robert said, 'Priscilla, I feel such a fool. I was jealous of Evelyn.'

Priscilla, enhanced by her gulp of whisky, said, 'He wouldn't half laugh if he knew and could see Juno's twins!'

Robert did not reply but stood looking out at Priscilla's view, lovely spring-touched country, a gentle valley leading seawards.

Priscilla said, 'And now? What?'

Gloomily Robert muttered, 'Love.'

'Love?' Priscilla sat down. 'The real McCoy? Heavens!'

'Yes.'

'But that's wonderful,' she said.

'It's ridiculous.'

'So it's caught up with you after all these years. When did it happen? When did it dawn on you?'

'I saw her footprints in the sand—'

This meant nothing to Priscilla. She said, 'And you still don't know who the father is?'

'That's immaterial.'

'I suppose it is. What a turn-up for the book.'

'You are enjoying this,' he said.

'No, I am not. You look too miserable, though why I can't think.'

'Priscilla, I am fifty-seven next birthday. She is barely eighteen.'

Robustly Priscilla answered, 'It's been known. Old John Morgan, who remarried at eighty, is having his fifth child. His wife is sixty years younger than he is. It works a treat, a very good marriage.'

'Ridiculous.'

'Unusual, I grant you, but have a look in the Old Testament.'

'No thanks.'

Priscilla drank some more. 'Losing sleep because you are in love, what a hoot!'

'I knew you would laugh—'

'I am not laughing, not really, of course I am not.' Priscilla put the empty glass on the table. 'And what does she say? Juno?' At the mention of Juno by name, Robert span round. 'For God's sake! She hasn't the least idea. That would be—'

'What?' Priscilla's mouth hung open.

'A disaster.'

The two old friends stood face to face. Priscilla said, 'I take it your cock and balls are in working order?' knowing she should have left the whisky alone.

Robert said, 'Of course they are. How can you be so coarse?'

Priscilla said, 'It's plain English, in the dictionary. Oh, Robert, sorry.'

Robert said, 'I feel I have no steering-wheel, no brakes.' He turned to leave.

Watching him go, Priscilla called, 'I won't even talk to Mosley.'

FORTY-FIVE

*J*uno had seen the envelope and, recognizing her aunt's writing, put the letter to one side. During a busy day she forgot it, but waking in the night she remembered and the thought of it lying unopened on the hall table nagged. She turned on her side and tried to sleep, but could not. After a while she got out of bed, switched on the light in the bathroom and by its glow put on Evelyn's dressing-gown and looked keenly into her children's cradles. Neither Inigo nor Presto stirred. Inigo lay on his back with his arms thrown back, Presto with one fist visible, the other tucked away. Both children slept with their mouths shut, breathing through their noses. Leaning to kiss them, she brushed the tops of their heads and straightened up, the sensation of silk on her lips. Then, leaving her door open, she slipped from the room and went barefoot down the stair.

In the hall she snatched up Violet's letter and went into the library, where she switched on a lamp and, crouching by the fire, laid a log and some kindling on the hot ash. Then, because she could put it off no longer, she slit the envelope and began to read.

Some time later Robert, in his bed at the other end of the house, was woken by the need to pee. He went to his bathroom and without putting on a light eased his need. Pulling back the shutters, he looked out at the valley to see in the moonlight a fox trot across his line of vision. Watching it until it was out of sight he grew thoroughly awake, and all the aggravating thoughts and doubts which plagued him by day crowded back into his mind so that he knew he would not sleep again. Staring out at the now empty view he thought of Priscilla and wished he had not spoken so freely. It had done no good to expose his pain. All she had done was make flippant allusions to the Old Testament which he, forgetting his Bible, had not followed. What the hell was she referring to? Something to do with old age? Some sexual connotation? His lack of recall niggled. Some old woman had conceived and born a child at ninety, was it that? Or the poor old bugger, who the devil was it, who had been circumcised at the same age. Good God, what barbarity! One should look it up. Then, nearer home, she had referred to their neighbour, John Morgan, who had married again in his eightieth year and fathered many children, to the irritation of his first family. Was Priscilla hinting perhaps that his plight was not unusual? Had she not enquired as to his state of virility? It was no concern of hers. It was not Priscilla's opinion that mattered, Robert thought irritably.

Back in his room Jessie stood by the door, asking to be let out. Sighing, Robert pulled on a pair of trousers and a sweater and followed the dog down the stairs where, reaching the hall, she did not make for the front door but padded towards the library, whose door stood open. A light showed and Juno sat on the hearthrug staring into the fire.

Surprised, Robert said, 'Juno?' and seeing that she wept, 'what's up?' He came forward and sat in his armchair. 'Tell me to go away if you want to be alone.'

Juno said, 'No.'

Robert leaned forward to throw wood on the fire. Juno folded the letter she had been reading and stuffed it back in its envelope. Robert said dryly, 'Somebody has written something hurtful, somebody has felt themselves encumbered to put it in writing.'

Juno said, 'My Aunt Violet.'

'And what's her dire news?'

'She thinks I should know how matters stand.'

'Yes?'

Juno said, 'I can't think why I mind.'

Robert said nothing.

Juno said, 'May I lean against your legs?' When Robert did not answer she shifted her position so that she sat facing the fire with her back against his knees. She said, 'She's a bloody old interfering bitch.'

Robert murmured, 'Go on.'

'She writes,' Juno spoke in a monotone, 'that after considerable soul-searching, she felt it her duty to write to my mother and apprise her of my twins, and that my mother has written back.'

'And?'

'She seems to have done some soul-searching, too.'

'And?'

'Having embarked on a new, successful and happy marriage – it appears she has given birth to a beautiful baby girl – well, I knew she'd had the baby – she is very much enjoying her new life and, although she gave me every opportunity of joining her, the twins do rather alter things. They do not fit with her husband Jack Sonntag's prominent position. She has given the matter a lot of thought, searched her soul; she has arrived at the conclusion that, since I have behaved so irresponsibly, it will be better all round if we go our separate ways. Oh yes, she wishes me well. I rather like that bit, it rounds things off.'

Robert felt the warmth of her spine as she leaned against his legs and said nothing.

Juno said, 'I should not be surprised. It's interesting, though. My mother never liked me very much although she tried, I think. She never liked my father, either. He was a mistake, I was another, but this time with Mr Sonntag she seems to have got it right. She tried, she was dutiful, and now she has snatched this wonderful opportunity. She is barely forty. I thought that was old, but it isn't, is it? What it amounts to is that I and my twins are an embarrassment. I knew we would be, that's why I had put off telling her. She doesn't want to be burdened with a lot of old clobber like that.'

Robert listened. He knew from her voice that her throat was sore from crying.

Juno said, 'It was nice of her to send me back my clothes and buy me nylons; she had not yet had the dire news, had not had the shock of discovering herself to be a grand-mother. I quite see that wasn't tactful of me.'

Robert said, 'No.'

Juno said, 'I should not really mind. I suppose I am angry with her as she must be angry with me, but I do rather feel she might have written to me herself, not left it to Aunt Violet.'

Robert kept quiet.

Juno pulled a handkerchief out of her pocket and blew her nose. She said, 'I shall just have to get used to the idea that I am not wanted.'

Somewhere in the neighbouring sky there sounded an aeroplane's growling flight. Alert, Juno turned her head to listen. 'A bomber?'

Robert said, 'A Beaufighter, I think, one of ours.'

In Juno's room Inigo and Presto whimpered. Juno leapt to her feet, threw Violet's letter into the fire. 'One of them is crying.' She made for the door.

Robert shouted, 'I want you. You *are* wanted. I want you all!' But she was gone, she had not heard. He swore, 'Bugger, bugger, bugger,' and reached with the poker to push Violet's letter, which had fallen short of the fire, in among the logs.

FORTY-SIX

*W*hen illness hit the village of Copplestone in 1942, its inhabitants stopped talking of Rommel's defeat at El Alamein and the Allied invasion of North Africa; if one of their young men was serving overseas they congratulated him on being beyond reach of the most virulent strain of measles in living memory. It spread among the schoolchildren until every child was afflicted and the school closed. It reached out to far-flung farms and remote cottages; it infected any adult who had missed the disease in childhood and even some who had not. Within weeks John and Lily's three children were in bed in the gardener's cottage, and in the house Juno watched Inigo and Presto like a hawk, while Ann made everybody wash their hands in disinfectant and insisted that callers coming to see Robert discussed their business out of doors.

All the children had recovered and life returned to normal when Inigo and Presto came out in a rash. Within hours they had streaming colds, coughs and high temperatures. They were not yet a year old. Standing between their cots, his stethoscope dangling round his neck, the doctor told Juno and Robert that they had pneumonia.

'I don't want to be alarmist but their best hope is for us to have them in the hospital.'

In the hall he muttered to Robert of complications, hinted at worse to come and cursed the fact that it was impossible to obtain the wonder drug penicillin; every dose was reserved for men in the services. Juno protested at the thought of hospital, feared separation and was

247

filled with alarm but, reading Robert's expression, gave in.

Ann packed the children, well muffled in shawls, into Juno's arms and Robert got into the driving seat. The doctor shouted, 'See you at the hospital,' and drove recklessly ahead. Robert followed more carefully, conscious of his cargo. When he looked at Juno's face beside him it was a mask of terror; she had not slept for several nights and, like Inigo and Presto, had a streaming cold. He said, 'They will be all right, I promise you they will. The doctor is being extra careful, that's all.'

Juno said, 'I don't believe you.'

Robert snapped, 'All right, don't,' fear reducing repartee to quasi-adolescence. The road to Copplestone had never seemed so long.

At the hospital cots had been made ready. Nurses in uniform snatched Inigo and Presto from their mother's arms. There was a smell of disinfectant, and shoes squeaked on lino. The matron towered, kind but firm: the hospital would take over, no parent was allowed to stay with her child. 'No, no,' and again, 'No.' Juno could not stay, rules were rules.

Juno protested. Inigo and Presto filled their phlegmy lungs and bellowed. Matron said, 'They will soon stop that, dear.' Robert caught Juno's arm, raised to strike. White-faced and sneezing, she continued to protest. The nurses whisked the babies away to their ward. Matron said, 'Visiting hours are three in the afternoon to five, dear, come tomorrow, Mr Copplestone.' Settled into identical cots, Inigo and Presto were surprised into silence.

The doctor joined Robert and Juno in the corridor. Producing his stethoscope, he applied it to Juno's chest. 'Stand still, Juno. Now let's listen to your back. Let's have a thermometer, matron. As I thought, one hundred and one. Take her home, Robert, put her to bed and keep her there tomorrow. I will give you a pill to give her last thing.'

Juno said, 'I am not ill. I must stay with my children, they will think I deserted them. They will never forgive me, they will die without me.'

The doctor said, 'What possible use can you be to them ill?'

Robert said, 'Stop this rubbish,' and dragged her out to the car.

When they arrived back, Ann said, 'I will light the fire in her room and fill a hot-water bottle and when she's in bed I will bring her some soup. She hasn't eaten for days.'

Juno said, 'Soup sounds familiar—' and let Robert lead her to the library and sit her in his chair by the fire where she sat stiffly, shivering and sneezing.

Kneeling by her, Robert took her hands in his and said, 'They are going to be all right, Juno, they are not going to die. They are going to grow up into lovely boys, fine men. I look forward to teaching them to ride and swim, shoot and fish. I shall teach them about birds and flowers. I love them. I saw them born. Please believe me.'

Juno said, 'Orchids?'

'Orchids, too, and peregrine falcons.'

Fumbling for her handkerchief, Juno snuffled. She said, 'I am so terribly frightened,' but said no more, for she could see that behind his brave words Robert was also afraid.

When she was in bed, Robert looked in. Ann had given her aspirin and there was a bowl of soup. He said, 'I will ring the hospital last thing, I promise. Now, drink your soup while it's hot and swallow this,' and gave her the pill the doctor had given him. She swallowed it. Then he said, 'Tell you what, I will telephone now and speak to that dragon.' Coming back ten minutes later, he said, 'Done that, she says they are both asleep. That's good, you know.' When she thanked him, he said, 'Try and sleep, too.' At midnight, when he came to tell her that he had telephoned again, Juno was deeply asleep thanks to the doctor's pill. He was glad, because he did not want to tell her that the babies had woken and were restless, coughing and still very wheezy.

Ann kept Juno in bed the next day and Robert haunted the hospital, braving the matron, ignoring the rules to sit for hours between the babies' cots, watching their fight.

Towards evening, the doctor came to make his examination, probing, listening, gently touching. Straightening up, he said, 'I think you can go home now, Robert, get out from under Matron's feet. You can honestly tell Juno they are better. I think, "turned the corner" is the colloquial term.'

Robert drove home to tell Juno, who was better too, and to eat a large meal, for he was ravenously hungry. After this, finding Juno awake and restless, he promised to telephone the hospital last thing before he went to bed, then he went out into the night and walked with his dogs across his fields and up through the wood to the top of the cliff, where he stood looking out at the sea considering his predicament.

It was long after midnight when he rang the hospital and asked to speak to the night nurse. He had undressed and stood in the cold in his pyjamas and dressing-gown. As he waited, his fear renewed itself; his heart, constricted by anxiety, thudded in his chest and he thought of Juno and the vagaries of love.

When the doctor himself answered the telephone, Robert felt complete panic. 'Are they dead? Have they died? You said they were better—'

The doctor laughed. 'Don't be a fool, Robert. They are sleeping like tops.'

'Then what the hell are you doing there?' Robert shouted, 'Why are you there—'

'I do have other patients. One of them is in labour, having a hard time of it.'

'Oh.' Robert was deflated. 'And the babies? Juno's babies?'

'As I said. Fast asleep, and by the feel of things their temperatures are normal. It's amazing how resilient these little creatures are. You'll have them home in no time.'

Robert groaned.

The doctor said, 'You still there? Thought you had passed out. You can tell their mother the crisis is over.'

Robert said, 'Thank God,' to which the doctor retorted that he and the nurses and even matron had not been exactly idle and, 'whoever their father was must have had a strong constitution'. Then the doctor let out a shout of laughter and said he must get back to the patient in labour. Robert replaced the receiver and went upstairs and on the landing stood for some minutes taking deep breaths.

Juno's door was ajar; he crept in. The room was chilly, the fire dying. He moved cautiously to put wood on the fire.

Juno said, 'I am not asleep, too anxious. Did you telephone?' She raised herself on her elbow.

Robert said, 'They are sleeping, their temperatures are normal. He says, I spoke to the doctor, that you can see them tomorrow. They are going to be all right.'

Juno said, 'Oh, God! Oh, Robert, you are crying.' She reached up and caught hold of him. 'Why don't you get in, then we can cry together?'

Demurring, Robert said, 'What about your cold?'

She said, 'I will give it to you,' and held back the bedclothes, so he got in and later, when she woke after sleeping in his arms, he thought he should make light, excuse what had happened. He said, 'Oh, darling, this is what's called one thing leading to another,' and she said, 'I thought it was called pleasure, a hugely enjoyable pleasure, I had no idea. What a surprise.' When again he prevaricated, 'You have a cold, I should not have – it was an aberration, I am too old, much too old –' she said, 'Oh really?' and, 'What nonsense,' and, 'Stop quibbling,' and, 'Have we time to do it again before we get up to go to the hospital?'

He simply said, 'Yes.'

251

1965
FORTY-SEVEN

*J*uno left her parcels in the restaurant cloakroom and came back to sit in the bar, choosing a table for four. Then, agreeably tired from a morning's shopping, she stretched her legs and looked about her. A few tables away a middle-aged couple were sharing a joke, in the far corner a group of men discussed business, a young couple perched close together at the bar, and at the table next to her a solitary man read the *Evening Standard* and sipped vodka and tonic. As Juno sat down he lowered his paper, then raised it again.

Seeing her arrive, the barman came across with a glass of champagne on a salver. 'Good morning, madam, Mr Copplestone's order, he's reserved a table for lunch and will be a few minutes late.'

Juno said, 'Thank you, that's just what I need,' and sipped the champagne.

The solitary man lowered his newspaper and said, 'Juno.'

Turning to look, Juno said, 'Jonty.' The street door opened abruptly and a party of people came in talking loudly. Juno quickly swallowed another mouthful of champagne.

Jonty said, 'What are you doing here?'

'Meeting my family for lunch, and you?'

'Meeting my daughter.'

'You married?'

'I married a girl called Sheena.'

'I remember her.' (I bet his mother was pleased. I must not say suitable, sexy or rich.) 'And how is your mother?' Pleased that her voice was steady.

'She died.'

Juno said, 'I am sorry. And your aunt?'

'She died, too, soon after my uncle. My father died ten years ago, heart attack.'

Juno thought, and the old labrador? He must have popped off first. She said, 'Oh dear, sad.' She sipped and replaced her glass on the table. Her hand was quite steady. She said, 'I didn't know. You have a daughter?'

'Yes.'

'Just the one?'

'Yes. Juno, what are you—' Jonty's question was lost in the brouhaha of another group, who pushed past on their way to the restaurant. When they were gone, he said, 'You look wonderful, you haven't changed at all.'

Juno said, 'You look pretty much the same yourself. What is your daughter called? Is she beautiful?'

'Victoria. I think her beautiful. She's late.' He seemed worried by this.

'Girls are apt to be.'

'She was meeting some boyfriends.'

'Girls do that, too.'

'It's the boyfriends I worry about.' He sounded pettish.

Juno said, 'Well, these days there's the pill.'

Jonty flushed and gulped the rest of his vodka. 'You are married?' He sounded aggressive.

Juno said, 'I am.' He had not changed all that much; broader, definite suspicion of stomach, coarser perhaps, the black hair was going grey and sliding away from this temples. It was considerably thinner, too. He was on the wane.

Jonty said, 'This is impossible. Can't we go somewhere quiet and talk?'

Juno said, 'I am meeting my husband, and you are meeting your daughter.' (The old Jonty would have

253

giggled and said, 'Let's arrange for them to have lunch together.')

Jonty said, 'We couldn't find you, we couldn't find your aunt.'

Juno felt a surge of rage such as she had only experienced once before, on the occasion when she quarrelled with Bert in the cowshed. She said, 'You can't have looked very far, she's in the telephone book. She is still alive.' She drank a mouthful of champagne. Then she said, 'I was only part of the furniture.'

And Jonty exclaimed, 'No!' so loudly that people looked round and stared.

'And Francis?' Juno said. 'What's happened to Francis?'

'Francis was killed in the war.'

Juno said, 'I did not know.'

A comfortless silence grew between them, to be broken by Robert swinging in from the street exclaiming, 'So sorry to be so late, darling, please forgive me. Did the barman give you a drink? Oh, good, he did. You must have another to keep me company. I'll wave to him.' He waved. 'We will have a bottle. The boys are coming, aren't they? I am terribly sorry, but I have to telephone, make two calls. Do you mind? Are you starving?'

Juno said, 'No.'

Robert said, 'I'll try not to be long,' and was gone.

Jonty said, 'Is *that* your husband?'

Juno said, 'Yes.'

Jonty said, 'But he is *old.*'

Juno said, 'But gorgeous. We took a short cut through the generations. It took me for ever to persuade him to marry me. He was afraid it would make me look ridiculous and him more so.'

'He is certainly not that,' Jonty watched Robert's departing figure. 'How old is he? Seventy?'

'Eighty.'

'And you are?'

'Forty.'

'And happy?'

254

'Oh yes.'

Sounding sincere, Jonty said, 'I am glad.'

Juno said, 'And you?'

'Oh, you know, so-so.' He looked, she thought, rather sheepish, as if he was about to say something along the lines of, 'We rub along,' but his face lit up and he said, 'Ah! Here comes my daughter.' And then, 'Good God. *Who is she with?*' and the blood drained from his face as Inigo and Presto hurried up to their mother, exclaiming, 'Ma, we are late, forgive us.' And, 'It's all Victoria's fault. This is Victoria; Victoria, this is our mother. We couldn't get her out of the shops in Carnaby Street. Look at all this, Ma,' and they waved Union Jack carrier bags. 'You should see the rubbish she has bought, and look at these which we bought for Bert, d'you think he will wear them?' They snatched from a bag Union Jack pants. 'The very tops, the true essence of vulgarity.' Both were in a state of high spirits.

Juno shook hands with Victoria, who was indeed beautiful, and said, 'What have you done with your aunt, boys?' She was not looking at Jonty, avoiding his eye.

'She's on her way,' Presto said. 'She said don't wait for her, start lunch. She's gone over the top, bought presents for everyone back home in Montreal, lashed out in a big way. We couldn't stop her,' he said, laughing. 'Didn't try. We are starving.'

And Juno, aware of Jonty beside her, giving him the chance to revive, said, 'He is talking about my sister. If you remember my mother went to Canada; she married again and my sister is the result. Two weeks younger than her nephews, another example of short-cutting through generations. My mother died a year ago. These are my twins, Inigo and Presto. Darlings?' She gestured an introduction.

Easy-mannered and casual, they shook hands with Jonty. 'How d'you do?' Their eyes, black and palest blue, wandering incuriously past him towards the restaurant, anticipated lunch.

255

Juno said, 'Sit down, for God's sake,' as the young people milled about her, 'you are making me giddy.' But Victoria exclaimed that she must go to the lavatory, and Jonty that it was time to leave, his wife would be waiting for them at Wilton's. He said to Victoria, 'Hurry up, then,' which she did, disappearing and reappearing just as Robert rejoined them, having made his telephone calls, but in time to register the scene and Jonty departing. Robert said, 'Hello, everybody, ready for lunch?' Noting her pallor, he very quietly asked Juno, 'Are you all right, darling?'

Juno said, 'I hope so. That was Inigo's father, Robert.'

Robert murmured, 'So I observed, and Presto's?' For Jonty, shaking hands with Presto, had visibly flinched.

Juno said, 'Killed in the war.'

Robert sighed, 'Ah – Watch out, he is coming back.'

Jonty, reaching the street, had turned about and, leaving Victoria standing on the pavement, came up to Juno and with his face close to hers hissed, 'If those two are fucking my daughter, it's incest.'

And Juno said, 'Yes, it is.'